Twisted50 Volume 2

To Mum and Dad,
Hopefully this is the first and
not the last time.

Thank you for all your love
and support. Without you both
this wouldn't be possible.

I love you both

Paul. x

TWISTED50 VOLUME 2

A second serving of 50 contemporary shockers

Freya Eden-Ellis, Ann M. Richardson, Ben Marshall, Bruce Thomas, Chris Jeal, Dean Marriner, Dee Chilton, Emma Pullar, Fiona Hunnisett, Fiona Leitch, Gordon Slack, Hillier Townsend, Jacky Dahlhaus, James Jay, Jessica Brown, Juliet Sneed, Karen Davison, Kendall Castor-Perry, Lee Betteridge, Lee Burgess, Leo X. Robertson, Lewis Rice, Lucy V. Hay, Madeleine Swann, Maggie Innes, Mark Walker, Maryna Gaidar, Matt George Lovett, Melissa A. Szydlek, Milethia Thomas, N.W. Twyford, Nick Yates, Paul Shearer, Penegrin Shaw, Phil Chard, Phil Town, Rachael Howard, Ricardo Bravo, Richie Brown, Robbie Mori, Scott Merrow, Simon Cluett, Stephanie Hutton, Steve Pool, S.V. Macdonald, Tom Nolan, T.R. Guest, Jane Badrock, Eileen Wilson, and Andrew Mark Perry

Create50 Press
London

CONTENTS

THANKS AND ACKNOWLEDGEMENTS

Twisted50 is the second book in the series to arise from the Create50 community and initiative. You can find out more at www.Twisted50.com.

Aside from the writers whose work is included in this volume, we must also thank everyone involved. Elinor, Jade and Cristina, thank you for working so hard in putting this book together. Also, Vicky, Lucy, Judy, Lucia, Tori, Lisa, Szofia and the whole team, thank you for pulling it out of the bag too. To the Create50 community, the writers, the readers, the proof readers, far too many to list, thank you.

Chris Jones
Create50 Founder
Follow me on Twitter @LivingSpiritPix
Create50 on Twitter at @MyCreate50
Facebook fb.com/MyCreate50

INTRODUCTION

Elinor Perry-Smith

What a dark and delirious pleasure it's been to work on the second volume of Twisted 50! I've enjoyed the stories and the editing process equally; working with Cristina Palmer-Romero on whittling the stories down to a shortlist, each of us fighting our corner for the stories we felt HAD to be in the anthology; collaborating with Chris Jones and the team at Create 50; but mostly I've grown to appreciate what a supportive community of writers we've been working with.

Practically without exception, writers have been receptive and responsive to our suggestions and that has been profoundly gratifying. We also noticed new themes emerging in this collection: what I (in my head) labelled as carer horror and disability horror, which highlights what I love about horror as a genre – it acts as a filter on a difficult world, using the distancing effect of human extremity to throw a light on harsh truths.

Often creepy, disgusting, heart-stopping and bleakly funny, the stories in this collection are proof positive that we all have a twisted tale to tell. It's my hope that our talented writers continue to develop their craft, using their well-deserved success here as a springboard. As Poppy Z. Brite once said, 'My dad told me that no one could ever make it as a writer, that my chances were equivalent to winning the lottery – which was good for me, because I like to have something to prove.'

Elinor Perry-Smith
Project Leader and Producer
Twisted50 volume 2

Twisted50 Volume 2 Team
Edited by Elinor Perry Smith
Create50 Team Leader: Chris Jones
Production by Jade Wheldon
GoodReads Librarian: Simon Caldecutt
Twisted50 Founder: Cristina Palmer-Romero

1

THE ROOKERY

Nick Yates

He always killed in the spring.

It was the rooks, he said. They spoke to him about that day. And that could not be good. If I'd pressed for details, he'd have told me, but I never did. Some things are best left unsaid.

When they started nesting; that was when the waiting started, and it was almost a relief to me when he took the first.

The great tall elms down by the river were the birds' favourite; slim, stark and black against the sky, transformed into giant charred poppies by the groups of tangled nests hanging in their upper branches. The Rookery.

I used to look up from my window at the dark silhouettes wheeling above, fetching and building; and I'd feel a chill creep into my bones. I didn't always know it had happened, not until I saw it in the paper or heard it on the news. Another child disappeared, another young life extinguished, another murder unsolved. A tragic mystery.

Most of the time though, I could tell just by looking at him across the table, head down, shovelling his dinner in great heaped forkfuls. His eyes were changed, brighter somehow, his movements more purposeful. Like his life had gained new meaning, driven by his obsession to change the past.

I walked the elms most winters, when the pain of those poor children was locked deep beneath the frozen ground. I'd stand there as the grey, swollen river oozed past and try to understand, stare up into the branches and wonder how it had come to this. Most people would mourn for a time, however long, until they found their own peace. But not him.

Love, in its lost logic, had chosen to chain me here, and I had watched evil take root and grow within him, until he had become unrecognisable as the man I married. There was no point trying to break that chain, forged as it was from the finest steel, over so much time.

This year he had started early, as if he felt their pull more sharply than usual; perhaps the rooks had started nesting early too. I don't remember. The date was March 21st, that I do remember. A gallery of daffodils, yellow and white, shuddered in the breeze, shaking their heads in silent dismay as he climbed back up out of the trees to the house.

It was the set of his jaw and the quickness of his step that told me the waiting was over. I let out a breath, realising I'd sleep better that night.

He chose his children when they came into the village shop, eyes wide, chattering to their friends, buying up sweets and pop. They ignored him; just the old shopkeeper in their eyes, a bland background to their urgency, all tattered apron and blank smiles. A study in musty forgetfulness perfected through the years. If only they knew.

I couldn't work the school shift; I couldn't bear to watch what he was doing. Eyes shifting slowly beneath that ever present cloth cap, weighing, measuring, studying, selecting. In the early years he simply hoped he might see them again, that somehow he might leap back to a time before that terrible day. Now his efforts were more calculated; designed to satisfy.

That night he had slept by the fire, empty whisky tumbler resting on his chest, rising and falling under a soft, troubled snore. That was when I saw it, glinting in the last light of the dying embers. A long blonde hair snagged in the cabling of his heavy woollen sweater.

She had been in the shop that morning, I was sure of it. He had visibly tensed when he saw her. New to the village perhaps, and so beautiful, white blonde hair caught up in a red bow. The similarities were strong enough to knock me off balance. God knows what it did to him.

I plucked the hair from his arm as he slept, studying it in the light. It could have been my little girl's; her hair had been that length before she was taken from us. I screwed up my eyes and tried to shake the image from my head; the laughing faces of my beautiful twins, their father beaming proud. All those years ago in a different life.

He stirred then and moved his head. I saw his cheeks were streaked wet. Still snared in a deep sleep, he let out a desperate groan of pure anguish and muttered the words I had heard so many times before.

'Why us? Couldn't you have left just one?'

I fell to my knees then, heaving sobs into my apron, picturing that Spring day seven years ago. One moment they were laughing and playing in the field, and, what seemed like the next, we were staring at their pale bodies, laid out on the riverbank. Beneath The Rookery.

The look he wore as he knelt to brush the strand of sodden hair from our boy's face remains etched into my heart. That, and the mocking cries of the rooks he said were taunting him for failing to keep his children safe.

Everything he had done since then was tied to that terrible time and his desire to see his children again. The birds seemed to influence him, as if they were daring him to make amends. Did he really think they would give him back his children, if he gave them someone else's?

I tossed the hair into the fire and turned away, shuddering. He had been a good man once; it wasn't his fault. Some things are best left unsaid.

He took his second child before the Spring was out, and to my eyes the shadows beneath those old elms grew darker than they'd ever been; cloaked in his sin. The rooks in their high castles looked on, bearing witness to his depravity, while remaining unburdened by his secrets. How I envied them.

One evening towards the end of April, he came home breathing hard, wispy hair wild about his balding head and a long red scratch across his cheek. His woollen sweater was torn at the shoulder, and his cap was missing.

I knew better than to question him, but I could guess what had happened. He was subdued the next day, full of nervous energy over breakfast. He asked me to run the shop for a couple of days, claiming he wasn't feeling well. He stayed in bed for most of a week.

When he finally emerged, it was already in the papers; a boy this time, as I knew it would be. He was well-known in the village, rugby-mad and captain of the local under-13s. The sort that might fight back.

The news faded eventually, the police stopped scratching their heads and went back to their regular work; soothing their ineptitude with easier wins.

He returned to the shop when the scratch had healed, wearing his identical spare cap. As spring blossomed into summer, he relaxed and something resembling hope showed in his face. It was as if a great burden had suddenly been lifted from his shoulders. His work for the year was done, the rooks rewarded, in turn to reward him, he believed, with the gift he so desperately craved.

The elms sprung into green leaf, and the austere rookery was swallowed up by new growth. Songbirds nestled in the upper reaches, their bright, undulating calls in contrast to the guttural cries of the rooks. The man I loved came back then, echoes of the quirks that had captivated me before our loss. He even brought me flowers like he used to; little white tulips that grew beside the river. I couldn't face them though, knowing where they had come from and what might have nourished them.

As the seasons turned again, I almost forgot who I was, who I was willingly sharing my life with, who I loved. We would laugh and joke, and he would talk of our children again, as if they might come bursting breathless through the door at any moment. He could be kind when he wanted to be, but it was always there, behind the smiles; I'd catch it in the occasional haunted look or flash of anger. If true evil can ever really be quantified, I think that was what I saw. A glimpse of Hell.

Then the storms came and changed everything. Autumn storms, more ferocious than I've ever seen. They reached their height one night in October, shaking the house and battering the windows with wave after wave of sheeting, frozen rain. By early light the devastation was clear. Tiles ripped from roofs, telegraph poles brought down and trees uprooted. Including one of the old elms.

The front door went at seven that morning. A firm, brisk knock filled with authority. It was just as he was finishing his breakfast, settling his frayed apron around his neck, about to go down and open up the shop, ready for the early morning rush of schoolkids. He looked at me surprised but just smiled and touched my cheek, whispering he loved me as he turned the latch. He didn't suspect a thing.

A police officer spoke his name, more a statement than a question. All my husband could do was nod; he kept nodding to himself when they took him away, as if he was already confessing. Not to the police though; but to the souls he had taken, to those families he had destroyed to fulfil his own deluded desires. To his own dead children.

It was the rooks.

They had kept his secret, but they had broken their silence. I like to think it was because even those dark, ethereal creatures had grown tired of his wickedness. Their sympathy for his loss had also turned to disgust at what he had become. Just like mine.

Workmen brought in to clear the fallen elm had discovered it. An old nest, exposed within the yellowing leaves. Part of The Rookery.

The nest was lined with fibres and hair, an odd collection, even for a rook. Red silk, blonde hair, scraps of rugby shirt in the local school's colours. And fabric from a cloth cap.

He was sentenced last week, just before Christmas; five consecutive life sentences. I'll never see him again, not even as a visitor.

Something snapped inside me when he was taken away, the love that shielded me from the horror had floated free, unhitched from the mooring that was no longer there, and sinking into those murderous depths.

I still have a photo that I keep locked in my family box. The four of us on a cold, bright day, a few days before the accident; carefree and untouched by tragedy. When it happened, I couldn't imagine it would get any worse, the pain of loss overwhelmed everything. That photo was the only thing that kept me going.

Now I know different. Carrying his secret and bearing responsibility for his actions has tarnished anything good that existed before. Even the memory of my beautiful children has been desecrated.

The police didn't push me when I told them I had no idea what he was doing. Perhaps they assumed I couldn't have been part of something so monstrous. Funny, if they had tried a little harder, I would probably have told them the truth.

I still walk under those elms each winter. I wait until a hard frost has frozen the ground solid; a wall to keep their screams from reaching me. I hear the harsh laughter of the rooks ringing out under leaden skies, and wonder whether they are mocking his cowardice, or mourning my fate. They know about the blood that stains my fingers, they know I have nothing left, not even memories. They know the truth about evil.

It's between me and the birds now. Some things are best left unsaid.

2

GRAMMA'S ISSUES

Ann M. Richardson

He crouched in his corner beside the big dresser, chilled, hugging his knees to his chest and pressing his lips against the dirty fabric of his threadbare jeans. He reached out to trace a finger along the spines of the magazines that more or less walled him in to the small space in the corner of the back bedroom. He could barely make out the print in the fading afternoon light that filtered through a dirty window at the foot of Gramma's bed. "January... February... March... April...," he whispered to himself. He stopped to tug the dirty blanket up over his shoulders.

Crowded stacks of magazines and newspapers towered precariously, nearly touching the sagging, water-stained ceiling of the old single-wide trailer. They were several layers deep on the floor, stacked in every corner, on every countertop. He quit reciting the months of the year to listen for Gramma. She slept on a small twin bed in the corner opposite Chris' small covey, but they couldn't see each other because of the wall of magazines between them. This past week, since her accident, she hadn't left her bed, that he could tell. The stench of human excrement stung his nostrils and made his eyes water, and he worried that he should check on her, but he was too scared to crawl out and go look. The blood on her face and sweater had scared him badly that day, and if he didn't look at her, it was like it didn't happen.

He knew she was still alive because each day in the late afternoon she began humming old songs and continued into the night until Chris fell asleep. This was of great comfort to him since he spent most of his time in this room, keeping away from his mother and her friends who occupied the living room in the front of the trailer. After the yelling and beatings, he was grateful for the relative solitude of his small cell and for his Gramma's humming.

Chris was hungry and wondered how long it would be before the adults would pass out in a drunken sleep, and he could sneak into the kitchen and scavenge for food. He ought to get something for Gramma, too. His mind began to wander, back to a few weeks ago when he'd come home from school, the last day of first grade.

He found Gramma sitting at the kitchen table, eyes vacantly staring straight ahead. His mother was passed out in the living room, hypodermic needles, hand mirrors, spoons and candles littering the low table in front of the sofa. He looked into Gramma's bruised face in alarm. Blood had trickled out of one ear and the corner of her nostril, and drops of blood spattered onto the breast of her dingy pink sweater.

"Gramma?" he said tentatively.

When she didn't react, he whispered a little louder, "Gramma."

She half-blinked her cloudy eyes and croaked out weakly, "Chrissy. Don't track mud… the floor."

Chris glanced at the small, grimy areas of the floor that he could see through the litter of magazines and newspapers. He looked back at Gramma, reached out, and took her frail hand in his. He rubbed the back of her hand, feeling the cold, papery skin and the purple-green veins under his sweaty palm. The fear began to grow in his chest, and his scalp and forearms tingled, raising the hairs. "Gramma… is you ok?" She did not respond. "Gramma!" he said more urgently, gently shaking her arm. Still she did not respond, but he heard the slurry mumbling of his mother from the living room couch, "Stupid… bitch… I'll teach you…" And then silence. He pulled on Gramma's hand until she rose and stood, and then he slowly, slowly pulled her with him as he walked backwards down the hallway, weaving around the stacks of magazines, careful so that she would not catch her foot on one of them and fall. They made it to the bedroom at the very end of the trailer, pushed open the door and shuffled around the wall of magazines to the foot of her bed. He gently helped her lay down on top of the covers, and smoothed her sweater with his shaking hands. "You'll be ok, Gramma. You'll be ok."

Gramma used to shuffle aimlessly through the maze of magazines and newspapers. She never was all 'there' but Chris felt she loved him. In the mornings she would be in the kitchen, humming a nameless tune and setting a plate of a few saltines or a small box of raisins in front of him on the table for breakfast. Unfocused eyes gazing off into space, she'd say in a dreamy voice, "Chrissy, best get yourself off to school and mind that you don't track mud in when you come back."

Chris heard a faint tune quaver over the tops of the stacks. He exhaled in relief. Each night for the past week he would pull his dirty blanket over his shoulders and listen to his Gramma sing to herself. Sometimes she would call out to him weakly, "Chrissy... Chrissy... eat your raisins." He lay down on his side on a layer of magazines, and pulled the blanket up around his neck. The wind had risen and now it was lifting the loose aluminum siding at the rotted-out corner of the trailer with a rhythmic banging. He absently wondered if he could crawl out through that small hole in the corner and run away.

Despite being drowsy and weak with hunger, sleep eluded him, and so Chris dully reached out to feel the stack of magazines nearest his dresser. "January... February... March... April... " Gramma was beginning the tune again when Chris heard the aluminum siding screeching and moaning over in the corner as it was pulled back from the trailer. A very cold breeze swept in and around the stacks of magazines. Gramma stopped humming abruptly. Two male voices hoarsely whispered to each other, arguing about whether anyone was home or not, and what the hell was that stench. They grew quiet and waited a moment, and Chris could hear them panting from their exertion. They must be listening for something. Chris held his breath and stayed very still.

Evidently satisfied that the trailer was empty, the men resumed pulling great chunks of wood from the rotted corner of the trailer's floor. Between grunts and breaking wood, Chris heard his Gramma calling his name weakly. "Chrissy... Chrissy... be still."

Chris grew stiff with panic. What if they heard his Grandma? The men grew more frantic in their efforts. Snatches of snarly conversation floated to Chris' corner; words like "cops" and "hide" and "stash" made his heart beat quickly, and he wedged himself beside the dresser and behind a stack of magazines, in case they came around to his area. They had forced their way through the hole and were inside the room now.

Sirens began to wail from far away and slowly grew louder, until they stopped. They must be very close because Chris could hear a dog barking inside a car. Soon there was the sound of a car door opening and slamming, and the barking dog sounded like it was just across the street. The men were not talking now, and Chris could hear their ragged breathing. For once he was thankful for the hoarded magazines that hid him and his Grandma.

"Chrissy... Chrissy..."

"Yes, Gramma" he whispered in terror, fervently hoping the men didn't hear him.

"Chrissy... be still."

"'K, Gramma."

Chris heard helicopters now, and the dog's barking was growing louder. The men were agitatedly moving around the stacks in the dark room, not speaking. They seemed to be searching for something.

"Hide it somewhere, quick!" one of them growled.

A body lurched around the stack of magazines, and Chris saw a boot standing right in front of his dresser. He clamped his mouth shut and put both hands tightly over his mouth. The boot stepped back quickly, and a large hand reached to feel around.

"Chrissy... Chrissy" Gramma called, her voice a little stronger now.

Chris remained silent as the hand closed around his ankle and jerked savagely. He was dragged out from behind the stack and hung upside down in front of a strange man who reeked of liquor and smoke. Chris continued to press his hands to his mouth.

"Chrissy... Chrissy," came Gramma's voice, stronger and louder still.

Even in his terror, Chris marveled at his Gramma's even tone and strong timbre. What would the men do if they found her? The man began to shake Chris, gritting through clenched teeth, "What the hell is this?" and calling to the other man, "Hey, we got a kid in here! Thought you said the back of this trailer wasn't used!"

The barking grew closer still, and the other man rushed around the stack and frantic with desperation whispered loudly, "We can use him as a hostage!" And the man dropped Chris on his head and stepped on Chris' chest with a big, dirty boot. Chris felt the air leave his lungs and began to gasp for breath as the man leaned heavily on his foot. The glaring eyes gleamed in the pale street light, filtering through the broken window and a sneer transformed the swarthy face as it loomed down close to Chris's.

"Chrissy... Chrissy!"

How was Gramma yelling now? Chris had only known her voice to be breathy and quavering. And what would the men do to her if they found her? How had they not heard her yet? The barking dog was almost at the trailer now. The helicopter's beating grew more intense, and the light streaming into the window grew stronger. The man leered down at Chris and pulled a gun out of his waistband. Chris wriggled under the booted foot, struggling for breath.

"Chrissy... CHRISSY. BE STILL!"

Chris turned his head toward the sound of Gramma's voice and watched in horror and fascination as the tallest stack of magazines began to slowly lean toward the man stepping on him. The stack behind that one moved, too, and a third one near the open hole in the floor began to lean as well. They toppled in slow motion, knocking the man off Chris's chest and smashing him to the floor. The other man was also crushed down by the volumes of newsprint and magazines, and as more stacks tilted and fell, they were silenced. The barking dog was now madly screaming up into the corner of the trailer, and the handler was yelling something. Chris felt himself fading out of consciousness as the sounds of angry policemen began to fill the air.

When he came to, Chris discovered he was bundled in a clean blanket, strapped to a bed being wheeled into an ambulance. He cracked open his eyes a slit and saw people in white scurrying around and calling instructions to each other. A police man near the bumper was talking with another officer.

"… both killed. Crushed under those friggin magazines. They must have knocked them over when they were trying to hide. Can't imagine anyone living in that shit. The whole friggin trailer was buried in magazines and newspapers."

The other officer was mumbling something but his voice was muffled, and Chris couldn't hear him very well. The first officer apparently couldn't hear him very well either and barked impatiently, "Take that mask off your face, we're out in the open now, you're not gonna die from any damn fumes! Now, what the hell were you saying?"

The officer spoke again, and Chris could hear the disgust in his voice as he said, "That poor kid was in there with that dead, old lady. I can't stand to think of it. Ya know, I got kids myself, and I can't imagine what that poor little kid must have been through. She's been dead over a week, and it ain't pretty…"

3

REPEATER

Steve Pool

The wailing siren and streaks of people passing through Peter's field of vision are the only things he is aware of, apart from the agony that he feels, centred somewhere around his belly. He can't move, so he can't see its cause. But he doesn't need to see to know what it is; he's been gutshot. The paramedics try frantically to keep him alive while the ambulance races on through an endless night. A woman wearing a pink beaded cardigan remains just out of sight but isn't far from him – Peter knows this because at some point she reaches over, grabs his hand, and begins to speak to him. For now, though, he is trapped alone within a frozen moment.

He begins to drift. He had been cold, colder than he can ever remember feeling. But now he is very warm. That warmth fills his entire being and makes him feel wonderful; it's as if he's been dropped into the perfect bath, and all of his aches and pains, including his searing bullet wound, have suddenly fled. The world above flashes, saturated with colour – green and red and white. He wants so much to sleep. Dreamless sleep fixes everything, some voice or memory in the back of his mind suggests. Who is he to argue…?

He jolts awake. Fire and lightning burn the sky and him with it. It is, by far, the worst pain he's yet felt. His eyes, however, desperate for the relief of darkness, stubbornly refuse to see. Somewhere, very far off, a voice echoes, "Clear…!"

He burns again. With a huge gasp, his lungs claw for air. His sight has also returned. A hard ball is hammering inside his chest, and the hole near his stomach combusts, provoking a terrible cry. A hand reaches over and settles against his forehead while another injects him with something. As his senses dull, his thoughts unravel. Sounds smear, and he struggles to comprehend their meaning. Someone mentions numbers – his vitals and his chances – but thinking about these only confuses him. The woman in the sweater finally reaches over. He can feel the long strands of her blonde hair drape across him, and he can finally see the beautifully fragile, grieving curves of her face. Her warm, vibrant hands close over his cold, numb ones, while she begs for him to hold on…

His shouts had drawn Peter's mother and father to his bedroom. Even though he was eight, he'd wet the bed and not for the first time.

"It's that damn nightmare he always has," his mother exclaimed to his father, who, with a look of pity and disgust, hovered in the doorway to Peter's room. "Just look at how he's shaking."

It was true; Peter was trembling, and the tears that streaked his face looked like scars.

His father sighed deeply. "I get it. I do…" He paused, looking for the right words that wouldn't make him sound like an insensitive ass. "But he's eight years old, Ellen. Old enough to not be doing this." He gestured with frustrated, helpless hands towards Peter's stained bedsheet. "Something's not right. We need to take him to a doctor."

"He's not sick, Gary!" Peter's mother placed her hands over his ears as she snapped at his father. "He's just having bad dreams again."

"When does he not have nightmares? Why doesn't he ever have any good dreams… like… like winning a big soccer game or going on an exciting trip or… I dunno… flying through the air… eating a big piece of cake…? Something positive."

His mother's hands pressed in harder, making Peter's ears and head hurt. "I don't know. Maybe it's because of something you're doing." She paused before speaking again, her voice lower from sorrow. "Or maybe it's something that I'm doing…"

As Peter watched his parents argue, he was no longer crying, but he was still shaking. He couldn't stop shaking.

Peter jolted awake and looked around. It was still dark in his room. Glancing across his shoulder, he squinted at the clock, which read 3:23. "Great," he thought to himself. There were two finals waiting for him at school later that day. Of course he'd had that nightmare.

His 'life-preserver', a bottle of benzodiazepine next to his bed, called out to him. But remembering his upcoming tests, Peter, instead, chose to find solace online. He yelped as he stepped out of bed, right into a bowl half-filled with melted ice cream that he'd neglected to bring downstairs, then wiped his foot off on a sock lying on the floor. Once on his computer, Peter pulled up a site, one that he'd bookmarked and looked at often, that posted information about psychosis. Lately, Peter had become obsessed with mental illness.

He was on his mother's couch when he snapped to, shuddering. The living room around him was full of friends and family who had come to his graduation party. Peter scanned for his parents.

After their divorce, his parents had gone through a long period of open hostility. There had been no escaping the criticisms and insults that they had, in the ensuing years, lobbed at each other, despite Peter's constant protests. It had been no comfort to hear that their separation had been in no way his fault. Peter had never believed that.

Jenny, his little sister, dropped next to him on the couch. "Hey, big brother! Or should I say 'Doctor Brother'?" A look of concern crossed her face. "You okay? Did you have another nightmare?"

Peter, a little fatigued, gave her an, "I'm fine." A pause. "Thanks for coming to my party, by the way."

"Yeah, totally. I wouldn't miss it for anything." Looking around, Jenny replied, "Sooo… this is pretty crazy. I cannot believe that you've finally graduated. Eight years is a long time to be in college. I'm so happy for you."

"Well, I still have my residency to complete, but, otherwise, thank you." Peter checked his hand for tremors before continuing. "Have you seen Mom or Dad? I was wondering how they were doing, being together in the same room and all."

"Hmm, yes," Jenny replied. "I have seen them, and I'm happy to report that both are on their best behaviour. I think it helps that Dad has stopped drinking."

"Really? I didn't know that."

"You would if you tried talking to him from time to time," Jenny said, scolding him but patting his hand reassuringly at the same time. "I have a great idea. Instead of sleeping on the couch at your own party, let's go find him and Mom."

"Good idea. Let's grab Keri, too."

Jenny smiled. "Have I told you how glad I am that you found her? She is so amazing. Don't you dare go and eff things up with her. I'm hoping she'll become the sister that I've always wanted."

"I'll try."

Jenny's eyes narrowed.

"What? Okay... I won't 'eff' it up. I promise."

Standing up, the two walked to the dining room where their parents were speaking pleasantly to each other. Seeing Keri in the kitchen, Peter waved her over.

Peter found himself staring up at an image that had been painted on the hotel room ceiling, Italian-style, of angelic children dancing around a circle.

Keri was still in the bathroom, getting ready. Peter was this evening's keynote speaker, his topic 'Visceral Symbolic Stimulus during the Sleep Cycle.' Standing up and patting himself down, Peter checked to see whether he had missed anything: dress shirt and tie in order, fly zipped, notecards for his speech in his shirt pocket. Everything seemed in place.

Keri called out, "Everything alright in there? It sounded as if you were having another nightmare."

"Did it? Sorry... I can't recall if I did or not."

"No, don't be sorry. That's good if you don't remember. So, anyway, the car just called. It's here to take us to the conference centre whenever we're ready."

She stepped out of the bathroom, wearing a stunning dress that Peter didn't remember having seen before.

"That new?"

"Yes," she replied coyly. "Do you like it?"

"It's wonderful."

Peter stood up and took her into his arms. She pushed back, but only a little.

"Not now. We have to go. Don't forget your jacket."

As the two of them left, Keri gave Peter a sly look. "Maybe later, though, you can give the dress a much closer inspection."

On the morning of Peter's and Keri's twentieth wedding anniversary, Peter had surprised her with plane tickets to Chicago. That's where they'd met as undergraduate students at Northwestern. She'd never once complained when both his residency and future practice had taken them to Washington D.C., but Peter had known that the Windy City had always been a dear place to her. After arriving at their hotel on the Miracle Mile, they had readied themselves for a wonderful celebratory evening. Peter had felt a strong urge to nap but had resisted, not wanting to risk having another nightmare and spoiling their evening.

The two had taken an early dinner at a Russian restaurant, delighting themselves with servings of borsch, kalduny, shashlik, and fine wine, followed up with bracing shots of vodka. Afterwards, eschewing a cab, they had walked to Millennium Park and its outdoor concert. When Keri had mentioned that she was cold, Peter had placed his jacket over her pink beaded cardigan. Neither had seen the two robbers racing out of the pharmacy across the street, guns blazing.

He burns again. With a huge gasp, his lungs claw for air. His sight has also returned. A hard ball is hammering inside his chest, and the hole near his stomach combusts, provoking a terrible cry.

A hand reaches over and settles against his forehead, while another injects him with something. As his senses dull, his thoughts unravel. Sounds smear, and he struggles to comprehend their meaning. Someone mentions numbers – his vitals and his chances – but thinking about these only confuses him. The woman in the sweater finally reaches over. He can feel the long strands of her blonde hair drape across him, and he can finally see the beautifully fragile, grieving curves of her face. He senses her warm, vibrant hands close over his cold, numb ones, while she begs for him to hold on. Peter stirs, and Keri shouts.

"Oh my God! Peter! Oh my God! I thought I'd lost you. Just hang on, sweetheart... we're almost to the hospital!" Peter moans and tries to squeeze Keri's hand. Over her shoulder, Keri shouts, "How much farther!? How long until we get there!?" Somewhere overhead, a muffled voice answers back.

A wave of fatigue washes over Peter. He just wants to close his eyes again.

"No, no, no, no, no! Peter! Stay with me! Please don't close your eyes!" She bends lower, dripping heavy tears, and strokes and kisses his forehead. He notices that his blood has stained her and feebly points, gasping out his words through his oxygen mask. "Your sweater... bloody..." His laugh is a cough. "Just... like... in my... recurring nightmare... right?"

Keri looks down, confused. Her words, soft and faded, follow Peter as he hovers once more above the darkness that waits impatiently for him. "I... I don't understand. Your nightmares... there was never any blood... or me... in them... was there...?"

4

DRINK TO FORGET

Madeleine Swann

The taste of breast milk faded all too quickly, and the mother's arms dissipated. Ryan was once again thirty, in a room unchanged since his teenage years (mess included) with a mother as much unlike the fake one as a mole rat from a kitten. He toyed with a plastic car on the computer desk. He didn't know much about cars, but his best friend Rhys had, before… "Guess it's the internet again," sighed Ryan, browsing science facts and boobs. No, it wasn't going to be enough.

He grabbed his baseball bat and returned to Maison du Morph, pressing his thumb – the one he had left – into the security sensor. Once inside the AC cooled shop, he hummed along to easy listening music and browsed shelves of jars filled with a colourful candy floss substance. He kept his back to George, the bearded shopkeeper, who watched the news on a small screen. "I can see you, Ryan."

"Oh, hi George."

"Used your memories already?"

"No, I mean, I used one of them, I've got one left, but I just prefer to have a back up for like, the weekend, you know?"

"You know I can't do that." George stood straighter, giving Ryan full view of his video game T-Shirt and sizeable belly.

"I'm not, like, just getting home and chugging them."

"I know," said George, but there was no mistaking his look of pity. "You gotta be careful, though, man." They both stared at each other, silently screaming, one in need and the other with his finger on a button. Finally George micro-shrugged. "OK, I'll give you one more, but that's it for the week."

"Oh, no, that's great," Ryan reigned in his gratitude to avoid suspicion, "It's good to have spare." His breathing almost returned to normal.

"Sure. Supplies are limited, you know. We need to slow down." Ryan nodded though he didn't believe it. He pursed his lips at the unconvincing ethically sourced label on the bottle as George handed it over. "Hell of a thing, huh?" George indicated the war screeching from the tiny speakers. "All those kids."

"Yeah," Ryan stared lovingly at the door. He didn't want to hear about war or any bad thing resulting from it. He told people he didn't care which elicited a look of contempt, but the truth was he cared too much. At night, despite the flat's boarded up windows, he heard soldiers crawling through the garden grass or terrorists hiding beneath his desk who, of course, weren't there when he checked. The faces of the dead were branded on his eyelids. "K, I gotta go."

"Take care," George waved him off helplessly.

Ryan, back in his room, cradled the jar in one hand and one wrist. He didn't want to drink it straight sway, it needed to be savoured. He trawled the internet again, narrowly missing an ad. "Tired of fluffy clouds and childhood games?" it yelled in flashing script. "Want something hardcore? Fall down the rabbit hole with SickMind." The words were punctuated with unnecessary pictures of wartime bodies, promising a really horrible time for memory drinkers. Unwillingly curious, he typed SickMind into YouTube. Hundreds of videos splurged up, each with a horrible tagline. 'Iceman Murder,' said one, 'Kitten Crush,' said another. Faces twisted in horror on the thumb nails. Ryan clicked on the one with the most views.

A teenage girl held up a jar of dark brown goo. "This is a memory from Elsa Lang, the soldier who killed her own people. OK, here goes." She drank the whole thing and chatted about annoying school friends before the effects began. Subtle darkness passed over her face, deepening into writhing revulsion. "I don't like it," she whimpered, holding her hands to her eyes and rocking back and forth. Ryan had had enough and paused it, checking the comments below. "Fake," proclaimed some, "that stuff looks just like blended beef."

"No," said another. "I've tried it, it looks just like that." This was followed by random insults, and Ryan didn't bother looking further. He pushed Rhys's car backwards and forwards across the desk, wishing suddenly and violently that his friend hadn't hung himself. The memory jar hummed in his thoughts. He pulled it from his pocket and examined it. 'New Puppy,' it was called. It wasn't his favourite kind of memory, he preferred cuddles with parents or stories at bedtime, but he'd take it.

"Ryan." His mum was at the door. He jumped so hard, he thought his skeleton would fall out. She didn't try to hide her disappointment in his nervousness, one of the things that had kept him from being drafted. "There's a swap sale over on third street. Will you come with me?"

"I don't know, ma. They weren't sure if there'd be an air raid, it might be better to go later."

"It won't be there later," she actually gnashed her gums, making Ryan want to look away. "You know they only last an hour. That reminds me; don't forget your baseball bat. I'll bring the knife and those bottles of lemonade we've had in the fridge for a month." Ryan fumed as he watched her head for the kitchen and grab the out of date sugary liquid and kitchen knife, then shuffle back to the front room to watch appalling comedy shows. Just when Ryan's disgust reached it's apex, however, she cackled along to canned laughter and uninvited love surged inside him. She wasn't a bad, old bird, he decided, just a little coarse.

He turned back to the memory. "I've got enough time," he mumbled, draining the jar of it's contents.

The soft fur of the puppy's head faded, and he was again sitting in his chair at the computer desk. That was it for a week. Ryan slumped onto the desk.

The swap sale offered goods many would have sneered at only a few months previously. Everyone had to bring something, and there was always someone who wanted what you thought was rubbish. The lemonade had gone in the first few minutes, and the pair searched through Ryan's plastic bag of meagre objects. "Whattaya think about that CD rack?" said his mum, pointing ahead.

Ryan shrugged. "You should just let me download music for you. I'll show you how to use the sites."

"Nah," she wandered to the next stall, "they steal your identity that way."

Ryan was too annoyed to argue so he crossed the lawn to have a look at some cardboard boxes. "Hey," said the man standing beside them. "Got some real good ornaments in there. Wanna see?"

"Sure." Ryan passed him a handful of knick knacks, "shame this place has no memories, huh?" His casual remark sounded worryingly needy. Picking up on it, the man leaned forwards.

"Ted's got some over there."

"Really?"

"Sure, ginger fellow with the facial hair." Ryan saw him and was there faster than he could say thank you. Ted rolled an eye over him, obviously enjoying the tiny bit of power he had left.

"Anything I can help you with?"

"Um, just looking, really."

Ted pulled out a crate of the fluffiest, sweetest looking memories. Ryan wanted to cry or hug him. Ted grinned, "how many? We gotta do this quick."

Ryan checked his bag, finding only a torn book and Rhys' car which he had included in a fit of despair. He stared for a good ten seconds before Ted began shifting from foot to foot, looking out for intruders. Ryan sighed. "How many will this get me?"

Ted plumped his lips. "Three bottles? OK, four."

"Thanks," Ryan smiled weakly, watching him remove four and place the remaining hundred back out of reach. His hand and stump twitched. The old man placed the jars into a brown paper bag and handed them to him, his smile taking Ryan back to afternoon barbecues doing forgotten things like laughing. Despite his theatrics, the old man was sweet and kind, and Ryan knew with a sense of doom that he was going to steal the rest of the bottles somehow.

His break-in plan for later turned out to be unnecessary when loud shouts rang across the crowd. Ryan couldn't make out the words but the black clothes of the interlopers now charging towards the tables meant only one thing – thieves. People gathered their stuff and ran, some getting away and others collapsing beneath the weight of bodies. Screams of people being stabbed burned Ryan, and he craned his neck to find his mother, eventually seeing her waving the knife at a small group. The muscles of Ryan's feet pointed towards her, eager to rush in and defend. His mind, however, was watching Ted pack up his memories. He swallowed. "Hand them over."

"This ain't no time for jokes, kid."

Ryan brandished his baseball bat in a way he'd never thought he could. Ted saw his intention and meekly handed over the crate, though the look in his eyes spoke of midnight visits with a dagger. Ryan didn't care, grabbing the crate with his one good arm and sprinting off before the thieves noticed he had something worth stealing.

He burst into the flat, barricading the door with every piece of furniture in the front room and kitchen which, by now, was only a comfy chair and two seater sofa. He slammed the door of his bedroom and touched the jars as if the feel of the glass had medicinal qualities. He checked the labels, one after another, then stopped. There was something odd in the swirl of the blue cotton cloud inside this one, something he couldn't explain, almost as if he recognised it. He gripped it tightly in the pit of his elbow and turned the lid with his hand, draining it in one go. Immediately he regretted it; the soft happy colour was synthetic and the ugliness within was already making it's way into his blood stream.

He was in Rhys' room, the way it looked before the green wallpaper tore and the carpet faded. His hands were around Rhys' throat and his friend's face looked like a rotting cherry. Rhys, waving his draft letter, had been about to tell everyone Ryan had purposely sliced his own hand off with glass from the window, so now Ryan was choking the life from the person who had been his friend since nursery school. He just wouldn't die, it had taken so...so long. Ryan couldn't even hear the choking by the time Rhys' pupils shrank and his face slackened. His best friend was no longer his favourite person in the world; he was a source of panic. Ryan placed one end of the rope around his neck and the other beneath the desk leg. He was certain people had done it that way before, he was sure of it, but he paced his own bedroom like a cartoon criminal until everyone cried suicide. Only then had he wept for what he had done while everyone comforted him.

Back in his room now, Ryan curled into a ball, barely hearing the noise outside, the rhythmic banging almost matching his heart. Fists, shoulders and other objects crashed against the front door until the sounds of splintered wood echoed through the almost empty flat. Footsteps thundered towards him, yelling like outraged wildebeest. They barged into his bedroom door, evidently expecting it to be locked, but after a minute or two one of them tried the handle and they walked right in, laughing. Ryan didn't laugh. He did nothing, making no attempt even to hide. He covered his head with his hands but no blows came. Instead, there was a second or two while they regarded him, then one reached for the crate, and Ryan weakly tried to block her, looking up to see a young girl within the dark disguise. A whirl of stabbings began, and relief filled Ryan as air left his body, and the invaders carried their prize somewhere quiet to drink.

5

THE MONTHLY MEAL

Gordon Slack

John scans the three guests as they tuck into their food; the atmosphere in the room is of quiet contentment and he is glad that his house is being used as the monthly meeting place.

He pours himself some wine then gestures to the others. They willingly accept, particularly as it is now the custom to stay for the night. And very much so for Oliver who is some two hundred miles away from his political colleagues in central London.

Paula swirls her large glass and takes a sip; this is a Château Margaux 2009 which, with its notes of crème de cassis and cedar, is judged to perfectly complement the meal. She picks up a meat portion with her fingers, the accepted etiquette for these meals, and slowly chews the succulent and slightly garlic flavoured meat off the bone. Finger bowls with lemon are readily available. And another deep scoop of the mushroom and truffle stuffing makes the meal complete.

"Luscious, luscious", she mutters repeatedly, placing the bone in her mouth and sucking gently as she pulls it out, extracting the last of the taste.

Oliver regularly shuts his eyes as he savours the food and repeatedly licks his lips; this is his first visit and he will be back next month. And like the others, he had requested that the meat be cooked very rare; no-one is disappointed.

"John, you are going to need some help," Peter says, putting down his knife and fork and cleaning his spectacles with a napkin. He has a large scar on his left cheek which he begins to rub. "You are a good host and this location is ideal. I have made arrangements."

Replacing his spectacles, he consumes a final slice from his plate leaving just a heap of bones.

"They will be made available; chosen for perfect tenderness."

The mood lightens. Paula, having left the table, returns.

"John's made our favourite dessert. I saw it in the kitchen." Peter smiles at her, rubbing his scar more intensely.

Paula sits, pulling down her short skirt as she adjusts herself on the seat. Oliver, noticing this, runs his finger on his plate then slowly licks at the gravy sample.

"Would you ever have babies?" he says to her. Paula smiles then leans into Oliver and whispers, "Best if it's born here. We could then eat the fresh placenta as well."

Standing to clear the dinner plates, John hesitates. "My apologies, more meat for anyone?" The response is satisfied faces shaking side to side. John nods appreciatively then picks up the plate of left-overs and takes them to the fridge.

"I'll now serve dessert."

6

ANGLERFISH

Lee Betteridge

Sperry runs off down the dark lane and Dad bends over and picks up the poo. Sperry's poo. He uses a bag obviously, with his hand in. Picks it up; turns the bag outside-in. The cold breeze blows a waft into my face and it stinks and my tummy feels a bit spewey.

"Mmm," says Dad. "Chocolate mousse." He always says that and it's not funny anymore. He swings the bag as we walk. The lane is so dark I can't see my feet. Trees and bushes and nettles squash in at each side, but there's a lamppost coming up so I don't mind. And I'm with my Dad, so I double don't mind.

Sometimes Sperry does her toilet in the dark patches and it's hard to find, but you have to pick it up because flies crawl all over it and kids can fall in it and the maggots crawl into their eyes and make them blind. All because lazies don't pick the poo up. When Sperry does it in the shadowy bits Dad always says, "I'll look for it next to the lamppost – the light's better there!" He always says that and that's not funny either. We never go on till we've found it though, even in the dark. We always pick it up; turning the bag outside-in.

The sky above us is very black and very starry. It looks awesome when we come out of town like this, my dad and me, and see the starry sky in the dark. Mum doesn't like it – too dark and cold – but me and Dad do. Sperry loves it too.

I called Sperry the name Sperry, but I kind of did it by accident. We called her Perry first, but then I drew her a card with a picture of her and me, and a man with a laurelandhardy hat, like in those grey films that Dad laughs at. I always draw the man with the laurelandhardy hat. I don't know why – sometimes the drawings give me the creepers cos his face is grey and his eyes are always too big and dark. But I drew this card, and wrote on it JAKE LOVES PERRY, but because I put the space in the wrong space, it looked like JAKE LOVE SPERRY. Mum and Dad said that name was even better, so Sperry got called Sperry from then on. Dad tells that story all the time. He thinks it's funny.

Sperry jumps out from under a bush where she was sniffing stuff or eating rabbit turds, and she makes me jump. As she rushes past my leg I go, "Waah!" like a mickey-moron and Dad says, "It's alright Jake. It's only Sperry." He's holding my hand with one hand, and in the other he's swinging the lead and the bag.

I say, "She just made me jump, that's all. I'm not scared."

Dad looks down at me, his face glowing orange because we walk under a lamppost, and he smiles. "I know," he says.

I try to change the subject quick. "Why'd it smell a bit fishy?"

"Why'd *what* smell a bit fishy?" asks Dad.

"Sperry's poo. I got a nose full just then and she hasn't even been eating fish, just dog food."

"That'll be her glands," says Dad. 'Glands' sounds like an interesting word so I say it again but like a question.

"Glands?"

"Yeah. Dogs have glands next to their bumholes that let out a smell that says, 'Hi, I'm Sperry,' or whoever-"

"That's a bit disgusting," I say.

Dad says, "It sounds it to us, but that's how dogs recognize each other."

"That's why they sniff each other's bums?"

"Correct! And sometimes the glands get a bit bunged up. Sperry's do, anyway. And smell a bit fishy."

We're walking through a very dark bit of the lane now, the bushes on each side rustling in the wind and making me imagine huge bristling beasts – like giant feathered worms. I shiver at that. I think I might draw one of them when I get home. Probably with the man with the laurelandhardy hat riding on its back like it's a pony.

"I hate fish," I say, mostly so that I'm saying something and not thinking about the man with the laurelandhardy hat. "I hate how they smell, and how they taste, and how they swim." Dad just laughs. The really dark bit of the lane seems to be going on for miles and miles and I squeeze Dad's hand tighter. He squeezes tighter back. We walk round the bend with the bin and Dad drops Sperry's bag in. Then we're round the bend and another lamppost is up ahead.

Dad says, "Fish are very interesting, you know. There's one called an Anglerfish that lives in the deep dark depths of the sea. It has a thing that hangs in front of its face with a little light on – like a fishing rod with a torch on the end. When other fish see it they swim up thinking, 'Ooh that looks interesting,' and then SNAP!" Dad grabs me and I jump and Dad laughs.

"The Anglerfish has huge sharp teeth and eats the nosey little fish."

I'm quiet for a minute, thinking, and what I'm thinking is what a nasty trick for the Anglerfish to do on the poor little fish that think they're going to see something pretty and nice and glowy.

Then Dad stands on something and he says, "For eff sake! There's some dirty effers about!" He doesn't say 'effers' though, he says the real eff word, but I'm not allowed because I'm still a kid. So he tries to wipe the mess off – not one of Sperry's but someone else's dog's – by dragging his foot about in the grass at the side of the lane. The bushes are rustling again and I don't like it because I'm thinking of feathery worms with huge biting teeth and the man with the laurelandhardy hat.

All of a sudden, Sperry starts to bark.

Sperry never barks so me and Dad are both really shocked, but she stands further up the lane, barking then growling then barking.

She's just outside of the orange circle made by the lamppost, and Dad shouts her back, but she doesn't come. She looks back at us, and her ears are all flat and her tail is tucked under her bum, then she starts barking again. Then the lamppost turns off and everywhere is dark.

Mine and Dad's hands grip tighter to each other while Sperry barks. Then she stops suddenly, and there are two different noises very quick. One is Sperry doing a cry like she did that time I shut the kitchen door on her tail – *prroww!* – And the other is a like the noise your own head makes when you bite crunchy toast – *scrunch!* But they're both loud and together.

PRROWWSCRUNCH!

Then there are no sounds but the wind and the rustling and my tummy feels a bit spewey again. Sperry doesn't bark no more.

"SPERRY!" Dad shouts. "SPERRY!" His voice sounds wobbly. "COME HERE GIRL!" But Sperry doesn't come here. It's like something in the dark has scrunched her.

Dad says to me, "Stay here," and he does the worst thing he could ever, ever do – he lets go of my hand. Then he does an even worse thing – he starts walking to where Sperry isn't any more.

"Dad! Don't!" I say. He looks back at me and I can only see his face a little bit from the lamppost behind me. He smiles, but it's not a proper smile, and when he says, "It'll be OK," I don't believe him because I know he doesn't believe him either. My shadow stretches towards him all long and lanky down the lane, and Dad's feet walk away from me, over my shadow-knees and shadow-groins and shadow-shoulders and shadow-head. I stand totally stiller than I ever have, and just before I can't see him anymore he stops and turns.

"It'll be OK, Jake," he calls, and then I can't see him no more.

I stand all alone in the dark with the wind rustling the bushes and I think of Sperry crying and the scrunch sound and Dad saying it'll be OK but not meaning it and mum at home on her own and me in the dark on my own and the giant feathered worms shivering on both sides of me and I try not to – I try really, really hard not to – but the man with the laurelandhardy hat pops into my head like he always does.

Then Dad screams, "RUN, JAKE! FOR GOD'S SAKE, RUN." He shouts so loud it sounds like the sound is ripping his own throat out.

I'm too scared to run though. I should run back to the lamppost, I know that, but my feet are too scared and won't move, and my tummy feels spewey and so does my throat, and my eyes are crying. I'm stuck all alone in the dark and the only time I've been nearly this scared was when I watched a DVD with an 18 badge but even then I was nowhere near this scared. The darkness where Sperry went and Dad went is the blackest dark I've ever seen.

Then a light comes on.

The little light – not the lamppost – is white-ish not orange, and it's lower down. I think it might be someone holding a torch. I think it might be Dad, and my scared feet suddenly start walking to the light.

The two giant bristly worms I'm in-between shiver and shake in the wind but I take no notice. The light is getting nearer me and I'm getting nearer the light and I think it must be Dad, but I can't quite see.

I start to get scareder with each step because if it is Dad he'd be saying something like, "Hey Jake, everything's fine," and he isn't, and I start thinking of the fish that Dad had said about – the Anglerfish – that lures in little fish with its light, and then SNAP!

And then I can see who has the light. It isn't an Anglerfish, but it isn't Dad either. My heart hurts sharp and I can't breathe because it's the man with the laurelandhardy hat.

His face is grey and he's holding up an old lantern. His eyes are too big and too dark and they have things moving about in there that look like flies all over a dog poo. He's whispering something really fast and really quiet so I can't hear – like a *shh-shh-shh* sound – a bit like the wind. But then I blink and he doesn't have no lips so how could he be whispering? He just has long yellow teeth and I think he might be an Anglerfish after all.

He smiles at me – not in a nice way like Dad smiles at me, but in a hungry way like Dad smiles at a sandwich – and in the lane in the dark the two huge bristling bush worms rear up behind him like giant cobra snakes. They have long brown teeth made of twigs and I feel a pee come out and run down my leg. It's warm but it makes me shiver.

The man with the laurelandhardy hat steps nearer and his eyes are wriggling with flies and maggots and his lips are whispering again.

He holds out his hand and I hold it with the same hand I held Dad's, but it isn't warm like Dad's. It's frost and shivery and its taking me away and making the whole world all wrong, like a poo bag turning outside-in.

The End

7

WHOLESALE FLESH CLUB

Melissa A. Szydlek

Welcome to Wholesale Flesh Club.

We are pleased that you have joined us.

We have what you want,

and can make any wish reality. Guaranteed.

Membership
1. *Take time to familiarize yourself with the terms and conditions of membership.*

1. *Initial Membership Fee*
    1. *474 grams of **your** blood. No substitutions. We will know. Can be drawn onsite or brought in.*
2. *Penalty for using someone else's blood is the tip of your pinky finger.*

2. *Lifetime Membership Required (Final and Forever)*
    1. *Annual renewals due within five days of anniversary date.*

2. *Membership cannot be cancelled or nullified for any reason.*
3. *Annual Dues – Late Fees:*
   1. *Six – eight days = one inch of flesh.*
   2. *Nine – 15 days = the tip of your thumb.*

- *16 – 20 days = two fingers.*

1. *21 – 30 days = your heel plus two toes.*
2. *More than 30 days = forfeiture of life.*

Shopping
1. *All sales final – no refunds/exchanges, no exceptions.*
2. *Prices **not** firm –negotiation encouraged. Final prices agreed upon by member and Club representatives.*
3. *Products/Services guaranteed. All representations made by Club representatives will be honored.*
   1. *Failure by Club representative to fully inform member of product/service/pricing means forfeiture of representative's life and member receives a waiver on their next annual renewal.*
   2. *Should Club representatives fail to deliver all products/ services the representative forfeits their life and member receives one annual renewal waiver.*
   3. *Currency is in flesh and blood. Only. Penalties for attempting to pay with flesh/blood that is not yours:*
      1. *First offense = one pint of your blood plus one finger.*
      2. *Second offense = your hand.*

- *Third offense = your hand and one foot.*

1. *Fourth offense = forfeiture of your life.*

1. *Payment in your flesh or blood can be brought in or taken onsite.*

Enjoy your time at Wholesale Flesh Club.

*

The jar of blood was too large for his small 10-year old hands and Ty struggled as he walked. The bandage on his left hand didn't help. He held the jar close to him, hugging it to his chest while trying to follow the crude map on the back of the Club's pamphlet. He found the pamphlet by accident during a soccer game with his friends.

A kick resulted in the ball rolling under some bushes in the park, and Ty volunteered to retrieve it. The ball had lodged deep into the bush, and the pamphlet had been stuffed inside, twisted, as if someone had wrung the paper between their hands. He popped the pamphlet in his back pocket and went back to the game.

The pamphlet fell out of his jeans as he got ready for bed that evening, and he read it by the glow of a flashlight in bed. He was immediately intrigued.

Any wish, thought Ty.

Still, it had taken him days to work up the courage to cut into his hand, in the fleshy part between his left thumb and index finger. He used his mother's food scale to measure out exactly 474 grams of blood, taking the weight of the jar into account.

The blood, sloshing in the jar, was still warm as Ty hurried downtown. He thought the whole thing very odd – using blood like currency – but he felt hopeless. He'd already told the policeman and teachers at school about his stepfather, and the *things* he did to Ty and his mother. But no one did anything. No one helped. The superheroes he read about in his comic books never saved him.

I have to save myself, Ty thought as he hurried down Hardy Street. He turned right at the dead end, and entered an alley. It was dark in the alley; the sunlight of the late afternoon all but obliterated, and was surprisingly devoid of trashcans or dumpsters. And it was quiet, not even the traffic from Hardy Street permeated the space. When he reached the end of the alley, Ty hefted the jar closer to his shoulders and looked around. He expected a door, or a sign, but there was nothing. He felt defeated, having cut himself and having come all this way. He set the jar on the ground, looking around. Red brick, no windows in the buildings around the alley, surrounded him. Finally, his eyes focused on a spot tucked into a grout line on the wall. There was a small button. He moved the jar along the ground with his foot, the scraping sound deafening, and pressed the button. There was no noise, but a portion of the wall moved inward, revealing a passageway. Ty grabbed the jar and cradled it.

"In ya go," said a voice.

Ty hesitated. Someone sighed, sounding annoyed.

"In ya go! We ain't got all day. Ya comin' or what?"

Ty moved forward, but didn't go in.

"Awww, Christ," said the voice. A large man, rotund and tall, moved into the alley. He was wearing tan pants, a white shirt, and a long white apron, stained red. He was bald, and had a large upturned nose that reminded Ty of a hog.

"In or out, pal? I gotta shut the door, yeah?"

Ty nodded and moved into the darkness.

The hog-man followed behind Ty, pressing a button on the inside of the wall. The bricks moved back into place.

"Straight back, kid," the hog-man said, pointing down the dark corridor.

Instead of walking forward Ty stared blankly at the hog-man, who glanced at the jar.

"Ya joining?"

Ty nodded.

"Jesus, kid, can you speak?"

"Y-yes, sir."

The hog-man laughed. "Sir, that's rich. Come here, kid."

The man frowned as Ty gave him the jar, but his frown projected less annoyance, and was more akin to 'not bad'. The man twisted off the lid and took a long whiff.

"Mmmm," the hog-man said. "So innocent. Just right." He poured the blood into a large bowl that sat atop an impossibly large metal scale.

"Perfect," he said. "Kid, I probably woulda let ya slide on an ounce or two. Blood like yours is worth that much."

Ty nodded.

"Well, go on," the hog-man said, pointing down the long corridor.

Ty turned and walked down the narrow corridor, his eyes widening as it opened into a huge, warehouse-like room. Ty walked into an open space, like an old town market. Where he had expected glass cases displaying goods, he instead saw crude wooden stalls, with almost nothing on display, and hundreds of people walking, many of them yelling at the vendors.

Vendors and customers stood haggling, laughing, and moving their hands about as they spoke. As Ty merged into the crowd he saw another hog-like man, this one much thinner and taller, sitting on rickety bench with a sign behind him that read, "*MEMBERS ONLY.*" The man looked at Ty, raised his head and with a long intake of air, snorted and then nodded. Ty glided through the crowd like a dancer. The people were in drab clothing, but the vendors stood out with their long white aprons.

"Like butchers," Ty whispered to himself, and shuddered.

He moved slowly toward a stall where a bulbous-nosed hog-man stood screaming at someone Ty couldn't see through the crowd. The hog-man suddenly stopped yelling and frowned, leaning over the stall and staring with wild eyes. Ty let out a small gasp when a disfigured man came into view. The man had one arm and no legs, and was leaning on a crutch. His face was a series of scars and scabs, eyes lopsided and surrounded by old, white scar tissue.

The man said, "Please, I need the power to tell the future. I should've asked that the first time."

"What you do have would kill you if I took it," the vendor yelled. "I told you! I *warned* you, didn't I? You got nothing worth taking. Can't do it."

Ty moved on, the pleas of the man ebbing away. The more he listened, the more desperate customer pleas became, the hog-men stoic.

"We got rules," said one vendor.

"Not enough," said another.

And on and on the voices ebbed and flowed like waves crashing in Ty's ears.

"Okay, why not?"

"You sure?"

"You son of a bitch!" came a cry directly in front of Ty. A man at a stall with a bottle of what looked like blood resting on the counter and something wet wrapped in a white cloth stood shaking.

"'Taint his!" The vendor yelled. "Not your first time trying to con us, is it?" The vendor jumped across the stall despite his heavy frame, meat cleaver in hand.

The customer dropped to his knees. "Please," he said, "I need this."

"Ain't your first scam here!" the vendor yelled. He grabbed the man's right hand, pulled it abruptly to the stall and pressed down, the cleaver separating the hand from the man's arm at the wrist.

The man dropped to the floor, screaming and wailing. The vendor took the wrapped piece of whatever it was the man had offered him and threw it on the man.

"And I'm keeping the blood," said the vendor, walking back behind his stall. Two other hog-men appeared from the shadows and dragged the screaming man away.

"Next!" yelled the vendor, wiping blood from his face with a dirty cloth.

Ty was scared, and wanted to go home. *I'll pay my yearly membership fee and never, ever come back to this place.*

"Whaddaya need?" came a voice from Ty's left.

A short, squat, hog-man looked at Ty from behind a stall.

"Step up," the vendor said. "I hear that you have some very, very special blood. What are you looking for?"

Ty tried to speak, his words catching in his throat.

"Come now," the vendor said. "No one comes here on a whim. If you've gotten this far, you've already joined. Whaddaya *need*? More than anything in the world, son, whaddaya *want*?"

Ty watched as the man unrolled a heavy black cloth. Shiny, clean, and sharp instruments – knives, cleavers, hatchets – sat on the stall. Ty's eyes widened.

"We always keep the instruments clean," the man said. "Now, whad-daya want?"

"I…," Ty said, "I want my stepfather to stop."

"Stop what?"

"I want him to stop hurting my mom. I want him to stop hurting me. To stop doing those *things*."

"Hmmm…" the vendor said. "Do you want him to stop hurting your family and move on to another, or stop forever?"

"Forever," Ty said, with no hesitation.

"What'll you give?" the vendor asked.

"What's the price?" Ty said.

"What'll you give?" the vendor asked again.

"Blood," Ty said, his voice shaky.

"That's a start, boy," the vendor said.

"I want my stepfather, and abusers like him, gone."

"Ahhh," the vendor said, his eyes widening. "A very *tall* order. Very…*pricey*."

"I want to protect families, especially the children. I want the power, strength, skills, and will to take care of them all for the rest of my life."

"My, my," the vendor said, a look of surprise on his face. "What'll you give?"

Around them, negotiations ceased; attentions focused on Ty. The hog-noses of the other Vendors wiggled in excitement.

Ty's hog-man leaned closer. "What'll you give?"

"A pint of my very special blood. And…"

"Yeah?"

"My soul."

Audible gasps from the crowd, many from other hog-men.

Ty's vendor looked toward the other vendors, who only offered a few shrugs of confusion. Finally, he reached for his tools and held his hand out to Ty. "Sold," he said.

#

8

CASSANDRA'S BEASTS

Maryna Gaidar

The cold and blustery London of 1888 started a new day. The shutters were opened; the piles of fresh newspapers were sold by urchins. Their cracked boyish voices travelled from the darkest corners of the city, reaching even the porches of the West End. And their daunting message made housekeepers shut the windows.

Among other stores huddling together in Southwark, the establishment of a taxidermist welcomed guests with a freshly painted sign, which read 'Cassandra's Beasts'. Two pairs of eyes stared at passersby through a big lattice window. A stuffed wolf lurked in the dark of the store, and an owl hanging by threads as if flying to grab its prey. Those eyes and claws made a group of children in school uniforms stop and marvel at the beasts, so that the first client of the day had to squeeze past them.

The door opened with a melody of Chinese chimes. A man entered and faced a whole army of stuffed beasts. They were everywhere in the store, each and every one of them looking at him with vacant eyes. The man was obviously the offspring of a noble family, which you could tell from his pomaded mustachio and smug look.

"Good morning, Sir Marlowe," Cassandra Woodstock said, the only living creature in this dark realm arriving just in time. She was carrying a yellow-crested cockatoo sitting on a twig.

"Ah!" the young man exclaimed. "Capital! Capital!"

In her mind, Cassandra kept track of how many times Sir Marlowe said "Capital!" She couldn't help smiling.

"It's fifteen pounds," she reminded the excited owner of the bird.

Sir Marlowe produced the notes from his purse.

"Thank you." Cassandra smiled again.

Something always made Sir Marlowe stay for a little while, with this slender lady clad austerely in black since her husband's death. He usually stood there, pinching the right wing of his mustachio, watching how deftly she dealt with the money. She would say something witty and he would giggle idiotically.

"How can you stay here alone among all those beasts?" Sir Marlowe asked in a patronising tone.

"Oh, there are many beasts! But not here, Sir Marlowe."

He laughed, though with a vague feeling that she was teasing him.

"Capital!" Sir Marlowe grabbed his bird. "I loathed this creature when it was alive and almost sighed with relief when it died. But now you have turned this feathered and noisy chaos into a serene piece of art."

Marlowe took Cassandra's hand hostage and didn't let it go, while talking about how beautifully this bird would decorate his study, how many books his study housed and how much he wanted a pair of lovely children.

Cassandra was still grinning when Sir Marlowe left with his bird. The opened door let inside the sounds of the street, the high-pitched voice of the newspaper-boy among them.

"Jack the Ripper strikes again! A new victim! Read about a new murder! Jack the Ripper! Read all about Jack the Ripper!"

The smile vanished from Cassandra's face. She opened the drawer of her writing table and took out the calendar in which she was marking the days. She circled 1st October and checked the time intervals between the previous murders. The next one would happen in a fortnight.

The calendar was locked again in the drawer, and Cassandra returned to her workshop where she was working on her special collection that was not for sale.

*

The days dragged. By the time 15th October arrived, Cassandra had lost her ability to sleep. Every night, driven by insomnia, she went downstairs to her workshop and stayed there till dawn. She was looking at her collection of beasts. And the more she looked, the more reassured she became. She was ready.

Cassandra locked the door of her store and disappeared into the smog of night-time London. A cab delivered her to Whitechapel. It was her third visit to this Hell on Earth in search of *him*.

Tense as a chord, Cassandra walked around the district, her heart pounding. The faces of strangers were hiding under the broad-brimmed hats and hoods. The backstreets reeked of piss and danger. On one of the corners washed by the flickering light of a lamp, Cassandra stopped and looked back longingly in the direction of her faraway home.

At the entrance of a pub, two prostitutes were showing their breasts to a gentleman walking by. God knows what he was doing there. Possibly craving opium or looking for other forbidden fruit.

Cassandra clenched her fists and made herself resume her walk through Whitechapel.

After almost two hours of futile searching, Cassandra wandered into a lane that was even quieter and darker. The very air of this place was draining courage out of her. And then she froze at the sight of a figure that slipped out of a crevice between two decaying houses.

That man was silent, elusive. Fear crept up on her. Cassandra approached to examine the crevice from which he had appeared, and gasped with terror when she discovered the gutted body of a woman. She was wearing cheap and gaudy clothes. Her hair was dyed red with a saucy, little hat atop. The victim was lying contorted on the ground, in an attitude of agonising pain. Her face was a mask of terror.

Cassandra hurried back to the street, praying that the killer wouldn't come back to find her sneaking around. The sound of her heels clacked through the deserted mazes of Whitechapel.

At the road crossing, she saw him again, wearing a heavy leather coat flapping behind him like the wings of a bat. He was walking in long strides, carrying one of those doctor's bags.

Cassandra followed him up to Regent's Park and saw him enter one of the posh mansions at the edge of it. The plate on the gates read 'Edward Kendal, Lord Dartmoor'.

*

The next day, Cassandra was waiting on the bench opposite the mansion. Two boys were playing at war near her. They were moving their soldiers and shouting commands to each other. Such an innocent delight in life.

In an hour or so, the door of the mansion opened and let out its young, handsome owner. He looked at the skies as if predicting rain and set off for the park.

On one of its secluded paths, Cassandra caught up with him. Well-built and handsome, he certainly attracted female attention. A lady walking her pug appeared to be his acquaintance, so they stopped to make small talk. Cassandra observed that the man's manners were more typical of some pretentious fop than of a serial killer.

The lady with the pug touched the man's hand before parting from him. In return, he favored her with the most charming smile. He continued his walk and Cassandra followed.

"Excuse me, sir."

"Yes?"

He stopped.

"Do I know you?"

"I have a letter for you, sir," Cassandra blurted, before she could change her mind.

She held up a sealed envelope. The seconds seemed to pass slowly. The man was staring at the envelope but Cassandra couldn't divine what was going on in his head. Her hand was trembling. Finally, he took the letter and broke the seal. As his eyes moved along the lines, Cassandra was mouthing the words to herself:

'Dear Lord Dartmoor,

I have been searching for you since last year. And yesterday, our paths crossed at last. But rest assured I have no intention of turning you in.

Instead, I would like to invite you to see my private collection of stuffed beasts, that I am sure you will enjoy'.

He raised totally different eyes to Cassandra. Darkness was swelling in them, absorbing her like an abyss.

"You are very brave, Miss... what was your name?" Dartmoor tucked the letter into his pocket.

"I never told you," Cassandra said stiffly when she finally found her tongue. "I'm a taxidermist. That's all you need to know, Lord Dartmoor."

*

The steps leading to the cellar where Cassandra kept her personal collection were creaking under their feet. First, only vague silhouettes could be seen in the darkness. But then Cassandra hit the lights and a dozen lightbulbs revealed seven stuffed... humans.

Dartmoor didn't realise at first what he was looking at. And when he did, he burst into laughter. Fascinated by the exhibits, he came closer and started touching their skin and hair.

"You are a genius!" Dartmoor exclaimed. "A virtuosa! What am I in comparison to you? Just a butcher!"

"This one is my husband," Cassandra said, gesturing indifferently at the figure of a man at the front. He was a tall, thin chap, wearing trousers and frock coat. Every curl of his hair was immaculate.

"Soon after our marriage, I discovered his true nature. He raped our maids. And he punished me for not being obedient. One night he stuffed some of his rusty tools inside me. I was bleeding. I went to my parents' house, I could barely walk I was in so much pain. I sought their protection, but they only sent me back because my husband was important and no one wanted to fall foul of his terrible temper."

"So, you were a beautiful flower that turned out to be deadly," Lord Dartmoor said, clearly feeling philosophical while walking among the dead. Then he got interested in the quality of the buttons on one man's sleeves.

"After my husband, there were other men whom I judged and sentenced to death."

Dartmoor came dangerously close to her. Cassandra felt his breath on her face, smelling of wine and death.

"We're so much alike," he whispered, caressing her cheek and leaning to kiss her lips. "I am also cleaning this reeking city from its putridity."

"You think so?"

It was a quick stroke. Cassandra pulled the blade out of his body and stabbed him again. Dartmoor, shocked, stared down to see guts bulging from his belly. He choked with blood, spraying Cassandra's with it. Her wild roar filled the silent cellar. The beast inside her was unleashed. She stabbed Dartmoor again and again, until his blood dripped from her face.

Dartmoor tried to grab her by the collar, but his hands were already weak like ragdoll's. He fell to the floor with a thump.

*

London was woken up by newspaper boys selling yet more shocking news.

"Jack the Ripper is missing! The serial killer doesn't strike! Where's Jack?"

Cassandra was behind the counter, drinking her tea from an elegant china cup when Sir Marlowe came in. Three of his servants were carrying something bulky, under a cloth stained with blood.

"Ah! Sir Marlowe!" Cassandra put her cup aside and let him kiss her hand.

"Miss Woodstock! Capital! Capital!"

It was his forty-first "Capital!"

"I killed this foul creature only this morning," Marlowe said, sounding very proud. "What a hunt it was! Do you hunt, Miss Woodstock?"

"Sometimes."

"Fox? Boar?"

"I prefer somewhat fouler beasts," Cassandra said, tucking a pencil into her hair bun, ready to embark on her new order.

9

SUPER NITS

Lucy V. Hay

Look, I'm only telling you what I heard. My cousin, Sue? Her lot go to the same school as them poor kids, she heard all about it. So this is bona fide, first-hand goss I got here, okay?

Yeah, I will have another drink, ta. Much obliged.

… Anyway. My cousin Sue, she said it all started with this woman. Mel, Melanie, Melody? Something like that. Mel had five kids. All boys, poor cow. She was one of them single Mums … You know the type, does it for the benefits.

… Slurp. Oh, pardon me. Manners!

Now, don't get me wrong, I'm sure Mel was a good Mum, salt of the earth and all that … But we all got choices, yeah? And sitting around on your arse having kids shouldn't be one. Hey, I'm only saying what we're all thinking. But you can't blame Mel, blame the government I say.

Where was I?

Oh yeah. Mel, the single Mum. Her kids – I don't know their names

– were all ranged between about one and twelve, apparently. One of the little ones, he started scratching. Yeah you guessed it, he had nits.

Not a big deal, it happens, kids are crawling with disease. It's a fact. That's why I never had any. The little buggers start school or nursery or whatever and before you know it, you got bubonic plague or some shit. Yeah, I'm serious. Germ factories, kids are. Not that nits *are* actually germs, but you know what I mean.

This beer's all head, reckon you can top it up? Cheers.

So Sue reckons Mel ain't too worried, at first. There are nice, mild potions and lotions to get rid of nits now. Remember that acid-like crap we had to put on *our* hair? It was like sticking your head in a bucket of Agent Orange. It would kill the bloody nits alright, but half-kill you an' all! Kids these days got it easy. Maybe if they had to stick their heads in that shit they wouldn't be so damn sensitive. Depressed, they reckon. Do me a favour. They got more than we ever had.

Anyhoo.

Mel buys the potion and runs the nit comb through the lad's hair and her others.' Like I said, she's a good Mum. Bish, bash, bosh – Bob's your uncle. All sorted. Imagine Mel's surprise then when two or three days later the little one is scratching again! And worse, a couple of the other bigger boys are now, too. Sue tells Mel she bets the nits have become resistant or something to the potion. Well, you hear of it, don't you?

So, Mel goes back to the supermarket and gets another kind of nit lotion. Gotta feel for her really, cos that shit's expensive, especially times five kids. Bloody pharmaceutical companies, holding us all to ransom. Someone ought to call Trading Standards. Mel spends yet another evening up to her elbows in chemicals and soap suds, putting this crap on her kids' heads and holding 'em still while she pulls that teeny-tiny comb through their hair. She tells Sue she's marked it up to experience: "these things happen, blah blah blah".

Yeah, another pint is just the ticket. Ta, love.

Anyway, Sue tells Mel she saw on Facebook that tea tree conditioner keeps nits at bay. Who'd have thought it eh. Dunno what tea tree is, makes me think of a cup and saucer with a little tree growin' out of it, but whatever. Mel thanks her and reckons she'll buy some.

(They've even got "nit repellant" these days, but if you look on the back at the ingredients, you can see it's lavender oil! But call it "nit repellant" and you can sell it at a stupid mark-up to The Mum Mafia. Capitalism. Brave new world, eh?).

Fast-forward another two or three days. All of the kids are scratching now and so is Mel herself! This is really starting to take the piss, Mel's on her last nerve. Being a single Mum to five boys is hard enough without nits taking up residence like your mother-in-law who won't take the effing hint. By this point, even Sue is avoiding poor Mel at the school gates. (Well, she don't want to get 'em does she? Sue's got her twin girls to think about, they both got ridiculously long hair. You can't blame Sue, not really. And it's not like she knew what would happen next! None of us did).

... A whiskey chaser? Oh go on, you've twisted me arm. Make it a double.

Mel's had enough. She trots down to Argos, buys some clippers. The boys aren't happy with that, especially the eldest. Reckons he wants to grow his hair like that Belieber kid or whatever his name is (I saw the boy once, okay? He did look like he wanted to be on YouSnooze in one of those vee-logs, whatever). But Mel puts her foot down. It's the only way to break the cycle, she says.

So, Mel shaves the littlies' heads and finally persuades the two bigger boys it's the way forward. She even clips off her own hair! It's the middle of winter. She can wear a hat for the school run or doing the shopping, otherwise she's at home. By the time spring comes around it'll have grown back enough so she can have one of those cute little pixie cuts. She's always been a good problem solver. Yes, Mel is feeling pretty pleased with herself, all told.

It took the school at least four or five days to clock all the kids weren't there, can you believe it? I wonder what we pay our bloody taxes for, sometimes. Poor little nippers. I'm surprised the neighbours didn't notice no one coming in or out, though. But that's life today, innit? Everyone keeps themselves to themselves. Not like when we were kids and everybody knew one another's business. It was said you could cough at the top of the high street and be dying of lung cancer by the time it reached the bottom. Awww. Those were the days.

So obviously, none of us know *exactly* what happened next. But Sue's eldest, he works down the garage and he reckons one of them police what was at Mel's place came in and told him this. I believe the lad. It's not like they're gonna put this shit on the news, is it? They don't want people freaking out. Besides, there's bound to be like, an injunction from the pharmaceutical companies, mark my words.

So Sue's Eldest said the policeman and his partner couldn't get any answer at Mel's place. Curtains drawn, place in darkness. Yet the letterbox was crammed with post and the kiddies' bikes were still in the garden. It didn't look like Mel had done a moonlight flit, but you hear of it. Single Mums can't pay the rent, so they do one.

But you gotta check. The policeman broke the panel in the front door. Well you can't blame him, there was kiddies inside. The two of 'em stopped in the hall and called ahead, hoping Mel would come out, guns blazing, wondering what the hell was going on. But the place was quiet. Like, eerie silent. Apparently the policeman and his partner said that's when they knew. Death hovered over the house like a bad smell.

The two of 'em checked through the house. Opening the door closest, they found the kitchen. Inside, it was the pits. Dirty bowls and plates, half-eaten food – everywhere. Mould. But worst of all, slime. Like a giant with a bad cold had sneezed all over the joint. The policeman told Sue's Eldest that shit glowed, like it was radioactive or summat. But that bit I reckon he edited in to his memory later. Been reading too much Spiderman. Whatever it was, it was grim. End of.

As they crept down the hall, the policeman's partner's foot brushed something. Musta been the jumpy type cos apparently he leapt five feet in the air towards the stairs! It was the size of a cat, the policeman told Sue's Eldest. And not one of them cute little cats you can keep in your handbag neither; one of them big, fat thuggish Tomcats you wouldn't want to meet down a dark alley. 'Cept it wasn't a cat.

... Yeah, yeah. Keep your pants on. I'm getting to that part, innit?

It was a shell. Not like an egg, but like an insect. Almost like a snake had shed its skin, I suppose. They didn't touch it. They'd never seen anything like it, all pincers and claws! They thanked their lucky stars that whatever it was had vacated its skin and scuttled off somewhere.

They found them all in the living room. The three little ones were on the sofa, like they'd been watching TV together. The older two boys were on the floor, like they might've been playing a game. Mel was seated on her armchair, a cup of cold coffee on the table next to her. All in all, a lovely little domestic scene, right? Except for one hideous little fact: *every single one of them was drained of blood.*

They were husks, all six of them. But not like that weird insectoid shape in the hall. Their bodies were crackly, like paper, as if they might fall to dust if you blew on them. I'm not having you on, I swear. It was said later the police's forensics lot found strange puncture marks on top of all of their bald heads.

Like teeth marks, they said.

Nits.

Nits the size of cats.

I'll let that sink in. And where the hell had the rest of them all gone??? Doesn't bear thinking about. Hopefully far away from here. I took some flowers down to Mel's house; put 'em outside in the garden. I'm pleased to say there were loads of bouquets there, all of us showing our sympathies, the town united. 'Cos children are the future, innit? Well, not these ones, obviously. But in general, I mean.

... Got any pork scratchings?

10

A KILLER EVENING

Chris Jeal

I once slaughtered a mini-van full of armed guards using just a potato peeler, now that took confidence. I slip my hands from the car's steering wheel and clap them together.

'Stop doing that, you weirdo,' says June from the passenger seat.

'What? I'm not doing anything.'

I'm not crazy, I promise, the whole 'clap' thing is a technique I found online for boosting confidence. I won't bludgeon you with details, but it includes thinking of a time you felt confident in the past and clapping your hands.

So far it's just made me look like a nut.

June places her hand on my knee and gives it a squeeze.

Have you ever met a girl who is so special you'd sleep on a bed of razor blades just to wake up next to her? June is that girl for me. We met six months ago on KillerCupid.Com. It's a dating site where serial killers can meet like-minded people, hang out and make memories together. On a side note, did you know there's a site exclusively for cat lovers? That's weird, right?

I turn the car into the driveway. The headlights unearth a small cottage from the darkness. I kill the engine, get out and look around backed by a soundtrack of screaming wind that's beating the shit out of the spooky looking trees – we're in the haunted arsehole of nowhere.

June gets out and makes her way to me. 'You nervous? You've been acting weird all the way here.'

'Have I?'

'You took a wee by the side of the road and gave yourself a clap. You must have been very impressed with yourself.' She pulls me close, flashes that killer smile. 'Relax, mum and dad are going to love you. Just like I do.' June kisses me. She tastes like peaches and electricity (and chicken strips, we got hungry on the long drive here).

She takes my hand, leads me towards the cottage.

Being a killer doesn't make meeting the potential in-laws any less daunting. I can't exactly murder them if they don't approve, at least not without ruining the evening. Also, it doesn't help that June's dad is the infamous serial killer known as The Tradesman (on account of him using a hammer to kill his victims.) Now, there's no king of the serial killers or anything, but if there were – it would be him.

June knocks on the door and shouts through the letter box, 'We're from the local church. We're here to talk to you about God and stuff.'

She straightens up, shoots me a wink.

Moments later the door swings open. 'June-bug!' a plump woman with a tea towel slung over her shoulder, gushes. This is Rose, June's mum. June-bug? That's a great pet name, why didn't I think of that? I call her Loony-June when she gets angry at me for putting my kill knives in the dish washer – it all gets sterilised, what's the problem?

Rose pulls June in for a squeeze, 'Hey, lovely.'

She turns her attention to me. I offer my hand but it's ignored, and I'm pulled in for a hug, too. She squeezes hard like she's trying to get the last remnants of toothpaste from the tube. 'Welcome to our house, Simon.'

'Thanks, it's lovely to meet you.' This is a dull response, I know. But when you have voices in your head screaming *flay the flesh!* and asking things like, *how many knives could that man's guts hold?* – dull is a win in social situations.

Rose ushers us inside informing us that she has a chicken in the oven before heading down the hall towards the smell of burning.

June whips her jacket off, looks to me for mine.

Her eyes snap to something hanging from my pocket.

She wrinkles her nose and plucks out the offending object, a mask I made from an old potato sack. I cut jagged holes for the eyes and used staples for the smiley mouth – fuck you, Blue Peter.

'Why'd you bring this?' she says, waving it in front of me just like the time she found a severed ear in the sock drawer.

'I feel naked without it.'

She holds it to her nose. 'When was the last time you washed it? It smells like wet feet.'

'Bug!' A voice booms along the hallway.

I pluck the mask from June and stuff it back in my pocket.

Frank hulks towards us. He looks even more terrifying in the flesh than he does in June's Instagram pics. I fight the urge for a confidence clap.

He scoops up June. 'How's my baby-bug?'

'I'm good, Dad.'

I stand awkwardly, waiting for their embrace to end so I can offer my hand. Frank turns to me. 'You alright, fella?' he asks, his voice sounding like gravel mixed with go-fuck-yourself. He grabs my hand and shakes it so hard I wonder for a second if I'll ever masturbate again. 'I hope you last longer than her last bloke,' he grins, eyeing me up. 'You'll be easier to bury, though, you're shorter than him.'

June nudges him. 'Dad, be nice.'

My mind races to find a witty comeback, something to charm, to impress... 'I'm of average height.' Shit. Fallen at the first hurdle.

Frank offers me a pity smile and turns to June.

I retreat inside my head, to my brain-cinema to think about what I should have said:

How I Wish That Really Went.

A daydream *by* Simon Getts

'You'll be easier to bury, though, you're shorter than him.' Frank grinned.

'I doubt that, old man. I'm no easy touch. You'd be in grave trouble if you tried.' Simon smiled, flashing that perfect smile. June swooned and got moist just by looking at Simon. He was handsome, hilarious and had an above average size penis. Frank spoke, 'I really respect you standing up to me. Plus, you are hilarious. You're like the son I never had.' Frank embraced Simon. Simon was the best.

The End.

… 'Oi, you deaf, I said do you want a drink?' Frank asks, tearing me from my thoughts.

'Er, that'll be great. Thanks.'

'Out here.'

I follow his huge lumbering frame through a doorway into a cold garage that smells of petrol. There's a workbench, power tools and junk poking out from under dirty sheets – this is probably where he comes to do 'bloke' things like taking engines apart and call stubborn bolts 'cunts'.

'In there.' He points to a fridge at the back of the room. 'I've only got beers. I ran out of Shirley Temples.'

Is that a joke? I think that's a joke.

I manoeuvre around the workbench, 'Hhurpp!' a groan from under one of the sheets. I jump back and instinctively reach under my shirt for my knives but remember they're at home on a 65° Eco-wash. Frank's laughter fills the room. 'Sorry, boy. Forgot to warn you about old Porkchop.' He pulls away the sheet. Bound to a chair with a rag stuffed in his mouth is a man caked in blood.

'You fuckin' bricked it, mate.' Frank tells me, his words riding on chuckles. 'He's a little project. Have to keep active, you know. Like they say; use it or lose it.'

'Good one,' I mumble.

I'm sure he did that on purpose. I feel like I'm ten-years old again, being sized up by the school bully. Frank sticks a kick into Pork-chop, 'Hhurrp!' then strangles two beers from the fridge. He hands me one; I half expect him to snatch it back before I can take it.

He nods at his victim. 'So what do you think?'

I take a sip of beer, assess Frank's handy work. Porkchop's arm is broken, and he looks like he's been sufficiently cuddled with a crow bar, but Frank's rope work is sloppy. I'm surprised Porkchop hasn't wriggled free and made for the woods. Of course, I lie: 'Looks good. I like how you've fractured his radius, thus rendering his right arm incapacitated.' I don't usually talk like this. I'm acting weird, trying to impress. Who knows, maybe I have?

'Fuck you on about? I just smashed him with me hammer so he was easier to tie up.'

I want to retreat into my head-cinema, but the projectionist has comfort eaten all the pic' n' mix and is projectile vomiting in the aisle.

Frank gulps beer. 'June reckons you've done twenty-one kills.'

'Yes, I'm hoping to double it over the next few years.'

'I had thirty-nine kills when I was your age.' Frank opens a drawer, removes a large blood-stained club hammer. He holds it up and grins at it. 'Me and the Persuader here terrorised London for years. Eighty-two dick heads I clubbed to death.'

I'm in a pissing contest I can't win. Best to just forfeit: 'Wow, that looks big and heavy. Bet it gives you arm ache.'

'I swing it, not wank it off.'

' ……..' I've got nothing.

Without warning, Frank whips the hammer up and slams it down onto Porkchop's hand. Bones crack, fingers rupture like overstuffed sausages. A muffled scream fills the room.

'I love that sound,' says Frank. He points to a smaller hammer on the workbench. 'Wanna have a punt?'

'No thanks. I'm more of a stabber-er-rer.' I say, jerking my arm back and forth, doing the universal sign for stabbing – *fucking* idiot.

'Boys, dinner's ready,' Rose calls.

'Grub's up.' Frank says. He heads out, the Persuader at his side.

In the kitchen, Frank sits at the head of the table and rests his hammer next to the mashed carrots. I sit next to June. She squeezes my hand and flashes me a grin, probably hoping that me and her dad have been having a back-slapping good time and he approves of me. 'Where'd you find this one?' Frank asks. 'Porkchop made him piss his pants.'

That's it, if I split up with June, the next girl I date is going to be one who's lost her parents in some tragic accident.

'I doubt that, Dad. Simon's got London in a panic. The filth are calling him the Night Terror.'

'Ha, Night Terror? Sounds wanky. Yer mother farted in her sleep last night, that was a night terror!'

'Frank,' Rose tuts.

Out in the hallway, a door bangs open, a disorientated Porkchop stumbles past the kitchen. He spies the front door – he's off. Ha! I knew those ropes wouldn't hold him. I win! I forget myself for a moment: 'Your rope-work is terrible, I knew it wasn't going to hold him, you old cunt.'

The room is silent.

June's fork drops into the peas.

I clap my hands.

Frank stares at me. 'Old cunt am I?'

Gulp '… yeah.' I hold his stare.

He cracks a smile, 'Ha! You got some front.' He slaps me across the back. Wait, what just happened? I insult him; he likes me now? Frank looks to the Persuader, then to me. 'Wanna see who can catch him first?'

I stand, whip my mask from my pocket and jam it over my head. 'I'll cut his filthy soul in half.' I look around for a weapon. I grab the carving knife next to the gravy boat and look to Rose. 'May I borrow this, please?'

'Why, of course, dear.'

Frank grabs the Persuader and stomps off. I go to follow, June grabs my wrist, gazes into my eyes. 'You show him what you got, baby.' I nod frantically, eager to leave, like a little boy desperate to join his new friend. She kisses me. I dart out of the kitchen.

As I leave the house, I hear Rose tell June she thinks I'm a keeper.

Best. Day. Ever.

11

RUMOUR HAS IT...

Jacky Dahlhaus

Rumour has it that I killed.

They put the cuffs on my wrists and ankles and yank the chain, just to make sure they are tight enough. I am rather small, and I think they're afraid my tiny hands will escape from the metal. I shuffle out of my cell and onto the prison block landing, one guard in front of me holding the chain, another guard behind me. They guide me towards the exit. My fellow female inmates hoot and yell. "Good luck!" is the only thing that I can discern.

Rumour has it that I killed five men.

They take me through the transfer formalities, papers get signed, my body searched. I am guided outside where the police van is waiting to take me to the courtroom. As I shuffle into the daylight, I try to shield my eyes. It's been a long time since I saw the sun. One of the guards pushes me along and into the van.

Rumour has it that I killed five men with the help of the devil.

After my chain is connected to the floor of the vehicle, the guards sit down on either side of me and the doors are closed. We drive off.

It is a short, bumpy ride. The guards don't talk to me, but, from the corners of my eyes, I am aware they're watching every move I make.

Rumour has it that I killed five men with the help of the devil, brutally.

When we get to the back of the courtroom building, the guards hurriedly get me out of the van. Paparazzi were lying in wait and their cameras are now flashing like strobe lights.

One of the guards quickly throws a blanket over me and they push me into the building. I stumble on the doorstep. A guard grabs my arm and pulls me upright. He overestimates my weight and nearly lifts me off the ground.

Rumour has it that I killed five men with the help of the devil, brutally, leaving them mutilated.

I am sat down in a little room and my lawyer comes to talk to me. His words go in one ear and out the other. My gaze wanders around the room. The lawyer cleans his glasses while he's talking. His words go on and on. After he's finished with his speech, he asks me if I'm ready. I nod. He indicates to the guard, and we're taken out of the room into a maze of hallways. The floor is made of green, marbled linoleum, like the one we had at school.

Rumour has it that I killed five men with the help of the devil, brutally, leaving them mutilated, their guts pulled out.

We enter through large, wooden doors into the courtroom. It is filled with a lot of people, most of them unknown to me. I see the jury on the far side, some family in the benches on my left. My Dad waves. My Mom cries. After I get seated at a table at the front, I turn to look behind me. The balcony is filled with paparazzi.

Rumour has it that I killed five men with the help of the devil, brutally, leaving them mutilated, their guts pulled out into the shape of a pentagram.

The judge enters. Everybody rises. We sit down again and the trial goes into full swing. As various people give their evidence, I study the jury. They are all sorts of people: old, young, male, female, some well-dressed, others not so well. They're all looking at me. I put my hand on the Holy Bible and swear that I will tell the truth.

Rumour has it that I killed five men with the help of the devil, brutally, leaving them mutilated, their guts pulled out into the shape of a pentagram, their genitals detached.

After the jury hears all the evidence, they retreat to their quarters. I am guided to a side-room. My lawyer paces the room, to and fro, again and again. Hours pass, and I can hear the clock tick. I wait patiently. We are finally called back into the courtroom.

Rumour has it that I killed five men with the help of the devil, brutally, leaving them mutilated, their guts pulled out into the shape of a pentagram, their genitals detached and stuffed into their mutilated mouths.

The judge asks the jury for their verdict. One jury member stands up and says, 'not guilty.' The whole courtroom goes up in cheers. The judge calls the room to order and has his final speech. He talks about how evil the nature of the crime was and how unlikely it is that a tiny, fragile woman such as myself could have committed such a heinous act. He ends his speech with the words, 'you are free to go.'

Rumour has it that I killed five men with the help of the devil, brutally, leaving them mutilated, their guts pulled out into the shape of a pentagram, their genitals detached and stuffed into their mutilated mouths, after they raped me again and again.

The guard takes my cuffs off. My lawyer embraces me, and I shake a lot of hands. Both my parents are smiling. They put their arms around me as they take me outside. The sun shines on my face. This time I direct my face to it, towards its heat. In the reflection of a window, I see a red glow in my eyes, and a wicked grin creeps on my face.

12

ME AGAIN

Scott Merrow

It was just before midnight — the witching hour they call it — on a dreary night in late November. Cold rain pelted the windows, but I was comfy in my favourite chair, wrapped snugly in a warm blanket, reading. A fire crackled in the fireplace nearby, helping to stave off the late autumn chill trying to invade my drafty old house.

Suddenly, *whoosh*, I felt a blast of cold air like I've never felt before. It seemed to rush up from the floor and pass straight through me from bottom to top. It was absolutely frigid, deathly cold; it chilled me to the bone — no, even deeper, it chilled my very soul. My teeth chattered. I shivered uncontrollably. Then it was gone.

Still quite shaken, I glanced around the room. The windows were closed up, but it was an old house, not as tight as it once was, and the wind raged mightily outside. It must have been a draught, what else? Just the same, it took a few minutes before I could settle down to my reading again.

I hadn't read more than a sentence or two when…

C-r-e-e-e-e-e-a-k.

What was that?!?

A creaky board above me. I cocked an ear upward and listened carefully. A few moments of silence. Then…

C-r-e-e-e-e-e-a-k.

C-r-e-e-e-e-e-a-k.

C-r-e-e-e-e-e-a-k.

Footsteps! Someone was in my attic!

I rushed to the stairs, livid that someone was violating the sanctity of my home. At the same time, I felt an acute sense of dread over what I might find lurking in the shadowy room above.

As I opened the door to the attic, I was instantly hit with an acrid smell — smoke! Fire! Abandoning all caution, I dashed up the stairs.

I saw him immediately. Across the room, a man appeared to be prying a brick loose from the chimney, creating a small hole. A thin wisp of smoke streamed out.

"Hey! What are you doing?" I shouted, as I darted toward him. Then I stopped suddenly as I noticed something very peculiar — the man's feet weren't touching the floor. He was floating a few inches above it. And I could see straight through him. He was a ghost!

At the sound of my voice, he turned to face me, and I felt an even greater shock — he looked exactly like me.

A shiver ran up my spine.

"What the…? Who are you?" I demanded.

"I'm you," he answered, matter-of-factly. "More accurately, I'm your ghost."

I stared in disbelief. It took a few seconds for his words to sink in.

"Impossible," I said. "How can you be my ghost? I'm not dead yet."

"True," he replied. "But we all die sometime, and so will you. What we don't realise while we're living is that 'when' doesn't matter. The one-way flow of time is an illusion."

"What? What on earth does that mean?"

"It means this: all moments of time — past, present, and future — exist together," he explained. "The idea of a forward flow of time is a human invention. It's the only way human minds can grasp it."

"How do you know all this?"

"A lot of things became crystal clear the moment I died. I suddenly understood, well, everything, really. Including the true nature of time."

"So, you're saying you know everything?" I was understandably skeptical.

"I think so."

"Well, when *will* I die, then?"

"Soon enough, I think. But that's why I'm here."

"Why?"

"To warn you. When I understood the flexible nature of time, I decided to seize the opportunity and come back to let you know about this chimney. It's dangerous. The bricks are loose. Sparks could escape and ignite all these books and old papers," he said, gesturing around the room with the sweep of an arm. "They're like tinder."

"So, is that how I'll die? In a fire?" I shuddered.

"I don't think so, but that's what I'm working on right now. I came to warn you about this chimney, but instead I thought I could just fix it and spare you the confusion of encountering your own ghost."

"Well, that didn't work," I reminded him.

"No. Sorry. Fixing this isn't as simple as I thought it would be. For one thing, I'm a spectre. I'm not exactly solid."

He gestured to his torso. I could see right through it.

"So it isn't easy for me to grab these bricks and move them. If I really concentrate, I can move them a little, but not enough to plug the hole. Maybe you could help me."

I stood on a pile of books near the chimney and reached up to help him. I grabbed a brick and realised instantly that it was a mistake — it was fiery hot. I pitched backwards off the stack of books. Unfortunately, I pulled several loose bricks with me, and the chimney collapsed. I crashed through the rickety attic floor, and plummeted downwards into the study where I had been sitting so comfortably just minutes before.

I crashed through that floor too, landing on the ground floor below.

A fraction of a second later, the hot bricks landed on top of me.

That's when I died.

Some time seemed to pass, but of course, that was an illusion. The next thing I remember, I was floating in mid-air, gazing down at my own dead body.

Then everything became clear. Everything. Including the true nature of time. I decided to go back and warn myself about the chimney. But I wasn't sure if my living self would understand the situation. Maybe I should just fix the chimney myself, I thought.

I willed myself to the time just before the accident.

I floated upwards, through the floor of the study, accidentally passing through my own living body sitting in the chair reading. I felt it shiver.

Up through the ceiling to the attic. I floated toward the chimney. I didn't have much experience as a ghost yet, but I was pretty sure I would need to be a bit more solid. Anyone who could float through a floor probably couldn't grab hold of a brick, much less move it.

So I willed myself some substance. It took some experimenting, but soon I felt the familiar pull of gravity, and I began slowly sinking. Then faster. When my feet made contact with the attic floor, I felt the floorboards yield slightly under my weight.

C-r-e-e-e-e-e-a-k.

It took a few seconds to adjust to my new mass. Then I walked the few steps to the chimney.

C-r-e-e-e-e-e-a-k.

C-r-e-e-e-e-e-a-k.

C-r-e-e-e-e-e-a-k.

I floated up and tried to move a brick. It was difficult.

Then I heard someone coming up the stairs.

A man's voice cried out. "Hey! What are you doing?"

I turned toward the voice.

It was me.

13

DEAD COMEDIANS

Simon Cluett

They're not laughing, thought Finch, *why aren't they laughing?* He could only see the first few rows, but it was the same indifferent expression that stared back at him. And what was that noise? *Click... click... clickety-click.* Was someone knitting?

The theatre seated five hundred but was only a quarter full. Disappointing, but if the crowd was on his side it might still have been possible to blow the roof off. Unfortunately, by the time he was just halfway through his first routine, Phil Finch knew the building's structural integrity was destined to remain intact.

"You see them on packets of cereal don't you? Tins of soup for example. There'll be a little picture on the label of some cream of tomato... in a bowl... with a spoon... and below it the words 'Serving suggestion.'"

Someone in the audience blew their nose. It was a loud *parp* that annoyingly provoked more laughter than he'd managed since walking onto the stage.

"*In* a bowl *with* a spoon mind you. Proper lah-de-dah."

Nothing. Not a sausage. And that was the best bloody line in the whole bit.

"It wouldn't have occurred to me to put a spoonful of piping hot cream of tomato in a bowl and use a *spoon* of all things to transport it from point A to point B. I would have clawed it into my mouth with my own bare hands."

"You're shit!"
As heckles went it was uninspired and Finch had a well-stocked arsenal of witty put-downs for just such an occasion.

"Listen pal, do I come over to your place of work and tell you how to sweep up? No I don't. So pipe down, I'm working here."

Bang! Zoom! And that, my friends, is how it's done.

Except it wasn't. The line was intended to belittle the heckler while getting the rest of the audience back on my side – but still no one was laughing. Not in the stalls, the gods or the boxes. The quarter-full venue was as silent as a place devoid of sound.
"Is this thing on?" Finch said, tap-tapping the mic.

"Tell us a joke, you twat!"

Finch grew up in the 70s and had fond memories of being snuggled up with his Dad watching comedians of the day lean against mics on primetime TV. With only three channels to choose from, the odds were good that someone like Bernard Manning would be on, reeling out gags about the Irish, Pakistanis, blacks, Jews or the Mother-in-law. And it had been OK to laugh, because there was no such thing as political correctness back then. That era of stand-up, and the laughter he'd shared with his Dad, had inspired Finch to become a comedian. It was why he went on stage, night after night, illuminated by a single spotlight, to amuse a crowd of strangers.

Bad gigs were an occupational hazard but Finch could usually tease out a few begrudging chortles before the curtain came down. This particular crowd, however, may as well have been at a wake. So Finch did the only thing he could in the circumstances; he dropped the mic and walked off stage.

The hotel room was the same as so many others he'd stayed in over the years. It was boxy, bland and offered only the most basic amenities. Room service was available at an over-the-odds tariff but ordering a sub-standard BLT was not high on Finch's to do list.

How best to kill himself? That was the question. The serving suggestion bit had failed in spectacular fashion and, in so doing, unravelled whatever shaky confidence he'd had in the rest of his act, his ability as a performer and his life in general. He'd found himself teetering on the brink of that dark precipice before. Plagued by self-loathing, he would force himself to compose a list of pros and cons associated with continuing the joyless grind of existence. *Angela* had always appeared high on the list of pros but alas, no more. He'd put the kibosh on that relationship after an ill-judged fling with a girl from Guildford.

Too much competition

Dwindling crowds

Low profit margin

Bad reviews

Zero TV interest

Old, tired & fucking sick of it all

Without Angela's name to tip the balance, arguments for seeing the deed through were compelling. But should he hang himself using his belt and a sturdy cupboard rail or run a hot bath, consume a cocktail of pills and booze, then drift away on a velvet cushion? Slitting his wrists had never been an option as he'd read it was necessary to draw the blade vertically along the wrist rather than horizontally. The latter was considered to be a cry for help, while the former severed multiple arteries to ensure maximum blood loss. Finch was a squeamish soul and so the velvet cushion seemed the more preferable option.

He twisted the taps, adjusting hot and cold to an optimal temperature and unpacked his bag of pills (in the form of barbiturates) and booze (in the form of a bottle of vodka).

"… I don't mind giving a reasonable amount, but a *pint*? Why, that's very nearly an armful!"
The telly in the bedroom-cum-living area had switched on, seemingly of its own accord. *The Blood Donor*, a classic episode of Han-

cock's Half Hour, was showing. *Suicide*, Finch thought as he locked off the taps, *could wait*. He smiled at the loveable curmudgeon, although the irony of watching someone who killed himself aged 44, was not lost on him.

The telly blinked off.

"Load o' fucking rubbish."

The accent was Mancunian and dripped with a rich, throaty smugness.

Finch's double-take was executed to perfection, only this wasn't some well-rehearsed theatrical technique for getting an easy laugh from a compliant audience; this was the real deal. The obese man was wedged into one of the room's two tub chairs. The curtains were drawn, and since the TV had been switched off, it was hard to tell where he ended and the chair began.

"Here's one... a Paki, a darkie and this little Jewish fella walk into a pub – "

"You're Bernard Manning."

"Give that man a cigar. Two nuns in a bath – "

"But... but... you're dead."

"Fuck me, if brains were dynamite, you wouldn't have enough to blow your own hat off. I'm a chuffin' ghost, ya prick."

Finch took a tentative step forward and flicked on the bedside lamp. Death, it seemed, had done little to change Manning; he still had the same bloated, jowly face, the same piggy eyes, the same ill-fitting suit and the same dicky-bow tie.

"Me grandad died in Auschwitz. He fell out of a machine gun tower."

"Why are you here?"

"I were in Bradford the other week. I felt like a spot on a fuckin' domino."

"I said, why are you here?"

"Alright luv, don't get your knickers in a knot. Heard you was thinkin' of doin' somethin' daft."

"Define daft."

"I mean toppin' yourself, you soppy bastard."

"And you're here to talk me out of it?"

"That's right, sunbeam. It's a fuckin' intervention."

"So this," said Finch, more to himself than to Manning, "is what a mental breakdown looks like." He turned away and headed back to the bathroom where his velvet cushion awaited.

"I went to see that Pavarotti last week. He were a right miserable cunt. He don't like it when you join in."

"'Ere Bernard, we're SUPPOSED to be giving 'im a good TALKING to... so stop messin' about!"

Kenneth Williams, now? thought Finch. "Seriously?"

"What do you think I'm doing, you chuffin' great poof?"

"How very RUDE!"

Finch ducked into the bathroom and locked the door.

Tony Hancock was standing over the toilet, pouring booze and pills into the bowl before flushing the lethal mix away. He looked around, startled. "Stone me, are you trying to give me heart failure?"

"What are you doing?"

"I would have thought that was perfectly obvious."

"But that's my stuff!"

"And clearly you cannot be trusted with it."

"That's rich, coming from you."

"Yes, well, do as I say and not as I do. Besides, I'm a tortured genius whereas you, Sunny Jim, are most certainly not."

Finch ducked out of the bathroom to find himself face to face with

Dick Emery, wearing the make-up and platinum blonde wig of his *Mandy* character. Finch looked down to see he was pressed up against a pair of ample assets that a fluffy pink jumper did little to hide. Emery gave Finch a smile that could only be described as mischievous.

"Ooh, you are awful... but I like you!"

The room was chock-a-block with familiar faces; Eric Sykes, Sid James, Frankie Howerd, Benny Hill, Peter Cook, Dudley Moore, Kenny Everett and even dear old John Le Mesurier in his Dad's Army costume.

"Please, just leave me alone. Let me finish it!"

"I say old chap, do you really think that's wise?" said Le Mesurier.

"You had a shit gig, well boo hoo," said Manning, "grow a fuckin' pair."

"I'm doing it, one way or another," said Finch, "and you can't stop me!"

Halfway to the lift lobby, Finch skidded to a halt. Blocking the corridor was Graham Chapman. He was dressed as his Monty Python character, *The Colonel*, with a neatly combed moustache and swagger stick tucked firmly under his arm.

"Stop that, it's silly!"

Finch veered left and took the stairs, bounding up the levels with scant regard for his own lack of stamina. The service door leading onto the roof was jammed. Finch huffed and grunted as he slammed his shoulder into it.

"Lemme give you a hand there buddy." The voice was American. A laconic southern drawl. Bill Hicks. Arguably one of America's finest comedians. Dressed all in black and puffing on an ever-present cigarette, he opened the service door with ease.

"You *want* me to do it?"

"Sure I want you to do it," said Hicks, "why wouldn't I want you to do it? One less asshole in the world. No one's missing out on a cure for cancer if your sorry ass is laid out on a slab. No my friend, you get out there and you go kill yourself. Kill yourself now. Do not question it, do not hesitate, just kill yourself you worthless fuckin' no-talent zero. Just be sure to get a good run-up."

Bill had spoken.

Finch ran across the rooftop towards a concrete balustrade overlooking the dreary seaside town. A patchwork quilt of twinkling lights conjured the illusion of streets filled with infinite possibilities, whereas the truth was closer to double digits.

"Steerrpp, in zerr nerrm errf zerr lerrr."

Peter Sellers as the bumbling Inspector Clouseau was in a Gendarme uniform, having been demoted following some typically hapless misadventure.

"Ceety ordneernernz, werrn terr ferr, cleerrly sterrts…"

Finch had no interest in what City Ordnance One Two Four clearly stated so he took a final step into thin air.

"Sterrp, yerr feerrl!"

The tarmac that rushed to greet Finch appeared to lack most of the qualities typically associated with a velvet cushion. As he fell, a thought revealed itself like a blossoming crocus. It was a moment of clarity in which Finch realised how to make the serving suggestion bit work. A wording tweak here, a change of tonal nuance there would make all the difference. Best of all, he could use it to set up a string of comedic conceits that would pay off later in the show; a series of callbacks to an initial idea that would form a through line for the entire show. It would no longer be just a 'bit' but a lynchpin around which everything else could be based.

In the cold light of day it was obvious.

But as ever in comedy, it's all about the timing.

14

STRATAGEM

Phil Town

What's a mother to do? A man kills your children and there's no trial, no punishment – our kind are killed all the time with total impunity. It shouldn't be that way but it is. So … revenge, right?

I watched on as he did it – he didn't see me, luckily. Snuffed them out, just like that, and laughed as he did it.

"You were their mother," you'll say. "How could you watch and not do anything?" So you think I'm a coward? Well, maybe you're right. But you have to understand that I was powerless. He's a big guy. What could I possibly hope to do … at the time?

Now's different, though. Here I am, outside the bedroom. I can hear him in there, snoring like there's no tomorrow. Let's see whether I can make that true for him.

I'll just sneak in the door. I don't know what I'll do if he wakes up and sees me. I'll be a goner, for sure. But maybe I can hug the wall and make it to the bed that way – then I'll have a chance.

I reckon choking, if I catch him still asleep and off guard. But I've got to get over to him first. I can be very quiet so I should be all right. I'm just worried that something else might wake him – a bad dream, a passing car, the dog next door … but what have I got to lose? Nothing. My children are gone. I really have nothing to live for – I understand that now. Be bold!

So, edging my way towards him. Softly. Softly. Hold on! A grunt from him, and he's stopped snoring. Damn! Wait. Wait.

No – it must have been something in a dream. He's started up with the snoring again. So I go on.

Closer. Closer. I see he's on his back. Perfect. He has his mouth wide open. Doubly perfect! That's it then. Here I go.

The way I figure it, if I can get far enough down his throat and lodge myself in his windpipe, there's a good chance I can choke him. If not, then at the very least he'll wake up with a mouthful of spider, and that'll put the fear of God up the cruel, murderous beast.

15

TUNNEL

Mark Walker

"Are we nearly there yet?"

The twin engines of Archie and Annabel fired up for the umpteenth time, filling the already cramped Prius with more tension than was healthy or necessary. The kids smiled to themselves; they loved games, especially this one. They knew it wound Mum and Dad up, which was the only reason to do it.

Karl and Kerry shuddered as the kids' wails bounced off the inside of the car. They still had an hour of driving ahead, and the roadworks they were currently limping through at 25mph was likely to make it that much longer. Karl's head pounded; it had been since they left home. He wondered, and not for the first time, how he'd ended up with kids. It all happened so fast. It still felt like yesterday that he was making his first, fumbling moves on Kerry back in University. Time waits for no man, he thought. He did love them, all three of them and with all of his heart but, jeez, sometimes he wished they would just fuck off.

He spoke sternly over his left shoulder without taking his eyes off the road. "Archie, if you and your sister can't be quiet, I am going to stop the car and make you walk the rest of the way to Grandma's."

The anger in Karl's voice was real, but Archie knew he wasn't about to make them walk along the side of the motorway. They were young, but they weren't stupid.

"Are we nearly there yet?"

"Seriously," Kerry countered, jumping in before things got out of hand. She cast a worried eye in Karl's direction as he pinched the bridge of his nose. "Can't we just sit quietly for a while? When we're at Grandma's you can make as much noise as you like." The combination of Grandma's military grade double-glazing and never-quite-right hearing aids meant the kids could run around all day in the back garden and not bother anyone. Well, perhaps the neighbours, but Karl and Kerry didn't live there and most of them were deaf as well, so it was win-win. As long as the kids worked out all their energy and knackered themselves ready for a night in the Travel Inn, then it was all good.

"Can't you play a game?" Karl asked. "I spy?"

"Played it," replied Archie.

"Car Cricket?" Kerry suggested.

"Several matches," reported Archie as he held up a small wipe-clean board with a pen clipped to the side of it. Several clumps of crossed tally-marks, like little picket fences, supported his claim.

"And I won them all," Annabel bragged as Archie dropped the board between them and punched her arm.

"I let you."

"No you didn't; you cheated."

"Didn't!"

"Did!"

"Did not!"

"You always do!"

"Shut up!"

"You shut up!"

"Both of you shut up!" screamed Karl, knuckles white on the steering wheel. He turned to face the kids, about to shout again, but the car swerved. Horns blared and he snapped back to face front, relieved the car was moving at a crawl.

"Karl, keep your eyes on the road!" Kerry yelled at her husband as she turned to face the back seat. "Kids, you need to be quiet, don't distract Daddy while he's driving."

The kids went quiet. Archie wouldn't admit it, but the swerve and horns scared him a little. He was only nine after all and some stuff still frightened him. But he had to be brave to look after Annabel. She annoyed the hell out of him most of the time and, although she was only a year younger, he was still her 'big brother' and he took his responsibility very seriously. As he did now when he saw her bottom lip quiver, in that way it always did when she was more scared than him. He reached across from his booster seat and grabbed her hand. She may have accused him of being a cheat at Car Cricket, but the smile she gave him made up for it all.

Kerry's heart melted as it always did when she watched Archie taking Big Brother duty seriously. And that led to the usual feelings of guilt that attacked her just after she had shouted at the kids. Neither she, nor Karl, would ever go out of their way to hurt the kids, let alone hit them. God forbid. But they had both done their fair share of shouting. It was part of being a parent she guessed. No one prepared you for the stresses and strains of being responsible for anyone other than yourself and, sometimes, you just had to shout louder than everyone else to reinforce the hierarchy. But, like now, every time that happened, she felt pained guilt immediately afterwards.

"I'm sorry kids, but you know... Daddy is driving and we can't distract him; it's dangerous." Her smile asked for some sort of sign that the kids understood, but they just stared back in wide-eyed, guilt-tripping fright.

Kerry watched cone after cone drift past the window as a new sign appeared by the side of the road, and she smiled.

"How about a new game?" she asked.

This got the kids' attention and they nodded, interested to hear what this new game might involve.

"Tunnels," whispered Kerry, "are full of monsters."

The kids listened intently, hooked.

Kerry kept her voice low and soft. "When I was a little girl, my mum played a game with us where we had to hold our breath whenever we drove through a tunnel." The kids hung on her every word and leant forward against their restraints to hear. "If you didn't hold your breath," Kerry continued, "the monsters would hear you, and GET YOU!" She shouted the last two words and made the kids jump and giggle.

"There's a tunnel just up ahead, we can play it then. When we get to the tunnel, I'll count 1, 2, 3, and we all have to hold our breath until we come out the other side."

"Daddy too?" asked Annabel.

Karl rolled his eyes and Kerry nudged him.

"Especially Daddy. Who's going to drive if Daddy gets eaten by monsters?" She knew he would play, he was too competitive not to.

"Hey, don't be feeding me to any monsters."

"It's okay Daddy, I'll protect you." Annabel smiled, she liked the sound of this game.

"I'll be okay, poppet," replied Karl, "I hear they are especially fond of little girls."

Annabel giggled.

The car continued on its slow tour through what, by now, felt like about a hundred miles of cones, barriers and other slowly moving cars. Karl felt like he had been on a conveyer belt most of the morning but, with the kids quiet, he could relax. His head was easing and he thought it was time to have a bit of fun.

"Okay," he said. "The tunnel is coming up soon. Mummy, get ready to count!"

The kids adjusted themselves in their seats and got ready for the tunnel.

"It's not a long one, so it should be easy," Kerry reassured them. "On 'Go'. 1! 2! 3… GO!"

A sharp intake of breath from all four players and the car darkened as it vanished from the glare of the morning sun. Kerry hoped she was right about this one being easy. It wasn't a long tunnel, but the roadworks had slowed them down enough to make it a little tougher.

Annabel struggled first. Her little lungs didn't pull in much air when she took her breath and she could feel that she was going to lose. But she didn't want the monsters to eat her. She turned her head to Archie, who seemed a lot more relaxed. He looked back at her worried expression and smiled with true, Big Brother love before he took her hand in his, reassuring her with a wink. He leant across with his other hand and picked up the board and pen.

Kerry clamped her lips shut, memories flooding back of her mum playing this game with her as a kid. Long trips out to see her Grammy and Grampy with her Daddy driving; also doing his best to avoid playing along. What goes around comes around she guessed, funny how we all end up being our parents. All those things they say and do that we think we will never, ever say or do ourselves, but always end up using them.

Karl's tightly-closed mouth curled up slightly at the edges as a plan formed in his mind. As the exit of the tunnel appeared up ahead, a bright spot in the gloom, he slipped down in his chair, disappearing from the view of the kids. Kerry had planted the seed. What *would* happen if Daddy disappeared, eaten by the monster... if he could just get low enough in his seat to disappear from view...

Behind him, Annabel and Archie concentrated on each other, not noticing what was going on in the front. Annabel really struggled. She held her nose with the hand Archie wasn't holding, her eyes wide with fear in her pale little face. She wasn't going to make it to the end of the tunnel.

Archie still smiled back and held her hand even tighter. Big Brother time, he thought. He grabbed the wipe-clean board and pen, rubbed the picket fences away with his fingers, and began to write. He was glad he was left-handed, with Annabel holding his right hand so tightly. He smiled at her as he held the board up.

'Its ok. monsters not reel. You can breath... ssssh!'

He knew his spelling was poor, but he was in a rush. He dropped the board and held his index finger up to his mouth in a "sssh" gesture and winked at Annabel.

Kerry began to hurt as her lungs burned. She dry-swallowed like people do when trying to ignore the fact they're not breathing, but their brain is telling them it is time to open up and let the air in. Whose stupid idea was this, anyway? she asked herself. She'd been crap at it when she'd played as a kid!

Karl was as low as he could get in his seat while still being able to see out. He looked up at Kerry, his mouth shut tight but grinning like an idiot. She looked down at him, smiling back. He can be short-tempered at times, she thought but, mostly, he's a good dad.

Kerry blinked hard as the car breached the end of the tunnel. She breathed out a sudden explosion of air, dragging it back into her lungs in two sharp breaths of relief. Karl copied her, blinking in the light, but still smiling to himself.

And then the screaming started.

Karl smiled to himself, pleased with his prank. Kerry hit him on the arm. "It's okay kids," she reassured them, "Daddy's still here."

Karl pushed himself up in his seat as Kerry turned towards the back seat. Karl concentrated on the car in front, smug with success. What's the point in fatherhood if you can't scare your kids from time to time? he thought.

Archie sat on his booster seat, screaming and staring at his sister's car seat. Or at least the space her car seat occupied when they had entered the tunnel. The seat had vanished and Annabel was nowhere to be seen. Her seatbelt still in place, locked into the clasp.

Kerry turned to Archie, a confused look on her face. Archie yelled as screams burst from his mother's throat and threatened to drown his out. They both stared in absolute terror at the no man's land between the kids' seats. The wipe-clean board sat on the car seat, Archie's message still upon it, but now punctuated with red spots of blood that dripped down from Annabel's hand, still clutched tightly in Archie's Big Brother grip.

16

BRAIN DRAIN

Lee Burgess

I was drowning, I knew it. The water was rising inside me. The creature, Hydrocephalus, had awoken.

I had finally made it, finally escaped that fucking place.

They had shipped me off. An eleven-year-old boy sent to a far-flung domicile of freaks and monsters. Physios, social workers, the evil creeping care staff, all awaited my arrival.

I read all their shitty primary school books in a matter of days. Back home I had read dad's impressive collection of horror novels. King, Herbert, Barker. Books for the big boys. Suddenly I found myself reading the kind of crap they had most kids reading at the age of five.

I remember sitting there, mechanically reading those stories, wondering if at some point, Roger was going to go all hillbilly on Billy's sorry arse. Or if Spike the dog would begin frothing at the mouth and rip out Jennifer's sweet abdomen.

Deep in my head, something was wrong. Something was breaking. Hydrocephalus was ready, ready to come for me. My mind was swimming, but it would soon be consumed, swallowed by the swelling creature inside me.

The units, those cold residential corridors that jutted off from the main school building. The units smelled of hospitals, bleach, and floor cleaner.

Those nights spent far away from home.

I remember the *lost* girls walking nude between bathroom and bedroom, lifting their night dresses as they sat, revealing things that I found enticing, but couldn't quite work out why. Breasts, thighs, and private places. I shouldn't have seen those things, not yet.

One night, Rebecca had forgotten to wear sanitary protection. Crimson liquid had pushed away the cleaning fluid. The floor had been spattered with tiny pools of blood, left unnoticed all night. The place stank like the meat stall at the old market. She had awoken that night smeared with her own menstrual juices. Everyone who was able had left their rooms to see what the screaming was about. Kids scrambled to their wheelchairs and crutches, pulling themselves up, into their seats, trying to capture a glimpse of the hysterical young woman.

So, so cruel.

A slow pattern, *drip, drip, drip.* Something was indeed broken. Hydrocephalus was but a whisper away now. This strange leviathan, hunting through my cerebral juices.

The boys were no better.

Peter, Peter just couldn't help himself. Some idiot had gone and informed him about shagging, and why the lost girls had "those bits." Peter was two years older than me, but mentally he was a small child, probably around ten. He was the first of the residents I had spoken to. They called him *Spazimodo.* He walked with a lurch and a limp. His heels never fully contacted the floor. That first night on the unit, I noticed horrific deep scars on the backs of his knees and ankles. Peter told me the scars were from surgeries where his legs had been ripped open and his tendons slashed to slacken the tension in his limbs. It hadn't worked. His knees were constantly bent, pulled tightly like elastic, ready to snap at any moment. His arms and fingers weren't much better. He limped and clawed his way along. Peter's deformities didn't bother me. The constant nightly fiddling did. I hardly slept for the sounds of Peter's nightly visits inside his own perversions. Most boys his age had the sense to do these things privately, but not Peter. For him that filter was missing, or had it ever been there? His nightly moans and whispers haunted me. In the dark, words floated up, moans and groans. "Ooh Lucinda" Then *those noises, rubbing, slapping, panting*. I told the staff, but they just told me not to make a fuss. So, I spent my nights with my ears plugged with cotton wool.

Dirty boy.

A year passed. Water pooled inside my skull. My eye sight began to dim, but the pain was yet to come. My monster, the being made from secretions from within, *Hydro* had begun the final leg of its journey.

This place, this institution for "special" children, was a kind of limbo. It straddled the gap between reality and another world, a kind of nether-dimension.

Deep within, a special place where vicious creatures dwelled. These were the physios, cruel beings with a taste for crippling experimentation. To enter this room was to know the deepest of agonies. The walls were lined with straps and harnesses. Hefty metallic frames stood free, awaiting some unsuspecting soul. They were clamped in, swallowed by these cold, horrifying beasts. Victims would be stood, sometimes just in underwear, ordered to perform humiliating tasks that hurt and degraded. For me, walking was grim but possible. My spine had never formed correctly so my legs often did as they pleased. My bladder was unstable, so sometimes walking made me pee involuntarily.

Here, I was forced to walk and to stand on wooden boards with balls carved into the base. These were devices designed for the torture of "special" children. I would stand, the boards would wobble and slide. Yellow liquid escaped me, warming my crotch, soaking my legs. The physios didn't care, the privileged monsters, they sneered and cackled as the stench of urine emanated from me.

This was hell.

Another year faded away. My mind was half immersed in the thick solution pumping from my spinal column. Hydrocephalus was almost there, waiting patiently. It took its sweet time. It teased as it expanded against my skull.

Lastly, my eternal nightmare. A thin clear tube and a tub of odd-smelling gel.

The nurse had shown me into the largest bathroom in the unit. She wore disposable plastic gloves. A young woman followed. I remember her. She had made me feel safe, but it was a false sensation.

The nurse asked me to undress, just the bottom half.

I trembled with my shoe laces, cotton joggers and boxers. Lastly, the young woman yanked my leg-bag from its rubber flange at my most private place. The nurse laid a towel on the tiled floor, she invited me to lie down. The young woman guided me gently onto the towel. She had cooed at me, told me to relax. Why? What did I have to relax for?

I laid there, exposed, staring at the ceiling. I felt a cold hand on my thigh as the nurse parted my legs, just slightly. She held the tube aloft, telling me to watch her every move. I didn't obey. I looked up, waiting, averting my eyes.

The radiant brunette woman lifted my t-shirt over my stomach.

She smiled down at me. Her eyes flashed, suddenly, dangerously. Who was she, a demon in training? I had seen her before, once, in that room at the bowels of the institution. Christ, she was captivating. She leant in, low, close. Her fingers gently brushed my elbow. Her smile grew. That movement, that touch, something stirred in my stomach. She took my hand and pressed it to her chest. I felt her beating heart as those fingertips stroked my wrist.

The nurse held the tub of glistening gel. With a gloved hand, the old hook-nosed hag smeared the tube thick with the curd-like oil.

I stared hard at the beautiful woman. I was thirteen, a young man. In an instant, the world blurred.

I felt a hand at my groin, pulling at the place that was sacred. My hands shot down, pushing the wretched woman's talons away. The younger woman pulled my hands up, resting them at my chest. Her lips pursed in a hush. *Shhh.*

The nurse's fingers went there once more. I felt glad for my lack of sensation. The young woman passed a plastic jug above my head. The nurse took it with her free hand. She lowered the glistening tube. I felt it touch me, *there*. No female had ever touched me there before. I felt violated. It didn't hurt, but I felt it. The tube slid smoothly into my urethra. The nurse held firm as she slid the catheter inside. I felt the plastic tip prod at the neck of my bladder. It pushed, pressing in and back, I felt harsh pressure. The catheter forced forward and down.

Then, something else, a throb, an expanding at my crotch. This was rapid. Of course, this was familiar, usually private, a stolen moment. Nobody saw, nobody touched, *usually*.

Shit, why now?

I could feel myself growing erect between the nurse's fingers.

I looked up, the beautiful woman held my gaze away from the abysmal act. Could she see this?

I held my breath.

I felt overwhelming compression on my lower bowel. The force increased as the tube pierced through the junction at my sphincter. I felt fierce scratching inside. The tube scraped and scratched. I raised my head. The nurse was looking along the exposed end of the catheter. She lifted my hand and curled my fingers around the protruding tube. With my other hand, I felt myself stiffen further against the violent force of the insertion. It began to push the tube out of place I pulsed and felt swelling shame.

The flexible plastic turned orange with a mixture of blood and urine. It shuddered. I clenched against the pain as my bladder shook.

The women waited, looking down with perverted fascination.

The younger woman purred as the liquid trickled from the end of the tube, splashing against the inside of the jug.

The catheter drained every drop. The young woman placed a hand on my shoulder. She smiled once more.

The defilement was complete. My unnatural arousal ebbed away. Still, the nurse held me. She placed the flange into place and returned the leg bag to its position.

That was my final humiliation.

Hydrocephalus morphed into a jelly-like beast inside my head. My brain screamed as the beast devoured it.

Here it had ended.

Or had it?

I awoke in a hospital bed. The light burned white-hot behind my bandaged eyes. My head had been split open. I felt pressure pushing outward. My skull was on fire. Blood clotted in my ears. Memories of that hellish place flashed up in fearsome detail. Those twisted faces, the moaning, the screaming. Those poor kids. They remained trapped in the grip of the cackling creatures.

A tall masked figure stood over me mumbling. I couldn't make out any real words. I thought I heard him say "brain drain". It wasn't clear. My ears pulsed. Again, the same phrase "brain drain". Was I still drowning? Had they taken my monster, had it escaped?

The masked figure walked away.

Then, *she* was there. The beautiful woman.

Her young face, those wonderful eyes were now sly, mysterious, black. She took my hand. She crouched in, kissed my forehead. Where were my parents? Did they know I was here? I wanted my monster, I wanted the security of death. Neither were present. I was alone with this menace.

There was no escape.

Hydrocephalus was gone, the brain drain had eaten it. My hidden beast was no more.

17

TARGET

Dee Chilton

You might think you know how it feels, especially if you've killed a few rabbits or deer... maybe even an elephant. Maybe even if you play that kind of computer game, you know, the ones where you have the power of life and death in your hands, where you feel the intense excitement of the hunt and the thrill of the kill. You might even get that same downer when it's all over and you have to return to the mundane ordinary world... until the next time.

Don't kid yourself; it's not the same thing. Trust me, I know. I was like that once.

Not any more though. You know how they say once an animal has tasted human blood it can never again accept a substitute? That's me. Blood lust they call it.

Yeah, that's it. A constant craving that nothing else can ever satisfy.

Oh sure, it gets a little easier to live with right after the kill. Sometimes you even think you can just stop, but soon enough it comes back... it always does. It eats away at you until it takes over your whole being. So how do you feed that without being labelled as a threat and hunted to death yourself? You have to box clever, my friend. You have to become one of them and pander to their needs. That's what I did.

Hell, I can show you, but you have to know you're on your own after that, as I've been since my first time. Some people are animals and you can't trust many of them. Anyway, you and me both already know that's the best way to survive and stay under the radar, don't we?

So, do you really want to feel it?

Think hard about it now, because there's no going back once you commit to this.

You do?

Well okay then, if you're sure. Let's do this.

Here, put on this eye patch. You see better with both eyes open, but a good cover helps you concentrate fully on the target. You don't want to miss anything.

And now the comms earpiece. That's it. We may police the law but we have to appear to stay on the right side of it too. Have to play their game, let them think they're in charge and we only want to be the last resort. We can't let them know how much we live for this. Stay cool, right? Short, firm answers, yes or no. Nice and calm. Easy does it. Don't give them any reason to doubt our motive.

Lie down. No, not like that, on your front. Nestle down and make a stable platform for your barrel hand. Yeah, there. Comfy? Good. Now, take the rifle, pull the stock in real close. Jam the butt right up into your shoulder. She'll kick you real hard if you don't hold onto her proper. Get your eye up tight to her scope. That's it.

Can you feel her? Like the taut skin of a powerful lover against your cheek.

Can you smell her? Sexy as fuck, don't you think?

Make her an extension of your own body, your soul even. You breathe, she breathes. You hold your breath; she holds hers. Cover her trigger, careful now, find her sweet spot and caress it. Nice and light. You don't want to go shootin' off too early.

You getting aroused? I know I am, just the thought of it turns me on. Just wait 'til you see what she can do.

Let's do a dummy run. Pick a target. Yeah, anyone will do.

Focus.

Three deep breaths in and out.

Breathe in and hold.

Steady.

Fire.

Hold again. Slow breathe out.

You got that?

Be sure to squeeze the trigger, don't pull it, and hold that aim after you fire. These babies are sensitive. Slightest movement will spoil your shot... and the experience.

And don't you go closin' your eyes after you fire. You want to watch close through the scope as that bullet rips into the flesh and your target explodes in a fanfare of brains, blood and bones. We should always savour every single moment of that. Okay, only thing left is to listen out for their order to shoot. We're all set for the kill.

I still remember my first one, clear as day. Thing is, lying there waiting for someone else's 'go' to waste targets from a distance, you do kinda stop feeling it. It's not much different to dropping a bomb, is it? Hey, do you know Oppenheimer's words after they dropped his nuke? Well not his words exactly, he took them from some ancient text.

Goes something like, *'the Supreme Lord said: I am death, the mighty destroyer of the world. Even without your participation all opposing armies shall cease to exist. Therefore, get up and attain glory. Conquer your enemies and enjoy a prosperous kingdom. All these have already been destroyed by Me. You are only an instrument.'*

Yeah. I like that. Coulda been written for us.

Thing is, you need really to be up close and personal, looking deep into your victim's eyes for the biggest buzz. You need to smell their blood, and their fear. Some of them shit and piss themselves when they know they're going to die. Their life is literally in your hands and you really do take it from them. That's what I figure.

You look worried. Hey, let me whisper something in your ear...

Shhhhhhh... Hold still.

Feel that? My new one true love. She's a real beaut. Vintage Ka-Bar. Standard issue to US Marines in World War two. Double-sided steel blade that consistently holds sharp edges. She sure knows how to please me. We're one and the same. She's an extension of my soul.

There. You can feel her too, now. Hear what she's telling you? *'I am become death. The mighty destroyer of the world. I am an instrument.'*

She makes me feel everything right to my core, as we slice deep into yours together. Like carving into an orange, just a little resistance as she meets the tough outer layer and... we're through and into the soft juicy flesh below.

Whoa, don't fight her! You'll just make us angry.

We like to use a ballistic cut, slip deep into your gut and up under your ribs to your lungs, then retract slow and steady but twist really hard as we pull back. That creates a much larger hole. More damage and bleeding. We love the sound of a sucking wound.

I'm sorry; it's no use pleading like that. She's in charge and I don't do sympathy.

Hey, you know where sympathy lies in the dictionary? Between Shit and Syphilis. Real rib tickler that, isn't it?

No? How about... that. Mmmmm, we liked that.

What's that you say?

Of course we'll get away with this, been doing so for years now. Who's gonna miss you? Nobody, right? I choose my targets wisely, so easy to do with fake I.S.P. addresses and social media accounts these days.

I hunted you, I baited you, and I trapped you with your own sick desires.

See, I'm a vegetarian, me. I believe we should never kill any animal unless it's for food. That's only fair after all, a life for a life. So that's what you'll be now, food. Every last damned morsel of you. Take-away meat, black pudding, pies and sausages. What's left goes for animal feed.

They sure love my products down on the market. My mate sells them on his stall.

I call them; you'll like this…'Boxed Clever' ready cooked foods. Humanely treated, fair-trade meat products from a sustainable source. You can sell anything if it says some crap like that these days, especially if it's cheap. So there you go, my friend. Nobody will ever know. Even the guys down the station can't get enough of it.

You wanted to know how it feels to kill someone.

Look into my eyes now. Breathe out your last; we'll breathe it in. There you go.

Here endeth the lesson, my friend.

18

THE AZRAEL

Juliet Sneed

It was the six-year anniversary of my incarceration in St. Vosper's Hospital when X came to me. He came in the form of a fat Black Widow crawling across my face. Panicking, I shrieked for the nurses (well, it was a *spider*). But no one answered.

"Nobody can see or hear me," said the Black Widow. "Unless I wish them to."

I plucked the thing off my forehead and examined the spider. It was really an animated skull on eight brittle, bony legs. My phobic mind had only thought it was a spider. Relieved, I stroked its head.

"What are you? What shall I call you? What do you eat? Are you a pet? Are you my pet? Maybe…"

The skull waggled its legs at me.

"I am X. I need your body."

The skull then scuttled into an eye-socket, burrowing until it reached my brain. I could feel it nestled against my frontalis. With a sizzle-wriggle-nibble, all my (correction: all of our) memories rose up as sores on my (our) flesh. Bursting, they released screams and shouts and sighs. Grey bone showed beneath.

I (we) were X.

"I am as cold as rain and as old as Earth. I kill all who take life. Who am I?"

Those were my first words as X, when I cast off Clive Witherwell – that mouldy old mask – and assumed my true features: an eyeless skull-face. I was not hallucinating at that time. I had just taken my Thorazine. I have always been a good patient. Always. Even though I did not deserve to be locked away. Those people are alive! Only I have the eyes to see them. My chorus of Mourning Greys.

My roommate, Thaddeus Hightower, scribbled in his notebook. He was always doing that, even if I had not spoken. Thaddie believed my thoughts took the form of tiny bats and roamed the interior of his cranium while he slept. The writing was his way of warding them off.

"Don't think so fast. Slow down."

He cowered in a corner, as if he feared I would hurt him. But I am good and peaceable. Not a danger to anyone. Really. It was just...

I could see into his mind. I knew what he'd done. The jars of eyes, the jewel-box stuffed with fingers... Thaddie was a Pseudo-X. One of the false Azrael; a human with delusions of grandeur.

More scrib, scrib, scribbling. He looked like a mouse, with his brown eyes all big and shiny and his little pink hands scuttling across the pages. "Please," he said. "Stop. I'm out of paper."

He threw the notebook away. I retrieved it, placing it in the hole where my heart once beat.

"Have you guessed my riddle?"

Mouse scuttled under his bed.

"I am sorry if I have offended you, Darkness."

I dragged my dear Mousie out from under the bed.

"That is not my name. It belongs to my cousin. Try again."

Mousie felt limp and moist; a sponge of a man.

"Unknown. That's you, isn't it?"

As a reward, I ripped his heart out – a quick death. He collapsed to the ground, and I squeezed his blood over my head.

Fully baptised into X, I shuddered with joy as I felt the pulling-groaning sensation of my wings coming in. Bursting through the ceiling and into the air, I hovered over the hospital. I hid my face behind a cowl of black clouds; and the crescent moon formed a sickle at my right hand.

19

COUNT TO TEN

Dean Marriner

"It's not my fault", sobbed the guard as he felt my blade push harder. He was slumped on the floor, his hands tied behind him, his head hanging forward. Tears ran down his nose and dropped into a salty pool on the floor. I knew he was telling the truth, but I enjoyed watching him suffer. It made me feel strong.
I leaned forward until my face was close to his and I calmly spoke to him.

"You have until I count to ten to tell me where the box is."

"I have a family," he pleaded. It made no difference to me. He had something I needed and fuck him and his family.

"One."

He lifted his head and his eyes filled with tears, his mouth flapped open but no sounds came.

"Two."

The knife was heavy, I'd been holding it for a full 30 minutes now; the handle was hard and dug into my hand. The blade was pushed up tight against his ribs. The soft material of his shirt, sodden with sweat, was the only protection against its honed steel.

"Three."

He shook uncontrollably as his body convulsed in fear. The smell of his sweat-soaked shirt filled my nostrils and made me feel exhilarated. All he had to do was talk.

"Four."

I took a hold of his hair and lifted his head. His eyes rolled around finding a point to focus on. He found me.

"Tell me and all of this goes away."

He said something, but honestly, I wasn't listening. I'd already decided the ending to this scene.

"Five."

The blade found an opening in the fabric and forced it aside. Slicing through the fibres until it met skin.

"Six."

The acrid smell of urine, filled my nose. I looked down as the dark stain spread across his leg and the floor turned yellow.

"Seven."

The blade punctured the skin; blood seeped from the wound. Like the piss-stained floor, it spread once it touched his shirt. A little blood appears to be much more than it is.

"Eight."

His terrified eyes bulged as he looked at me. A scream caught in his throat and stopped.

"Nine."

The blade slipped deeper into the flesh, slicing, past skin and deeper into fat and muscle. It required all the force I had left. The blood ran down the blade and over my hand, warm and sticky. The ferrous smell filled my nose.

"Ten."

Breath rattled and gargled in his throat, little splatters of spittle peppered my face. The blood was hot on my hand and spilled over the floor, mingling with the piss. I held the blade in place for a minute then slowly retracted it. The flow pulsed as I lay him down on the floor, his clothes soaked in his bodily fluids, his eyes fixed on mine. I watched as his life slipped away and I felt a power and a thrill just like the last time. I enjoyed the feeling of killing.

I kissed his cheek and whispered softly,

"It's not my fault."

20

ONE STEP, TWO STEP

Kendall Castor-Perry

After five summers, the poppies in front of the derelict cottage have grown too dense to walk through.

You mums and dads, you're all screaming and weeping as you pull at those thick stems, their milky sap leaving stains on your clothes. Yes. Like *those* stains.

You haven't forgotten Reverend "Like A Teddy Bear" MacDougall. You all knew what the stains on his cassock meant.

You whispered among yourselves about his inappropriate "Walky Round the Garden" games with young boys, but did nothing.

He "helped the Police with their enquiries" following each tearful accusation. The pigs did nothing.

You all saw him leering at the butcher's boy — Liam, ten, remember him? — but you did nothing.

Then one day, Reverend MacDougall disappeared. And young Liam never returned home.

You put two and two together. Knew things had gone too far. But you had done nothing.

Until the letter. "Dig there."

You couldn't wait for the Police. Now you're crowded into the cottage's garden, with your shovels and your wailing, two feet down into rock-hard clay, poppy stalks strewn about, crushed underfoot.

Faster. Faster.

Until someone hits bone. Now it's dinosaur-dig slow, tears splashing on grey, trembling hands.

There.

Streaked black with dried blood, a furry leg juts out from deep within the decayed remains of the Reverend's crotch.

Into which his Teddy Bear has been neatly sewn.

Fuck you. All of you. Liam *did* something.

"Walky round the garden,

Like a Teddy Bear.

One step,

Two step,

Tickly under there."

21

FOR THE RECORD

Ricardo Bravo

From: SIO David Treadwell (David.Treadwell@yorkshire.cid.uk)

To: Prof Tom McLaughlin (thomas.mclauglin@dpls.ucl.edu.uk)

Subject: RE: Carson Incident

Prof McLaughlin,

Unfortunately, I don't have access to the original tapes as these are being held as part of the IPCC investigation. I only managed to get a copy of the interrogation transcripts (see below). I hope you can help me make some sense of what happened that day.

Thank you in advance for your help.

Best regards,

SIO David Treadwell

Yorkshire CID

****

Interrogation Transcript RB/395/20160824-001

DS VINCENT ERICSSON (V.ERICSSON): This is Detective Sergeant Vincent Ericsson. It's eleven eighteen-

JESSICA CARSON (J.CARSON): This is all a huge misunderstanding, I don't-

V.ERICSSON: Please, Ms Carson. Just state your name for the record.

J.CARSON: Erm... Je- Jessica Carson.

V.ERICSSON: Ms Carson. You were seen today dumping a shopping bag into the river. This bag was later discovered to contain a severed human foot. Would you care to explain?

J.CARSON: I... I had no idea it contained a foot. I thought it was just rotten meat.

V.ERICSSON: Well, then... how did you end up with that bag?

J.CARSON: I was coming back from doing my shopping at [REDACTED] when I found the bag just there, by the river. At first I thought it was a present, you know, like in the adverts where a kind soul leaves some groceries for an older person. You know which...

V.ERICSSON: I've seen the adverts.

J.CARSON: Good. So I picked it up. But when I was on the bridge, I noticed this... horrible smell coming from the bag. I've never littered in my life, but the stench, it was repulsive. I had to get rid of it, so... I did. I'm so sorry.

V.ERICSSON: You didn't look inside the bag?

J.CARSON: Of course not. Can I please go home?

V.ERICSSON: Calm down, Ms Carson. I'll talk to the S.I.O. We'll clear this up in no time.

J.CARSON: Oh. Thank you. You are very kind.

V.ERICSSON: Can I bring you anything?

J.CARSON: Some tea would be nice.

END RECORDING

Interrogation Transcript RB/395/20160824-002

SIO DAVID TREADWELL (D.TREADWELL): The time is three twenty-five pm. Present are myself, Senior Investigating Officer David Treadwell, and Detective Sergeant Vincent Ericsson.

DS VINCENT ERICSSON (V.ERICSSON): Please state your name, age and address.

JESSICA CARSON (J.CARSON): Erm… I already told you.

V.ERICSSON: For the record. Please.

J.CARSON: Jessica Carson, 68 years old, [REDACTEDREDACTE-DREDACTED]

D.TREADWELL: Ms Carson. At this point I would like to point out that we have obtained a warrant to enter your house.

J.CARSON: Oh *(inaudible)*.

V.ERICSSON: Sorry, you said something?

J.CARSON: I hoped you wouldn't do that.

D.TREADWELL: Now, before we proceed any further, we would recommend that you get in touch with your solicitor as-

J.CARSON: No solicitors. There is no need. I can explain everything.

V.ERICSSON: Ms Carson, I would really suggest that you-

J.CARSON: Please. I've never had a problem with the police before, not even a parking ticket. I am a good person. I want to explain.

V.ERICSSON: One moment, please *(inaudible.)*

D.TREADWELL: *(inaudible)*

V.ERICSSON: Yes, sir. So, Ms Carson, did you know P.C. Michael Johnson?

J.CARSON: Mickey? Yes. He was a good kind man. Always help-ful... I really liked him.

D.TREADWELL: P.C. Johnson's remains were found in your house. Could you please explain the circumstances surrounding his decease?

J.CARSON: I beg your pardon?

V.ERICSSON: How did he die, Ms Carson?

J.CARSON: Ah. Well... he visited my house to help me move some furniture. After a while he was feeling quite out of breath so I asked him to sit down for a while to... to regain his strength. I prepared some tea and some of my famous strawberry scones. You know, they are quite the sensation at the village fête. Mrs [REDACTED] is always after my secret ingredient but I'll-

D.TREADWELL: Ms Carson, stick to one topic.

J.CARSON: I'm sorry.

V.ERICSSON: It's okay. Please, continue.

J.CARSON: Well I prepared a tray. He complimented my scones. Everybody does. I would make you a batch but unfortunately my kitchen is not-

D.TREADWELL: Ms Carson.

J.CARSON: Was I rambling again? All this is very new for me.

V.ERICSSON: You were saying?

J.CARSON: Well, I went to the kitchen to get some more jam when I heard something breaking in the living room. I ran back and found poor Mickey lying on the floor, eyes bulging out, hands on his neck, a cup and saucer of my best china broken to pieces. I inherited that set from my grandmother, you know.

D.TREADWELL: Ms Carson. In a moment like that, any normal person would have called 999. Why didn't you?

J.CARSON: *(inaudible)*

V.ERICSSON: Please, Ms Carson. A bit louder.

J.CARSON: I was... embarrassed.

D.TREADWELL: Embarrassed.

J.CARSON: Yes, embarrassed. If anyone ever found out that a man ate my scones and... died, well I would never hear the end of it. People would say he died from eating a dry scone and I do not make dry scones, thank you very much. And that nasty Mrs [REDACTED] is just waiting for an opportunity to take over my stall at the village fête where my strawberry scones have received the first prize every year for the last thirteen years and –

D.TREADWELL: Wait a minute. You really expect us to believe this? Strawberry scones and tea?

J.CARSON: But – but it's the truth. What was I expected to do?

D.TREADWELL: Certainly not dismember the body.

J.CARSON: Well, I may have... overreacted.

D.TREADWELL: You don't say.

J.CARSON: I didn't know what to do. I thought that if I could get rid of his body –

D.TREADWELL: Why did you kill him?

J.CARSON: W – what? I didn't kill him! He was very tired after moving the couch so maybe he had a heart attack. Maybe he was allergic to strawberries. I don't know.

D.TREADWELL: Well, unfortunately with what's left of the body we will never know, will we?

J.CARSON: I... I think I would like to talk to a solicitor, please.

END RECORDING

Interrogation Transcript RB/395/20160824-003

DS VINCENT ERICSSON (V.ERICSSON): It's seven o... two pm. This is D.S. Vincent Ericsson with S.I.O. David Treadwell. In the room, Ms Jessica Carson and her legal counsel... Mr Murphy Elliot?

MR ELLIOT MURPHY (E.MURPHY): That's Elliot Murphy, Junior Associate at McCall and Associates.

SIO DAVID TREADWELL (D.TREADWELL): Good for you.

E.MURPHY: Well I... I would like to state for the record that you have tricked Ms Carson into acknowledging this most ridiculous charge when it is clear that she is not in her best state of mind and –

D.TREADWELL: Mr Murphy, please relax. Your client waived her right to representation before she confessed to disposing of the body of P.C. Johnson. We are now trying to ascertain whether his death was premeditated or not.

E.MURPHY: Well... I, er... I will still make a complaint against your superiors. Against you, with your superiors.

D.TREADWELL: Please do. Now, we have some additional questions, if you don't mind.

V.ERICSSON: Ms Carson. As you can see from these pictures, the forensics team have found DNA traces in various of your... kitchen appliances. Would you care to explain?

E.MURPHY: *(inaudible)*

JESSICA CARSON (J.CARSON): It's okay, young man. Well, I... thought it would be easier to dispose of Mickey's... you know... insides by throwing them in the toilet, but they kept blocking it. So I popped them in the blender to –

E.MURPHY: Oh, God. I'm... I'm gonna need a... a minute, I – *(inaudible)*.

D.TREADWELL: Mr Murphy. Not in here!

END RECORDING

Interrogation Transcript RB/395/20160824-004

DS VINCENT ERICSSON (V.ERICSSON): It's eleven forty pm. This is D.S. Ericsson with Jessica Carson and Mr Elliot Murphy. Ms Carson, are you okay to continue?

JESSICA CARSON (J.CARSON): I'm fine, thank you. It's just that… I really made a mess of things, didn't I?

MR ELLIOT MURPHY (E.MURPHY): Please, not another word. Detective Ericsson, it's late and from the looks of it, you will not be able to determine cause of death or intent. All you have right now is a forced confession obtained under duress from a weak old lady. So, either charge her for illegally disposing of a body or –

SIO DAVID TREADWELL (D.TREADWELL): Please sit down, Mr Murphy.

V.ERICSSON: S.I.O. Treadwell has just entered the room.

D.TREADWELL: Ms Carson, I think it is time for you to come clean.

J.CARSON: What do you mean?

D.TREADWELL: You don't know where I'm going with this?

J.CARSON: I… I don't.

D.TREADWELL: Okay. Have it your way. The forensics team in your house have made a very interesting discovery. They found other human DNA traces not only on your knives and your blender… but also inside your oven… your pantry… your freezer.

E.MURPHY: What are you implying, Inspector?

D.TREADWELL: I am not implying anything. I only seek the truth. Oh, and for the record, Mr Murphy, when I said they found other traces, I meant that these samples did not belong only to P.C. Johnson but to some other person or persons unknown. But, you already knew that, didn't you Ms Carson?

E.MURPHY: *(inaudible)* is he talking about?

D.TREADWELL: The forensics team are combing through your house and garden right now and I think you know what they are going to find.

E.MURPHY: What are you… I don't think that that is… it's not appropriate to –

J.CARSON: Could you please leave us? I want to have a chat with the inspector.

E.MURPHY: Madam, as your legal counsel I would strongly advise you to –

J.CARSON: Leave. Now.

E.MURPHY: *(inaudible)* is highly irregular.

D.TREADWELL: D.S. Ericsson and Mr Murphy have left the room. Do you wish me to –

J.CARSON: No. Please, leave it on. For the record.

D.TREADWELL: As you wish.

J.CARSON: Tell me something, do you think you have won here, Inspector Treadwell?

D.TREADWELL: I beg your pardon?

J.CARSON: Do you really think it was by mistake or luck that I got caught? I've been doing this for many, many years and you and your police force have been none the wiser.

D.TREADWELL: Is this an impromptu confession?

J.CARSON: No, love. I came here to deliver a message.

D.TREADWELL: Oh! And what message is that?

J.CARSON: That the time is almost upon us. You see… He is coming.

D.TREADWELL: And who might… he be?

J.CARSON: Are you really so naïve, Inspector? Can't you see the hell that is upon your doorstep?

D.TREADWELL: All I see is a crazy, old lady who is preparing her insanity defence.

J.CARSON: Oh no, Inspector. I know it makes you comfortable to label me as such, but I'm not crazy. I simply answer to a much higher power than the laws of this country you blindly abide by. I'm a soldier in an army of thousands, slowly paving the way in preparation for His arrival. For every soul we consume, He grows stronger, and He... has a very big appetite.

D.TREADWELL: So do you, apparently.

J.CARSON: Don't mock me, Inspector. This is a courtesy call.

D.TREADWELL: Okay, if what you say is true, and that is a big if, why tell me? Why warn us?

J.CARSON: Ah! Because He likes a challenge. You see, the more prepared you are, the better you will fight. The better you fight, the more you will hope. And the more you hold on to hope, the worse it will be... when you fall.

D.TREADWELL: You really are something else, lady.

J.CARSON: Well, it's been a pleasure, Inspector, truly. But now you'll have to excuse me. I'm... expected for tea.

D.TREADWELL: Who switched off the lights?

J.CARSON: *(inaudible)*

D.TREADWELL: Detective, get in here. NOW.

V.ERICSSON: The door is locked.

D.TREADWELL: Break it down.

V.ERICSSON: The lights are – Jesus Christ!

D.TREADWELL: Get a doctor!

E.MURPHY: Oh, my God. What did you do to her?

D.TREADWELL: I didn't do anything, you stupid man.

E.MURPHY: You're covered in her blood.

D.TREADWELL: Get him out of here! Stop the-

END RECORDING

22

MURMURATION

James Jay

Brey snake-eyed her GPS through the howling storm. It had finally gone whacko, so she scoured the terrain for landmarks and by some miracle she stumbled on an abandoned camp-site and knew then that the Bird, Butterfly and Bee Research Station, her ultimate destination, was close.

She'd made her last call home before the electro-magnetic skies closed in and her mother gushed how proud she was, the whole world was proud. Brey said it was no big deal. Her mother, in tears, said no one had done what she was about to do and her name would go down in bloody history.

Brey knew when her mother was upset, she swore. Ever the comforting daughter, she said yes she had enough food, yes her feet were fine. No, no frostbite.

"I'm not wearing stilettos," said Brey.

Brey asked about the news. The usual, said her mother, Climate Change, World leaders at odds, Scientists' dire predictions, all that stuff. Well there's still time to take care of that, said Brey and don't worry, we will, humans can be dumb, but we will sort it. Well I hope so, said her mother, better we sort it than Mother Nature, you know what mothers are like, and they both laughed.

Brey said she'd be home soon and then there was silence, some mumbled goodbyes and love bounced back and forth halfway around the world between aching hearts.

She trudged through the storm thinking about her family, her friends and marvelling at the evolution of human beings into this creature of huge imagination that acts of its own free will and yet could work together. She thought of billions of people swarming over the planet and patching together beautiful patterns of life and love. What was that word that described flocks of starlings weaving the last light of the day into the silky dusk of night? Murmuration? Yes, that was it.

Murmuration.

Blackpool, summer. Dai lit one up and chuckled at the family gorging on fish and chips. He knew this one, he'd seen it before and it never failed to make him laugh. The kid blows on a hot chip, a seagull swoops, grabs chip, flies off, kid blubs, Dad laughs, Mum comforts kid and scolds Dad.

Sure enough, a seagull planted itself next to the kid, but like a thief with a conscience it didn't make the food heist, instead it took off and crapped on the kid's upturned face. Mum wiped the poor hysterical kid's eyes whilst Dad bolted after the gull as it hopped down the promenade, squawking as if mocking him.

That's a first, thought Dai. He tracked the gull to the top of the Tower then lost it. Unseen by human eyes it sat bellowing to the world and then fell silent, watching the eternal tide roll in, infecting him with waves of an indeterminate nature. Bacteria rushed from his gut to his brain and re-aligned the quantum-entangled specks in his eyes that were his navigation system. He looked down with contempt at the unsuspecting masses below as gulls gathered around him, engorging certain unspoken commands.

New Orleans. Deke, the heavy-duty construction guy, wound himself up to swing his lump hammer just as Mrs Growtthe appeared in the shadowy cellar.

"Tough goin'?" said Mrs. Growtthe.

"There's a damn tin box stuck in here for some reason," said Deke. "Installing your tumble dryer's gonna take some time. Stand back."

Deke's arm sprang forward like a sling-shot just as a budgie flew out of nowhere and hovered between the tin box and Deke's unstoppable hammer. Mrs Growtthe screamed, "Charlie!"

Brey's compass spun like a crazy casino wheel as she fought the intense nausea that the swirling invisible force summoned up. It was gathering strength and infecting her with each step she took.

Mexico. Hernandez was Spiderman. His mother, proud of her seamstress work, watched him pose on the back of the last flat-bed truck that rolled through the streets of Zhaituano on this 'The Sacred Virgin Maria's Holy Day Parade.'

It was a riot of colour and music, and as the column of trucks petered out, the crowd was hushed by the last one that stopped, its engine ticking like a time-bomb. The driver flashed a wicked smile though a pig's-head mask, whilst Hernandez stood looking to the skies.

On the back of the truck sat a clown tied to a chair with wire – barbed wire that punctured his skin, blood oozing from the wounds and spreading like rough red patchwork. Hernandez and half a dozen kids dressed as Superheros surrounded the clown. A raven swooped, wheeling and cawing, and as the kids pointed their replica guns at the clown, he wet himself, and piss spread from his crotch down his baggy trousers, spreading like litmus paper, dripping onto the floor of the truck.

Brey willed herself on, each step resisting the force that opposed her as if it were God's own hand that was pushing her back.

In Blackpool the donkeys plodded along the beach, each one laden with an ice-cream licking child.

The sun shone and frothy waves lapped the deckchair-strewn beach as bucket and spade castles rose out of the baking bronzed sand.

Nearby, a bee danced, but not an 'I found pollen' dance, a dance to the beat of a different drum. It shook, spun and reeled out its message then took off with the swarm following, collecting troops along the way, the Queen Bee giving her blessing to the soldiers who seemed to have no sense of purpose, until sandy beaches appeared.

Under the Tower, children laughed and screamed at a Punch and Judy show where Mr Punch relished his shrill swazzle 'that's the way to do it' voice as he bashed the head of his foes with his club until only one remained. The Devil. Punch raised his club to strike when a seagull landed with a thump on the stage. Punch stopped and the seagull took off, shitting foul crap onto the skyward-gazing kids, stinging their virgin eyes. Mothers desperately wiped their children's burning faces whilst Punch and the Devil were locked in a face-off. From between them a figure slowly rose, the puppetmaster dressed as Mr Skeleton, dynamite strapped to his head, a bloody 'KISS ME QUICK' slashed into his brow. Dai laughed at the insanity of it all and looked around for a film crew. There was none.

Brey broke through the storm and entered a heavenly blue, silent world enclosed in an invisible bubble. Her watch had stopped, time was at an end. She slid on a titanium-coated helmet to stop neuron interference and dragged herself towards the Research Station that was just a snowball's throw away. She'd never had a religious belief, but now it was as if someone or something was playing games with her. If they were, she hoped it was God.

Mrs Growtthe nestled Charlie's crushed body in her hands.

"He just hovered there, like he meant to," said Deke.

Mrs Growtthe shuffled away whilst Deke, curious about what Charlie was defending, put his head inside the hole. He wrenched open the tin and something fluttered inside. Deke tried to back out but he was wedged tight.

"Holy shit," said Deke, as pretty blue butterflies fluttered out of the tin. Deke broke into a nervous laugh as the butterflies saw light behind Deke's head. Mrs Growtthe did not hear Deke's cries for help as the butterflies gnawed their way through his gasping gaping mouth and throat, munching towards the light.

Mrs Growtthe watched as blue butterflies drifted past her window, billowing like the sails of a galleon, floating down to where a lithe young girl lay naked in her garden, sunbathing, dozing, dreaming, eyes closed, lips apart. Mrs Growtthe heard an ice-shattering scream as the naked girl, now coated in pretty blue butterflies, clutched at her groin, like she was trying to rip off a blue fluttering swimsuit of death.

Hernandez and the Superheros opened fire, not with replicas, but savagely real guns, ripping through the Clown, blowing him off the wagon as it rumbled down the street, leaving the circling birds to enjoy a warm, ready-made meal. Ravens pounced on the crowd, blinding them, tarring them with feathered blackness as their wings stuck to sticky human blood.

Brey saw the shimmering metallic blue buildings and a flag. She had made it.

Parents dragged their children away from the demonic show as Punch neared Mr Skeleton's head with his swinging club. Closer, closer, BOOM!

Mr Skeleton's head separated raggedly from his body, his neck a paint-spray machine covering the kids with bloody measles, his head a cannonball that impaled itself on a spiky iron railing, the seagulls feasting on warm eyeballs whilst Mr Skeleton's torso thrashed about in its death throes.

The bees hummed down the beach chasing the donkeys, their infant passengers screaming as they clung to their braying charges until each child was immersed in bees stinging, bees buzzing, bees dying, bees clinging, a cavalcade of donkey-laden, bee-stung dead children, a caravan of dwarfed death.

Dai turned his eyes to a growing black cloud of birds dancing, reeling, circling. Feathered beasts, the descendants of dinosaurs, their DNA awoken, moving as one, a million shape-shifters weaving a wondrous web of woe. He plunged inside the old Essoldo cinema, jammed the theatre door and shakily lit a smoke. He was safe. Then Dai heard banging and turned to see the projectionist's face slide down his window, his mouth full of furious frenzied bees.

Brey entered the site and saw a banner, 'Congratulations Brey Scott,' strewn amongst the after-effects of what appeared to be a very wild party. Where were they? Were they playing a trick?

Dai sunk in his seat, whilst the film, stuck in a loop, repeated the same line over and over, "The greatest trick the Devil ever pulled was convincing the world he didn't exist." Dai covered his ears to drown out the sound of beaks on the door, hammering a single word into his brain; murmuration, murmuration, murmuration.

Brey looked around. Not a soul in sight. A diary; open at yesterday's date, was nailed to a door, a scrawled note read, 'Brey, make this your home.' Didn't they mean make yourself at home? She cried out with pain as intense electro-magnetic waves surged inside her guts. She took out her compass and crawled to the flag. The needle spun dementedly. She counted.

"5, 4, 3, 2, 1."

The needle swung away from Brey then pivoted back towards the flag. The South Pole flag that was now the North Pole flag. Her calculations had been right. The demonic forces lifted. She stood, wailed the national anthem and cried, knowing she was the first to stand where was, for just one brief moment, both the North and South Pole before they switched.

A shadow caught her eye. A dog? No, a wolf. It pounced in the snow and sniffed for lunch. Lunch popped its head up. A hare. Brey smiled then frowned. What was a wolf and a hare doing here? An Arctic wolf and an Arctic hare? In the Antarctic? What was happening? What had happened?

A phone rang. She ran to the Bird, Bee and Butterfly Hall and picked up.

"Hello?... Yes this is Brey... Hello Mum, Mum what is it?... Mum speak up... What's going on? Murmuration? What do you mean, Mother?"

Brey turned around. In the middle of the hall was a huge pyramid of mangled bloodied bodies stretching from the floor to a smashed skylight. No mercy had been shown to the scientists as they had tried to claw their way out faster than whatever it was that wanted out more quickly than they did. Blood oozed, dripped and bled down the human fountain of distorted Rodin-like bodies, flesh torn to shreds by beak, mandible and stinger, like a Biblical plague.

Brey screamed down the phone.

"MOTHER?"

"MOTHER!!!!"

23

THE VIOLIN CASE

Jane Badrock

Marion walked to the train station and waited on the platform at the exact spot where she stood every working day. This aligned her perfectly with the entrance of one very particular carriage. It was after several years of travelling that she had finally been welcomed by the merest hint of a nod of acknowledgement to this exclusive sanctuary. Here there were rules which had to be obeyed. The first of which, silently decreed, was that absolutely no conversation or phone call was permitted except in the event of a derailment; and only then if strictly necessary.

Marion had quickly perceived and happily adopted the second rule; an unstated dress code of inconspicuousness. As the train began its approach, she instinctively checked the neat bun her hair had been scraped into and tightened the belt on her plain taupe raincoat. She enjoyed this unostentatious attire; it made her entrance at rehearsals so much more flamboyant. She would walk in with a loud sigh, strip off her coat then let loose her hair, tossing her head to unleash the flaming locks. She was, after all, a performer; a violinist in the strings section of a highly reputable London orchestra where passion and exuberance was as highly regarded as ability.

The train came to a halt and Marion held her violin case tightly against her body. Heaven forbid she should accidentally knock someone with it. Once, when a young lady with – in Marion's opinion – an oversized handbag, bumped the arm of the bald headed man wearing the pince nez, there was uproar. Someone actually tutted!

As she boarded the train, Marion immediately sensed a less than amiable atmosphere. Someone half raised an eyebrow in warning. She turned to take her usual seat and was shocked to see it already occupied by one of the regulars who blushed slightly when he saw her. His eyes rolled sideways for a split second. Furrowing her brow a little, she followed the usurper's guilty glance across the aisle. Open mouthed she took in the apparition; a young male of about twenty wearing an unspeakably loud bright red T-shirt was sprawled out with his muddy shoes plonked on the seat opposite. Marion, unable to stop herself, did the unthinkable. She spoke. "Young man! Put your feet down immediately!"

The youth, aware of her stance more than her utterings, took out his earpieces, looked at her and muttered.,"You what?"

Marion puffed herself up and continued. "Remove your disgusting feet. People need to sit there you know. And that," she pointed, "is his seat."

After a taunting, fleeting look in the direction of her finger, he responded. "Fuck off you old bag!" And with that, the earpieces were re-inserted.

"Well I never!" Marion exclaimed. What did he mean old? She was barely fifty.

The other occupants of the carriage, still shocked by her utterances, were otherwise unmoved either in expression or position. There was just the merest hint of sympathy, by way of an almost indiscernible nod from the spectacled man now occupying her seat. She sat next to him, gingerly managing the violin case on her knee, and spent the rest of the journey deep in contemplation.

It was a subdued and restrained Marion who meekly took her place in rehearsals that day; she was not herself at all. Even her fellow musicians, who normally tried very hard not to notice her, couldn't help but stare as she sat down. And when she began to play, her legato was disjointed, her tremolo tremulous and her pizzicato was simply the pits. After missing her entry, the conductor sliced his hands through the air bringing the performance to a halt.

"Miss Stapes!" he boomed. "Are you ill?"

"No, it's just…"

"Do not, I repeat, do not tell me of your trivial problems. Once you come through that door you are mine, body and soul. You can have no other thought in your head other than to aspire to perfection. No, to exceed perfection. Go home now and do not return until you can perform as I require of you; with *sentimento*, with *sciolto* and most of all with enthusiasm…with…" he searched for the word, "with **gusto!**"

Well it wasn't a technical term but Marion knew exactly what he meant. And more importantly, here it was his rules that counted. She glanced around the hall; she'd seen it all before but never been on the receiving end. The kindest reactions were the smug glances. The cruellest were the loud phone calls to friends and family advising them of a forthcoming vacancy in the strings section. It was a competitive business and Marion knew she had to perform at her best to keep her place. She maintained her dignity as she put her violin away, vowing to herself that she would not be beaten, but when she got outside, she sloped away dejected and exhausted.

The following morning Marion boarded the train with trepidation. She had not slept well but was determined to try harder. If only her seat was available she could perhaps forget all about it and get back to her bestissimo. But her worst fear was confirmed. There, once again was the horrible oik sprawled across the seat, feet firmly on the blue striped seat. In blind panic, she pushed her way off the train and sobbed all the way home.

Once safely inside her house, and after a good few cups of chamomile tea with a little splash of brandy, Marion took out her violin. She played and played until she could do no more and she sorrowfully concluded that the conductor was right. She could do timid, which might just pass for *sentimento* and she could do keen, if not quite *sciolto*. But when it came to **gusto**, well, she was just completely feeblissimo. There was no way she could show her face at rehearsals. At least not until she had found a route out of her depression.

The weekend arrived and Marion took solace from gazing out of her window looking at her small but well maintained garden. With a frown she realised from the leafless state of the old cherry that it had succumbed to the death kiss of the ivy. Then, with a smile, she recognised that she was just like the tree; constrained and suffocated by an unwanted presence. Her poor old violin was no use. What she needed was a new instrument, something that would cut her free from the strangling vines of her new situation. With renewed fortitude, she went straight out to get one.

For the rest of the weekend Marion practiced and practiced with her new purchase until she felt she had mastered it. She was also delighted to find that it fitted into her old violin case.

On Monday morning she woke early and checked her schedule. There wasn't a rehearsal that day but so determined was she to prove to the conductor she had overcome her problems, she decided to go into London anyway. No bun today, she took out the brand new red raincoat that she had been saving for a special occasion and headed off to the station.

This time Marion boarded the train with such authority, people almost looked at her. She was determined to uphold the carriage rules even if it meant breaking them. She turned sideways to look for the offending feet on the seat and was not disappointed. I'm in control now, she told herself, but maybe I can, should, give him one last chance. With a deep breath, she squared up to him and spoke.

"Please put your feet down. Or else," she added with just a hint of menace. Her warning was met with a casual shrug. "I have warned you, young man."

The man with the glasses could no longer resist looking up. Gracious was that...? And what is she doing? He gazed in wonder as Marion snapped open the catch on her violin case. He'd never seen her do this before.

"Mind your own business." The lad snarled. Another woman turned her head just a fraction, ears sideways.

"I'm giving you one last chance." Marion announced, beginning to lift the lid.

Now the man was peering over his paper in fascination. Was she going to play to the lad? Music soothing the savage breast and all that?

"Get a life." Came the reply.

Marion took out her instrument. Her spectator frowned. Gracious. It was one of those modern metal thingys. He'd had her down for a traditionalist.

Marion now stood next to the lad who hadn't quite realised what she was holding.

"What the fuck is that thing?"

The young man's question really should have made Marion think. It wasn't the same response; it wasn't even the same voice but the die was cast and after all, it was the same sin.

Waving the chain-saw in the air, she pulled the cord and in a jiffy held it to the lad's ankles. It wasn't that different from the old tree branches she had practiced on but it was a good deal messier and the bone crunching noises were a little unpleasant. Not quite perfect, Marion told herself. As his screams began the carriage fell into panic.

"How unfortunate," said someone.

"I've got blood on my shoes," said another. Marion, ignoring the commotion, sensed the presence of someone else approaching the scene.

"You mad fucking cow!" said the more familiar sounding voice. She turned to see the original youth standing there, right in front of her his arms outstretched. In a jiffy she'd whisked off his arms, one above and one below the elbow.

"Jesus fucking Christ!" he yelled as the severed limbs flopped on the floor, rivulets of blood pouring from the stumps. Better but still not right, Marion thought. Where is my *legato?* I'm all *tremolo.*

"I'm moving further up tomorrow," a voice said.

"I think she's lost it," said another.

"What is wrong with you people?" Marion exclaimed. "This is a quiet carriage and I am performing. Is this how you behave at a concert?"

The man with the spectacles slowly got to his feet. "I say, old girl. You are making a bit of a mess."

Marion looked up at him in amazement. She hadn't realised he was so tall. Now the conductor's words were reverberating in her head. Louder and louder. What should she do? This passage didn't need *sentimento*. It didn't need *sciolto*. She smiled to herself. I know precisely what is required. She looked the man in the eye and with a glint in hers, lifted her instrument high in the air. As he stared back in bewilderment she swung it with flair, with accuracy and most importantly with unquestionable gusto and chopped his head clean off.

Applause at last! Marion bowed to the sound of escaping feet as the carriage emptied. When she looked up she was astonished to discover her audience had disappeared, yet she could still hear the sound of voices. This won't do at all, she said to herself. But now I've rediscovered my prowess, I can bring my genius to everyone.

Wielding her bloodied instrument like a sword, Marion followed the noise to the next compartment.

24

CARING FOR MOTHER

Karen Davison

Jane woke with a start.

The echoes of her mother's shrill voice were followed by the inevitable thud of her stick striking the wall. The red digits of the alarm clock read 3:29 am.

She threw back the blankets, swung her legs out of bed and pushed her feet into her slippers. The air was cold, her breath misted in the orange glow of street lights which seeped through the thin floral curtains.

Another thud on the wall.

Jane pulled on her pink flannel dressing gown as she stepped out onto the dim landing. The grandfather clock in the hallway below chimed the half hour as she shuffled along the threadbare carpet to her mother's room.

The door stood ajar, light from many scented candles cast a deceptively inviting glow. She took a deep breath to steady herself before pushing open the door.

The fetid stink mixed with the cloying sweetness of perfume turned her stomach, but she was careful to hide her revulsion. Her mother sat propped up with pillows, her features pinched in anger, her small eyes chips of ice below furrowed brows.

'You're too late. I'm sitting in my own filth!'

'Sorry mother.' Jane mumbled averting her gaze. Even in her weakened state, the old woman still made her feel worthless.

As she worked, her mother's sharp tongue chastised her: she was too rough, the water was too cold, she was taking too long. By the time she had her cleaned and settled on crisp white sheets, it was nearly 4 am.

'You can take that cup of tea away, it was disgusting.' The old woman snapped.

Jane picked up the cup, her shaking hands causing the fine bone china to rattle, filling the rose print saucer with the cold contents. Out the corner of her eye, she saw her mother shaking her head in disgust.

'Useless! No wonder your father left us.'

The usual feelings of guilt accompanied Jane to the kitchen. If only she had been better behaved, less clumsy, a more worthy daughter…

As she washed the cup, she studied her reflection in the window.

Dark circles under her eyes looked stark against her pale flesh, her hair hung in lank strands about her shoulders. She looked like a ghost.

When was the last time she had dressed and left the house? She couldn't remember, the only contact she had with the outside world was her weekly phone call to Mr Patel to order the grocery delivery.

But tomorrow, she would be going out.

It was all arranged.

Their new neighbour was going to mind mother so she could take a break. Sophie was a retired nurse after all, so mother would be in safe hands.

Jane felt a knot form in her stomach, a mix of fear, excitement and guilt. She wouldn't stay out long, just a stroll along the high street. She looked at her frayed sleeves; perhaps she would treat herself to a new dressing gown.

*

Next morning, Jane waited anxiously in the hall, her hair still damp from the shower. Mother was asleep, the breakfast Jane had carefully prepared, untouched by her bedside.

The creak of their old iron gate signalled Sophie's arrival and Jane opened the door. In a whisper, she explained that mother was resting and not to disturb her.

'Don't you worry about a thing,' Sophie gave her a warm smile, 'I looked after my own mother for many years and I know how important it is to have some time out.'

Jane glanced up the stairs, she hesitated, nerves churning in her stomach. She jumped as Sophie laid a gentle hand on her arm.

'Off you go now, everything will be fine. I will be here when you get back.'

Jane nodded, turned resolutely away and stepped across the threshold into freedom.

*

Jane woke to total darkness. Had mother been calling her? Sitting up caused an unfamiliar creaking of bed springs. Pushing back the covers, she swung her legs out of the bed. The shock of cold concrete beneath her bare feet caused a surge of panic. Where *was* she?

Her head throbbed, making it difficult to think.

She had gone out, hadn't she?

She remembered the door closing behind her, the wind whipping at her hair. Her steps along the garden path had felt heavy, as if the force of her mother's will had been reluctant to let her go.

But she had gone. The echoes of her footfalls quickening as she went. She had felt exhilarated, empowered, free.

And then…?

A whimper escaped her lips as the memory of her abduction hit her with terrifying clarity.

They had grabbed her off the street, four men, all in black. She had tried to fight, but they had been too strong. They had bound her hands and bundled her into a van.

What would happen to Mother if she wasn't there to care for her?

Sobbing with fear, her frantic hands searched the walls of her tiny cell until she located the door.

'Let me out!' she pounded with her fists, 'Mother needs me!'

A hatch slid open. Light flooded in, blinding her and driving her back against the wall to shield her eyes. Keys jangled and hinges groaned. She could feel panic stealing the air from her throat.

Two figures loomed, faceless silhouettes against the brightness. Ignoring her frantic pleas, they grabbed her and forced her onto the bed. Jane felt the sting of a hypodermic needle.

Before oblivion took her, she thought she heard mother, calling her name.

*

The police had taken Sophie's statement and finally allowed her to go home.

Exhausted, she dropped the keys in the dish on the hallway table and went straight to the drinks cabinet in the lounge. Pouring a measure of whiskey, she downed it in one, closing her eyes against the scorching heat, taking pleasure from the discomfort. She poured another and made her way over to the window.

They would be taking the old lady away soon.

Sophie sank into the armchair and closed her eyes. The lights from the emergency vehicles pierced her closed lids with pulsing, hypnotic light. Each strobe brought an image, an old movie reel of captured moments.

Her hand on the banister.

Her foot on the landing.

Fingers reaching to open the door.

The freshly cooked breakfast on the bedside.

Then, dear God... the eyes! Staring out from the shrunken figure, propped up with pillows, its flesh marbled and putrefied.

Sophie could still smell the stink of decay in her nostrils.

The stab wounds which had caused the old woman's death had been inflicted weeks before.

Jane had been arrested as she returned to the house. It had taken four officers to get her into the police van. Even after they had closed the doors, her screams could still be heard, calling for her mother.

25

THE
ANNIVERSARY

Robbie Mori

When I turned fourteen I saw what comes out of a skull when squashed. My mother's brain laid bare for all to see. On the floor of the kitchen where she fell. A pool of blood easing out from behind her head. Flooding, like gravy from a burst meat pie, gloopy, dark and intoxicating, her blonde hair turning pinky red. 'Grab the child! Don't let him walk in!' But I was too quick for them.

I stood there, glued to the terracotta tiles, a warm streak of piss snaking down my leg. Strip lighting humming, me in a trance. That's when they all poured in. Everyone rushing around: 'Call the police!' 'Call the Priest!' Passed me around, like some kind of trash you don't want to hang on to, and I resented them calling me a child. Ollie had whacked *Mother Dearest* at the back of the head with the pan she just washed and handed to him to dry, the one with the red heat spot in the middle. I can almost imagine the scene, her at the sink with her back to him, going on and on. Him looking at that pan and imagining what damage it could do. The red spot staring at him, mocking him. The shadow people whispering in his ear 'Go on Ollie, one quick heavy swipe and she'll shut up for good. Then you'll only hear the tap dripping in the sink. Tick, tick, tick. And the humming of the lights. Hum, hum, hum.'

The look of surprise forever locked on her face.

My name is Ben, did I say? I am fifteen now. I hate everything and everyone, especially my father and his most peculiar ways.

Today is the anniversary. Walking up the hill towards the church, in the spraying rain, I struggle to keep up with father. I catch my reflection in the dirty window and flatten my wiry hair. Red as a fox. I wince, as I feel the burn of his slap at the back of my neck, which is sore from the sunburn I got riding my bike by the beach. 'Straighten up, don't slouch, don't make a show of me, don't sit next to that bloody waster from the flats.'

Father bloody hates when I talk to Deano, Dean Cullen from the flats at the bottom of the hill. Says they're all drug dealers and prozzies living there. Forgotten by God. I think we're the forgotten ones, God has no place in our house, not with what goes on in there. Deano looks like a convict today, his head badly shaved and full of nicks. His little brother Karl probably has nits again, that's when the whole family looks like those pictures of Nazi concentration camps, that and the fact they live on frozen chips and pies from Iceland. The supermarket, not the country.

Deano is not what you would call a good influence but he is my friend, in fact he is my only real friend, well, the only one that hasn't shunned me since *that* day. I was even dropped from the football team, not that I was any good, but it was good to belong to a group even briefly. Once I was dropped I was forgotten by everyone. Just like that.

When we sit in Sunday school, we're told Jesus walked amongst the lepers but something tells me even *He* wouldn't go near this family. We're damaged stock. Damaged from birth, Ollie with his Tourette's that tells him to say, 'Fuck you' and 'Dirty titties' to Mrs Welch next door, and her just taking it, saying 'God bless him, he doesn't know what he's saying.' Father with his drinking, abusing Mother Dearest. And me, the runt, nothing I can see that's wrong with me but I am sure it's just a matter of time.

In the church, it's stifling with the sweet smell of pollen and old people's clothes. Moth balls and old lace. Everyone's eyes are on us; I can just imagine what they're all thinking.

'A nice lad like Ollie, whatever made him do it? Oh, he couldn't help it, the poor lad.' It's enough to make you sick. I catch Deano's eye, I nod and I get another slap on the neck, making the sunburn really sting. The priest tells us all to pray for Mother's soul, one year on. One thing I know is: praying doesn't work. Deano told me his sister prayed and prayed but she still got pregnant. Praying didn't do her any good. Deano's father beat the baby out of her one night, and now she doesn't leave the flat.

First chance I get after Mass, I tear my tie off and fling it to the wind, and father lands me one at the side of my head. I run home. Neck still stinging, I shut my bedroom door and watch the gap beneath it. I do that every night. Sometimes father comes in, and makes me read passages from the bible until my head bobs forward, drunk with sleep, sometimes he just stands outside my door, but the threat of what he might do instead is worse. Sure enough, I see the shadow of his feet come to rest outside the door, for a moment. He walks away and I hear the familiar hiss of a beer can. I don't think he is the same man as when Ollie and I were small, as before the *accident* even. When night falls, father goes around and shuts all the windows tight. 'So, they won't come in' he says. 'God will protect us' he says, 'See us right.'

I don't believe him.

I never see God. I see things that shouldn't be there. They are just the shadow people, I tell myself, I prefer to call them that than ghosts, so I don't get scared. They can't hurt me, they won't pick on me like they did with Ollie. And whispered to him until he cracked, and carried out what they told him to do. I will never understand why they picked him. He was the *good* boy, not me, never me. I'm better off hiding.

Once they grabbed my feet in the bath and pulled me under. I didn't have a bath for a month after that, but I stank, so now I just soap and rinse myself under the shower, Oh and I don't pull the curtain. I try to be good and think about what father says: 'God will find you even in the darkest of places.'

I can't sleep tonight. I can see my mother's glassy eyes in my waking dreams. They have the same expression as the stuffed fox in the window of the Fox and Hound. I wonder if that's what happens to you when you die. Do you just freeze as you were and your eyes turn to glass? I tell myself I have been stupid, and notice father turned on the light in the hallway.

I glance at my watch. The one I got for my communion that has a button on the side which, when you press it, turns a little green light on so you can read the time when it's dark. Very handy. I sit up, torn between panic and the need to find a better hiding place. I am up, and lift the floorboards under the bed. Ollie's knife sticks out of the stained yellow duster I wrapped it in. That's the first thing I did when they came to take him away. I took his knife for myself. And now it might be time to use it.

The light is still on and I see father's feet outside my door again. 'You in there, son?' I grab my knife tighter. He never called me that before. At this moment, I do not know if that's him out there, and I am glad I put the latch on. Why would he leave his room?

He taps. 'Ben, open the door. I need to talk to you.'

'What about?' I kick the pile of dirty clothes next to me. I shouldn't have spoken.

'Open and I'll tell you.' His tone has changed. He sounds mocking. Now I know he's not himself.

I hear him tap again as I wonder if I'd survive a jump out the window. I think it's too high; I would at least break a leg and the shadows would get me. But the drain pipe is sturdy looking. Iron pipe, no plastic. I could climb up to the roof and stay there until he is gone.

Tap, tap, tap. 'Son, open the door or you'll be in trouble.'

I slip on my beaten trainers and slowly lift the window trying to make as little noise as possible. 'What are you doing in there?'

Shit, he heard. No matter. I make a leap of faith from the sill, hoping I don't crash down, and grab the pipe. I scrape my knuckles on the wall and it hurts like hell. I settle myself before the climb, which is not as bad as I predicted. As I flip my bruised legs and body onto the roof I see father standing in the garden, in a pool of light coming from the kitchen. He is looking at me. When I say looking, I mean his eyes are fixed on me but they're dark. I struggle to recognize my father. Blood on his shirt, from a neck wound perhaps. Somehow, I don't think he is alright.

And then I know he is not. Two shadow people are standing next to him whispering in his ears and staring at me. Their hands are bony. I don't know what they are, not really, but I know Ollie was never the same after they got to him. And now they're talking to father.

I must leave, I think, as I wipe sweat off my eyes. I look back, he is no longer there and I start to panic but then I see him and he's back in the garden pacing up and down, but this time he's holding a bread knife. I freeze in disbelief then I recall the scene I walked into when I was 14, what Ollie did, and I know he's after me.

Suddenly I remember the discarded mattress at the front, father put it there months ago, for the Council to collect, but then he never rang them. I could have a go. Leaping into the unknown is somewhat exciting. I try to land on my feet but I crash flat on the mattress. A shooting pain in my ass makes me wince. I remember the knife in my back pocket. I feel for the wound and my hand is wet with blood. I stumble to my feet. I get this urge to confront father and so I wait and look around until I see him. He's in the kitchen staring out at me. I run at him with my knife but the room turns black and my legs go from under me. I get up, I am in the hallway, how did I get here? I smell a puddle of vomit next to me which seems to match the stain on my t-shirt. I begin to walk away awkwardly, but then my steps steady and I break into a run. I keep going and I don't turn back until I get to Deano's. His dad answers the door and I collapse in a heap at his feet.

When Deano's father makes his way to our house with the Old Bill, they find father hanging from the ceiling in the kitchen, from a belt, with a fallen chair next to him. Nobody questions a thing, not even that it wasn't his belt but mine. That's both of my parents dead in our kitchen, Ollie in prison and me free as a bird.

I said I wasn't the good son.

26

SAIGNANT

Fiona Hunnisett

The amber glow of a streetlight pierces the dark Parisian backstreet. A student, Paul, searches impatiently, checking each door, each window. His footsteps echo. No, not an echo, it is the sound of other footsteps, slow and labored. Behind him, another man emerges from the shadows, his rattling breaths rasping the silence. Paul swivels round, eyes wide.

The young man, Dan, bends double. His sausage fingers splay against the wall, as he supports his flabby frame. He shakes his head, struggling for breath.

"Can't we just go to McDonald's?" he finally wheezes.

Paul gapes in horror. "I did not come to Paris to eat a Big Mac. Besides, it's got to be around here somewhere."

His face lights up as he points above Dan's head. "That's it! The sign for the restaurant."

Dan raises his eyes to the large iron meat cleaver hanging above him. He swallows hard and steps back from under it.

"Either that or a butcher's," he mutters.

He shuffles after Paul who is already down the adjoining alley, peering at a door.

"Saignant." Paul points to the brass name-plate on the door. "Just how I like my steak."

He knocks. The door creaks open a fraction and the black hooded eyes of a small moustached man peer out suspiciously.

"Hi, er, I mean bonsoir," stutters Paul.

The man stares. Paul and Dan exchange uncertain glances.

"Er," Paul continues, "the owner of the hostel has booked us a…"

The surly face switches to a smile.

"Ah, bien sûr! The two English. Bienvenue. Welcome to Saignant." The Maître D' swings open the door and ushers them into a tiny vestibule, hung with heavy ruby-red curtains. The pungent aroma of roasted meat dilates Paul and Dan's nostrils. Their mouths salivate and ravenous grins stretch their faces.

"May I take your coats?" asks the Maître D'.

They slip off their hoodies. Unnoticed by them, the Maître D' looks them up and down, paying particular attention to Dan's rounded frame. A smile momentarily twitches his moustache.

"And your portables… mobiles?"

"Our phones?" Paul and Dan both hesitate.

"Oui, monsieur. Here at Saignant, la viande, the meat, is our God. This restaurant is its church and nothing is allowed to interrupt our worship. We keep the mobiles here." He points to a row of small lockers behind him. "You will have the key. No one can touch them."

Paul glances at his phone. "No reception anyway," he shrugs, and hands it over. Dan reluctantly does likewise. The Maître D' locks the phones away and hands them the key. Then with a theatrical wave, he pulls aside one of the curtains to reveal stone steps descending into darkness.

Dim lights buzz on above them as Paul and Dan follow him down to a wooden door, thickly painted in crimson. He knocks briskly three times, pauses, then pushes it open.

A medieval-like scene greets them; The room is a low, brick-arched cellar, its far end dominated by an open stone fireplace and a large metal spit. Four chefs tend to a carcass that turns above the licking flames. Their silhouettes obscure the roasting meat from view.

In the contorting shadows people feast, hunched over small tables, each with its own flickering candle. As Dan and Paul enter, the diners turn to stare, their greasy lips glistening in the candlelight. An imperceptible nod from the Maître D' and the gnawing and slurping resumes.

The Maître D' installs Paul and Dan at a table furthest away from the fire, hidden by one of the vaulted pillars.

"Wow, that was a bit Slaughtered Lamb, wasn't it?" grins Dan.

The Maître D' reappears with two shot glasses.

"An aperitif, Messieurs, on the house. You must, how you say, down the hatch."

Paul and Dan beam at one another and knock the drinks back.

"It is good, n'est-ce pas?"

They nod, their eyes watering.

"Your meal will be served momentarily."

"Isn't there a menu?" asks Dan.

"Non. Here it is juste la viande, just the meat, saignant. You will never eat better again in your life, that I can promise you."

The Maître D' fills their glasses from a large earthenware jug; The syrupy wine trickles from its spout.

"Cheers." Paul and Dan chink their glasses and gulp it down.

A chef places two large metal plates on the table and, with a bow and a 'Bon appétit', he and the Maître D' take their leave.

Paul and Dan drool as they behold the chunks of succulent meat before them. They search for cutlery. There is none. Then glance around the restaurant. Everyone is eating with their hands.

"Best restaurant ever!"

They tear into their steaks with caveman ferocity.

"Bet you're glad we didn't go to McDonald's now?" mumbles Paul as he tears off a slither of flesh.

Dan grins contentedly as blood and grease drip down his chin.

For the next hour they gorge themselves in a carnivorous orgy of gluttony – tearing, guzzling, devouring. Every time they finish, another pile of roasted flesh replaces it.

Eventually, Paul and Dan sit back, satiated smiles on their shimmering crimson faces as, around them, the sounds of feasting continue. They both yawn, made drowsy by the heat of the room and the food and alcohol inside their swollen stomachs.

As if by magic, the Maître D' appears by their side.

"Messieurs. How did you enjoy your meal?"

"Magnifique!" slurs Paul, rubbing his bloated belly.

A burp reverberates from Dan's lips, accompanied by a thumbs-up.

"Before dessert, it is our custom to invite our new guests to visit the kitchen. The Head Chef awaits you."

They sway as they follow the Maître D' through the restaurant, too intoxicated to notice that the other diners have stopped mid-bite to observe them. They pass through the kitchen, oblivious to the cleavers and knives, blood and bones. At the end is a large doorway hung with a thick curtain of wide strips of opaque plastic. The Maître D' waves them through with a bow.

In the dining room, all is paused, waiting, listening… A yell, followed by a blood-curdling scream that's quickly stifled.

In the kitchen, a spurt of scarlet splatters the plastic curtain.

A short while later, two chefs, their white aprons smeared red, haul out Dan's fat, naked body, blood still dripping from his freshly cut throat and an apple stuffed in his recently screaming jaws.

The diners watch in fascination, as the chefs heave up the trussed corpse to hang, upside down, from a sturdy hook in the centre of the vaulted ceiling. Its bulging stomach flops down.

The Maitre D' holds a glass goblet beneath Dan to collect the warm blood that oozes from the gash in his neck. When the goblet is full, he holds it up to the light of a candle, examines the liquid's rich hue, then swirls it gently around the bowl of the glass before breathing in its bouquet, like a sommelier appraising the finest Burgundy. Finally, he takes a sip, closing his eyes and savouring the taste of the crimson nectar.

The Maitre D's eyes open wide with pleasure. He beams at his expectant audience and lifts the goblet in the air.

"Mesdames, Messieurs. Let us raise a toast to the newest member of Saignant."

The diners raise their glasses, as the Maitre D' hands the goblet to Paul, who licks his lips hungrily.

27

MARKET RESEARCH

Richie Brown

Veronica strides briskly across the pedestrianised town-centre, permed, dapper and purposed, her errands foremost in her mind: bank, optician, and coffee.

She sees a woman selling 'The Big Issue,' and veers.

As she pushes the magazine, unread, into a waste-bin, someone speaks.

"Excuse me, madam. Would you mind assisting me with some market-research?"

A suited young man, very smart, holding a clipboard, proffers a laminated identity card, very official and so clearly in order that Veronica waves it away.

Veronica is most amenable, always ready to impart her opinions and beliefs, though seldom asked, and the young man is really quite handsome: tall, slim and blonde, with pale green eyes.

And so engaging!

The young man smiles

and he is beautiful.

"I'm Clive. Thank you for your time. Just a few minutes, and I know you'll find it interesting!"

Veronica, eternal spinster of the universal parish, desperately lonely beneath her brisk facade, relishes the contact. She is about to ask Clive for whom the research is intended when Clive nods discreetly at a nearby group of obese shoppers, dressed incongruously in various forms of nightwear.

Clive winks at Veronica.

"I do appreciate this. It's a treat for me to speak to a discerning respondent, such as yourself, than…"

He winks again.

"That's very uncharitable of you, young man!"

Clive flushes.

"I'm so sorry! I hope I've not caused offence."

Veronica accepts, graciously, Clive's apology.

"I think it's so important not to judge others. We're put here to help, not to condemn. I believe that with all my heart."

Clive nods gratefully, but flustered he fumbles and drops the papers from the clipboard. Veronica helps retrieve them as Clive stammers apologies.

Veronica waits patiently and Clive finds, eventually, the right page.

"Right! And let me apologise one last time for… Anyway, let's start, and we'll soon have you on your way. I really do appreciate this. First question: when contemplating a new brand/variety of cheese, are you adventurous/mildly adventurous/mildly conservative/very conservative?"

Veronica answers fulsomely (mildly adventurous; British cheeses) and almost truthfully, given that pre-sliced, generic cheddar is the sole cheese choice on her sparse shopping lists.

The questions run on, covering a wide range of products and services and Veronica responds with comprehensive answers, considered opinions, and earnest anecdotes. Clive laughs appropriately, and writes everything down in a most satisfactory manner.

Veronica enjoys this rare attention and barely registers it when Clive says:

"This next question may be a little embarrassing..."

Veronica giggles.

"Oh, you won't shock me, young man, I assure you!"

Clive flicks his papers.

"I hope not! So... Would you swallow my cock here in public/behind a skip/only in the privacy of your cat-infested house?"

"I beg your – What did you say?"

Clive grins, and hefts his crotch.

"My cock's a beauty and the cats won't bother me. If I whipped it out now, you'd be kneeling and gagging. You dirty bitch."

Tears of anger prick Veronica's eyes.

"I will not be spoken to like this! I shall find a police constable at once!"

Clive shrugs.

"Good. You can tell him you killed your mother."

A beat.

"How dare you!"

Clive laughs, and his pale eyes gleam.

"Oh dear! A teeny-tad too slow to be convincing! You can tell the nice policeman how you pushed mummy down the stairs. Bump-bumpitty-bump, incontinent arse over saggy old tit, all the way down. Mummy twipped and got an ouchy and Jeebus took her for a fucking sunbeam. Because you killed her. Not a hint of suspicion, seeing how frail your dear old mum had become, and how dedicated you were, nursing her, for years."

"I did not hurt her!"

Veronica hears the cracking, crumbling, lumping thumps and sees the thin, white, limbs in a flurry of nightdress, tumbling down the stairs.

She hears herself laugh.

"No-one can blame me," blurts Veronica and claps her hand to her blabbing mouth.

"Untrue! I've got quite a lob-on, and your dog's-arse mouth is making me so bloody horny. But in a lovely, gorgeous way."

"How do you know?"

This easy acknowledgement of her terrible, destructive secret; it is almost cathartic.

"Market research. We know everything. How long did she take to die, at the foot of the stairs, whilst you waited?"

Clive consults his clipboard, rustling the papers.

"You sat, to watch in comfort, I believe. A chair from – "

A chair from the dining room.

Veronica dragged the chair into the hall, and made herself comfortable, moving back once as her mother stared uncomprehendingly at the ceiling, brushing Veronica's foot with a frantic hand, seeking help that never came. How long? Probably ten minutes, before Mother's breathing and itchy, rodent-like, pointless twitching ceased.

Clive pulls a heavy fob watch from his jacket and flips the cover.

"Two hours and forty-seven minutes. Your poor, sad eyes, to witness such a thing! Mama was in agony throughout, but you know that. Everyone was soooooooo supportive afterwards. Such a shame that support was lacking when needed most: when you fed her and wiped her – ooh! Hang on!"

Clive makes a pantomime of leafing through the clipboard.

"Well, it seems you had constant offers of help but turned it all away."

He stares at her, eyes wide.

"Why?"

Tears course Veronica's face.

"I loved her. I had to look after her. She was my mother, but the strain…"

Clive laughs.

"What a saint. Let's see what you were really up to, you minxy minx!"

Veronica begs Clive to stop, but he is intent upon the clipboard.

"Your starter for ten is–"

bird table

One dreadful, winter morning her mother was not in her bedroom, and Veronica ran through the house, seeking her, and then from outside, someone calling. The French windows into the garden were open and in the snow and east wind her mother, in a thin nightdress, by the bird table, cramming, stuffing, and gorging suet, seed, and stale bread. Veronica ran outside, knocking the filthy stuff from her mother's hands, wrapping her mother in her own cardigan under the scrutiny of the interfering bitch next door.

Later, Veronica visited the neighbour, suitably tearful at mother's incessant decline and the neighbour was comforting and solicitous.

"Poor Mother", Veronica had said, "she forgets she's eaten."

The neighbour was tearful too and told Veronica she was a treasure, an angel. Veronica smiled faintly, glad that Mother was sleeping now.

So peacefully.

Clive snorts.

"No she wasn't. You locked her in her room and gave her a suet block to gnaw. But you got smarter after that and didn't starve her quite so much."

Veronica nods blankly, and stares around.

Everyone looks at her. People have stopped, and every blank and vapid face gawps at her.

"Ignore them. Let's see. What else?"

Dressing her inadequately, or – better – leaving her naked and turning off the heat. Terrifying her by pounding upon her door, suddenly, in the night. Washing her with icy water. Screaming into her face...

Clive flicks through the papers.

"Plenty of verbal abuse. Pretty much non-stop. But nothing to leave a physical mark. Clever you! When buying flowers would you select roses/chrysanthemums/carnations/freesias?"

"White lilies, for the funeral," whispers Veronica.

"But mummy hated lilies; at least, she did when she knew what lilies are. That's why you chose them. I'll put you down for gladioluses – gladioleas? – gladileas? –bollocks, let's say 'bindweed'."

"What do you want of me?"

Clive beams at her.

"Just your reaction. It's very valuable to my employer and your support and assistance is greatly appreciated. Oh, and why? Why did you do it, for so many years?"

Clive waits, pen poised.

There is nothing

nothing

to write.

"OK, I'll put you down as a 'Don't Know.'"

"You can't prove any of this," Veronica mumbles.

A thumbs-up from Clive.

"Abso-bloody-lutely correct! But I don't have to prove anything.

Because we both **know**. And for the *cognoscenti*, like what we are, knowledge outweighs proof."

Veronica nods, miserable, any relief she felt previously now gone.

"When contemplating the purchase of a coffin do you select the cheapest/the most environmentally-sustainable/the one best guaranteed to impress your acquaintances? Not 'friends,' You have none."

"Oak. Solid brass handles and a silk lining," murmurs Veronica.

"I'll just say 'several black bin-liners and tape' – that best reflects your true intention."

Clive's pen, busy across the clipboard, records everything.

On the night of the funeral, after the scant, mealy-mouthed mourners had scavenged the funeral tea and skulked away, Veronica returned to the cemetery, and scaled the low wall. In the chill darkness and the drizzle, she pulled off her knickers, straddled and then squatted over the fresh-turned earth, and pissed on her mother's grave, the reek of her steaming urine mingling with the sickly scent of the pallid lilies in the wreath kicked viciously aside.

Clive sighs.

"Indignity and hatred even after she was buried."

"What are you going to do?" asks Veronica, unconcerned and hopeless now that the darkest secret of her life lies bare and souring in the light.

"Why, nothing! Nothing at all. You have been very generous with your time, and your responses are most valuable to us."

"Who do you work for?"

Veronica saw Clive's identity card but had not recognised it, and the logo was a slashed, red symbol.

"You'd rather not know. But you should thank him for this. Confession is good for the soul and your soul needs all the good it can get."

And Veronica does not wish to know. She gazes around the sunny precinct, and does not wish to know anything. The doors to the shops are large, cavernous and menacing, and the people gross, stupid and vacant.

Clive winks at her.

"Your secret is safe."

And Veronica sees he is not good-looking. His face is too thin, and the pale-green eyes flicker above hollow cheeks and beneath a heavy brow.

"If you want to spill your guts that's your business but all you'll achieve is to be thought a crazy old cat-lady."

"What shall I do now?"

Clive shrugs.

"Dunno. Carry on with your day and your life. Do some shopping. Buy something nice, because you're worth it. Ooh, I know! Get some cats! They'll suit you. And keep skirting around the place at the bottom of the stairs where Mumsie died. Terrified, broken, un-helped and in pain."

He consults his clipboard.

"Blimey! And all befouled. Feculence everywhere."

Veronica, previously busy, bustling, ever occupied, no longer cares.

"I'll go home now."

Clive's smile is even more saturnine.

"Excellent idea."

Veronica turns slowly, unsure of which direction to take, and begins to wander away.

Clive calls after her.

"One more thing. There will be a follow-up visit. Another representative will come to you to confirm some aspects of our discussion today. But between ourselves – and I should not say this, I **really** shouldn't – I think it best if you do not open the door. Not if you value your skin and your sanity. And your eyes."

Clive's smile grows broader, darker, and uglier.

Veronica trudges away, avoiding the gigantic, ruinous, static wrecks of the blank eyed, slack-jawed pedestrians, her errands forgotten. She wanders, lost in empty streets she does not recognise, glimpsing sallow faces staring through grimy windows, flinching from dark, sudden-rustling hedges, starting at febrile movements seen from the corner of her eye, but there is

something

nothing there.

An unknown time later she claws into her dark house, slams and locks the door and then skirts, as always, the

patch of carpet at the bottom of the stairs.

She longed for that push, that shove, for years, holding back, savouring the anticipation and the denial, and when she did, when she pushed, she wondered if there was any feeling in the world as good

she wondered if it was like love.

Veronica drags a chair

the chair

from the dining room and sits upon it at the foot of the stairs, hands folded upon her lap

and she never answers the door again.

28

TRAUMA ONE

Maggie Innes

White. Dazzling white. Shiny tiles. Steel. Bright lights.

Far below, a blur of moving shapes, muted in greens and blues.

And slicing through the spongy soundscape like a scalpel through skin, the high-pitched scream of a heart monitor. Flatlining.

Eeeeeeeeeeee

What happened to me?

Denise's thoughts are calm, detached. Almost peaceful.

Free-floating high in the corner of Trauma One, she observes as defibrillator pads are attached above a glistening, gaping abdominal cavity.

"Charging... clear!"

Denise knows the Re-sus drill inside out. She must have done it a thousand times herself. But she feels nothing as the body – her body – convulses off the bed like a rat snapped in a trap.

Eeeeeeeeeee

"No output."

I was...

I was in an accident.

Staff in theatre scrubs mill around below, heads bobbing and pecking like curious, hungry birds. Denise can recognise some familiar hospital colleagues. It's touching to see the concern on their faces. But any warmth is doused by an icy reality seeping in through the frayed edges of her consciousness.

Baby...

Heads are shaking. Faces falling. The lightness and brightness in Denise, around her, darkens and grows colder. Heavier.

My baby!

"Charging..."

The theatre doors ricochet open.

In strides Mr Andrew Gordon, swathed in his usual fragrant haze of golf club grass and expensive aftershave. His inferiors scatter like snooker balls, parting the eminent surgeon's path to the bed.

Ahhhhhh

All eyes rest on him. He raises his gloved hands, a godlike hero preparing for performance. As he scans the monitor, Denise feels a sigh of pure emotional energy ripple through her and radiate out, reflecting off the bright-tiled walls

It's bright and beautiful.

It's hope.

Andrew

She joins with everyone else in Trauma One, watching and waiting for The Great Man to work his world-famous magic. Make the miracle happen.

Thank you

Mr Andrew Gordon stands, still and self contained. Frowning slightly in a way that jolts Denise's memory. She's seen it before. She knows what it means. He is weighing up his options.

Andrew

The monitor screeches on, a demented chainsaw.

Please

Eeeeeeeeeeee

I'm sorry

Two straight, squat lines of conscience crease the surgeon's winter-sunned forehead.

I didn't mean it

Through his pristine, unbloodied latex gloves, the faint golden glint of a wedding ring.

I won't say anything

Mr Andrew Gordon pulls his shoulders back. Decision made.

I promise

He reaches out.

Andrew

He switches off the monitor.

Our baby!

Silence.

For a few blissful seconds, Denise savours it.

A brief shadow of surprise darkens the faces of Trauma One personnel. Then they quickly bow their heads in worshipful deference. Thoughts already buzzing. Gossip brewing. RIP Theatre Nurse Denise – dark horse that one! Five months gone and no one had a clue. Did she even have a boyfriend? Hit and run, wasn't it? Poor cow.

Denise realises, in one dread, dizzying instant, what the silence means.

The light dims to grey, to black. A terrifying chill consumes her and – disorientated – she tumbles. Sucked spinning, swirling and spiralling down, down down… towards the motionless, mutilated meat prison laid out below.

Powerless and voiceless Denise plummets, while her soul screams in silent anguish.

NoNoNo

NONONONO

Her empty corpse sucks her in and swallows her up like a swamp – cloying fleshy mud, suffocating earthy stench.

As the viscous darkness closes over, one intense image burns. A pale, embryonic hand, reaching out. Five waxy doll-like fingers. Still and streaked with cold-clotted blood.

NO

The vital essence of what was, is and always will be Denise thrashes and spins, chokes and scratches, lunges and spits. Struggling in frenzied furious vengeful agony to metamorphose. Spiritual energy into physical. Love into hate.

No

Her grey-blue eyes groan open into glittering slits.

And stare straight at Mr Andrew Gordon.

Unforgiving.

Unforgetting.

Undead.

29

MUMMY-MOLLY
PUDDING CLUB

Stephanie Hutton

It is nearly bong-bong-bong-bong four o'clock, which is Mummy-Molly Pudding Club time. Mummy has got out our special mixing bowl, wooden stirrer and the shiny red scales. Now I am big I can do the measuring all by myself. Mummy's face is a bit twisty which means she is worried in case we make a mess or if daddy comes home early even though he never does. Daddy does not like mess. Or puddings. Or Mummy.

I am feeling extra happy today because in last lesson Miss White leaned right over my workbook and said I wrote the most beautiful letters she had ever seen. Her hair was swishy and smelt like a Bounty bar. She had her white flowery dress on that twirled a bit every time she turned to the white-board.

Mummy comes back into the kitchen. She is wearing trousers that look like pyjama bottoms but are not. She shuffles her feet like an old person. Mummy is pretending that she is not checking on me, but I think she is doing sideways eyes at me to see if I am measuring the right numbers. That is silly because I know I am better at numbers and letters than Mummy is. Mummy doesn't even know it is called numeracy and literacy but I don't tell her she is stupid because Daddy does that a lot.

I have already got the mixture just right. Today we are making our lots-of-colours cupcakes. I always make Mummy's cupcakes with special toppings and mine just with icing. I will put different coloured sugar flowers on her cupcakes when they are ready which will keep me happy inside because it will make me think of Miss White's dress.

*

Mummy does not feel like doing Mummy-Molly Pudding Club much anymore but she knows it is very special so she does it anyway. She makes her face look happy when I look at her. Just like Mr Potato Head, she can change the shape of her mouth. But she is still just Mr Potato Head underneath. Her skin looks a funny colour, not just where the bruises are. There are hair-spiders all over the house and Mummy cries when she brushes her hair and more come out. I hear her puking a lot, but then I sing songs from the school show and I don't hear her any more. I am in the show, I will be singing one part by myself in front of everyone. This makes me feel warm and dizzy.

Mummy is getting more poorly. She looks like she put her eyeshadow on under her eyes instead of on top by accident. Her belly is not so fat any more but that doesn't make her happy. She mostly stays in bed and groans and moans holding her tummy tight like a monster is trying to get out of there. Proper people with selfies round their necks have started to come to my house to visit mummy. They say I'm a good girl for getting to school all by myself.

I throw away all the Pudding Club stuff from the back of the cupboard. I don't throw away my secret ingredient, even though I know I should. But it is special so I hide it in my wardrobe inside my Cinderella bag.

*

It is not just old people and rats that die. Mummy went away in an ambulance – I didn't even hear the whoo-whoos, but in the morning she was not at home. She never came home. Aunty Lynda came to look after me because daddy still had to work and was extra cross. I did hear the next whoo-whoos – that was the police who came to get Daddy. It was a Thursday and I didn't know what to say to the kind police lady because I felt shy. She might see I had put some of Mummy's nail varnish on. She didn't come to my bedroom or ask about Cinderella bags or puddings. I saw Daddy's face in the back of the police car. He waved a bit. I didn't wave back.

I heard Aunty Lynda saying Daddy would go to prison where he would rot which is what he deserved. I think rot means like an old brown apple – maybe he is now wormy and changing colour? Everyone came to the school play and the whole school cried when I did my song by myself. I looked up at the ceiling and made teary eyes by thinking about when I got a stupid teddy-bear birthday cake instead of a princess one. I had an even lovelier dress than for Mummy's funeral.

Now the grown-ups have to think about Long Term because Aunty Lynda is really a Great Aunt, which does not mean brilliant but means too old to look after me forever. I know who is not too old. I know who does not wear baggy trousers, or cry in the toilet, or shake like a jelly when daddy talks. Miss White needs to be my new mummy. Miss White knows that I am clever and special and said I can be whatever I want to be. She is right. Now I need to let her know she can be my new mummy. But first I must get rid of my special ingredient. I run upstairs to look inside my Cinderella bag and fetch the round tub out which has little blue sprinkles in that get rid of rats. Or other things you don't want.

30

Eileen Wilson

Dark. Bumping… by a railroad, maybe?

God, help me!

My hands are tied. And my fingers…

A metallic blood smell combines with fumes. Drag spews from a noisy exhaust. Why did that ring a bell? Did he follow me?

Deja-vu, a trailer… A dark vehicle rolls by. It exits when that tingling sensation crawls up the base of my neck to clutch at my throat. I stop and turn sharply, exposed a second. I shiver.

Someone's watching.

Human resilience, we convince ourselves, it's nothing. Even if I do walk that bit faster. Chill in the sunlight, safe in my cosseted world, I credit the prickles as over-sensitivity, not sixth sense, unconfined I feign confidence and shimmy home as if there's no target on my back.

He must have done it before, otherwise how would he know I would be there? Known other girls would be there?

It's the nightmare where the phone rings and the caller disconnects as you answer. That moment you wait, knowing someone listens, holds their breath and awaits your reaction. He wants to know you're weak, unsure. Knows he can control you, how you think and act. Patience. The poker player conceals his hand until you show yours. He senses weakness. You have to disconnect, or play that game of 'Hello, who is this?'

Then, he has you. He knows if you're defiant, someone who'll cave, or someone ready to play cat and mouse, a deviant like him.

The car's slowing, if I vomit, I'll choke. He'll win.

He sensed deviance and liked it. Deviance prevails.

It's a game, a game of control.

Eyes smarting, head spinning nausea prevails. That squeamish feeling edges from the pit of my stomach, ambles towards my oesophagus and makes me retch. Bile rises as I identify other smells, some type of cleaning product?

It's strong. What is that? Chlorinated and familiar, bleach maybe?

And vomit. There's vomit. Not my vomit.

My cheek splits open as the car bounces, rending the skin apart in a jagged tear. I hunker down and my nose touches liquid, sick, not my own. Worse. Someone else was here, in make-up.

My fingers are agony but I think I was unconscious when he cut me. The cheek makes me cry. Peachy skin tears on something sharp to the side of the boot. It's a hook of some sort, small.

A bra-hook?

Acrid goo edges up my nostril. My mouth tastes of pennies and puke, osmosis through masking tape taut over parched, broken lips. Lips, I think, he kissed when I woke. Like some perverted 'Sleeping Beauty' where the heroine wakes in a claustrophobic nightmare with the devil himself.

It was hazy but I think he has a beard. Close shaven, not bushy, something trim like his build.

This can't be happening. Not to me. This is something for some voluptuous boob-jiggling blonde. The horror; the baby-sitter spied on by the creepy voyeur, the hospital patient confined to bed in the maniac's ward. The live body in the morgue...

The smell. It's bleach... Formaldehyde?

Formaldehyde!

What the hell is he going to do with me?

Heart racing, I lie on a coarse wool blanket. I think it's red but blood trickles from the head-wound as he caresses my breast with the bread knife and lifts me carefully into the trunk, a broken doll, his prize, something to play with and replace when a new toy takes his fancy.

His hands are rough but gentle and I smell sawdust. I feel him tower over me as he runs his fingers through my hair and pulls my head back to look at me. Semi-conscious, he drifts in and out of close up. He notes my pain and smiles.

Cold, blue eyes seem... what... amused?

I stare back, groggy, unrepentant, naked but for lingerie. Keep him interested. Stay alive.

I think he's entertained. He licks his lips and eyes me up. Resigned to the bad-dream, all I can do is stare unflinching as I see the sheen of blurred scissors come up from his side-pocket.

Then come down. It rains gold.

He cut my hair. Long honey locks fall around me in clumps. My hair. It worms into wounds but I stare at him, incredulous, hurt and annoyed. He wants me to cry but I refuse. My neck is damp with sweat and fear.

He pockets the scissors. Then manoeuvres me round and back in the boot.

'You're strong. Interesting. I like that.'

The torch-beam dims, it's dark again.

'He liked that.'

I feel warm. Stockholm syndrome. Pleased for any kind word, I will him not to leave me in the dark, hurt and alone.

Still. Then music, the car engine. We have turned a corner. It makes me feel sick and bangs me into something hard and metal. What's he hit me with?

Abduction was easy in hindsight. I made it easy. Gave him every-thing on a plate, then some. Where I went, what I did, whom I met and ultimately, where I lived. Facebook, Twitter, Linkedin... how easy was it for him to know me, my whereabouts?

Fooled myself I was a writer. Want to swap a script?

Send me ten pages and I'll show you mine, if you show me yours! Name, address and details present and correct, Sir! If you'll just stalk here...

I was a patsy and my finger-pads were gone. It hurt like hell but not as much as knowing I let him do it.

Fucking idiot.

No fingerprints, no typing, how to kill a writer dead, unless he was an agent, then again, they'd done that for years.

He may be some crack-job psychopath, but I played myself for a fool.

Keep interesting. My mantra. Skin could heal, plastic surgeons could repair you but death... you didn't come back from that one. No brainer.

We're stopping. The engine dies. I hear the driver's door open.

Even through the trunk, the enormity of the light hurts my eyes, there's no shield and even closed they hurt. Purple blood vessels undulate, fighting spots in my already aching head.

Spotlights. There are spotlights. Huge black monsters hold beams directed at me. Lights, camera...action! Broken, defiant me, in my torn 'La Perla,' bloodied, woozy and lifted onto sheepskin.

His face zooms partly into focus. Those blue eyes catch my own and a wry smile works its way onto his countenance.

I know him! Hindsight, a great thing when some maniac has sliced off your finger pads with a bread knife. He hits record as the rat arrives, the pet that eats my skin in ravenous, feral bites.

Blue eyes waits and watches, holds my chin and says 'He loves me' but 'I need to perform,' and if he 'pushes me,' I can 'live forever,' have 'character.'

Maybe that's why he has the camera.

I'm over forty. I have a life, a job, a family. My weeping digits smart whenever I change position. The sheepskin is no longer white. When he tells me to 'smile for the camera.' The pain's excruciating but his expression's worse.

I lie still and let him manipulate me like a mannequin. Pleased with his shots he bends to look at me.

Why has he taken me and what's the tarp for?

Remember to say 'I love you, darling.'

He's slowing down. The light is going.

I have to stay calm, slow my breathing and stop my heart bursting from my chest.

He moves closer, eyes my body and unties my hands. In one swift pull he yanks the tape from my mouth and I want to scream, scream at him, 'I'm not dying for you, posing for you, doing any of this for you!'

I shiver, upset and he puts his arm around me. I can feel his chest warm against my own as the bread knife glints and bends towards my back.

'Sssh. It's all right, rest'.

I sense someone else enter the room. I smell perfume.

I peer into his eyes and see him watch me, await my response. Resigned I feel a woman caress my shoulder and a silk robe fall across my body but I stare at him steely-willed. I won't break.

I am a strong, confident woman, he can take my body but he can't take my mind.

He kisses my cheek and smiles as if he knows what I'm thinking. He knows how I feel and what I will do, how I'll play it.

He wants a victim, so he can take his time, use me, or replace me and there's nothing I can do to change how he does it, but I am the hero of this story and I stand defiant.

I challenge blue eyes to the outcome, chin thrust forward, eye to eye.

This is it. The end.

And the director says 'Cut…same time tomorrow.'

31

MILLY AND MAX GO TRICK OR TREATING

Ben Marshall

MILLY and MAX are twins. They are 5 years old. Today is Halloween and the twins are very excited. They are going to play a game called 'TRICK or TREAT' for the first time.

Mum helps Milly dress as a CAT and Max as a BAT. Mum even paints their faces. Black whiskers for Milly and a black nose and eyes for Max. Milly wants a pink nose because pink is her favourite colour. "You're supposed to look spooky," says Mum, but the twins can't stop smiling.

Milly and Max can't wait to scare Dad and creep up behind him. Dad is slumped in his chair. He looks heavy and very still. "Is Dad sleeping?" Max whispers. "Let's spook him," Milly whispers back. The twins tiptoe in front of Dad. His head hangs down and his eyes are closed. The twins reach out. Dad suddenly lifts his head and opens his eyes with a mean stare. He grins with white toy fangs and the twins scream and run away. They love it when Dad plays monsters.

Max runs quicker so Dad grabs Milly and tickles her. Milly shouts that she hates to be tickled but really she likes it very much.

It is very dark outside and the street is busy with other children all dressed up too. Witches, little monsters and even children under white sheets who moan like ghosts. The twins skip to the first house. "Look," cries Milly, pointing to "a Pumpkin!" yells Max. The pumpkin sits outside the house next door where Mr Glover lives. Dad has told Milly and Max to only go to houses with a pumpkin outside. "That way we know they are playing the game too," Mum had explained.

Mum and Dad wait at the top of the drive. The twins slowly follow Dad's torch light to the door. Milly on tip-toes like a cat, paws clawing. Max flaps his wings. They both knock nervously. Mr Glover opens the door and acts very shocked. "My Goodness. A cat! A bat!" he says, pretending not to recognise the twins. "Trick?" asks Milly "or Treat?" asks Max. Mr Glover thinks about it then offers the twins a lollypop jar. "Wow," says Milly, taking a pink sherbet lolly. "Thanks," smiles Max, taking a lemon one. They each drop the lollies into their goodie bags and run back to show Mum and Dad.

Most of the houses are playing the game. By the time the twins reach the end of their street, Milly and Max are getting very good at being spooky. Their goodie bags are bulging. Mr Glover brings out mugs of tea for the Mums and Dads and all the children play and swap sweets. Milly and Max are upset to see that some children have more treats than they do. Milly and Max want more. As Mum and Dad chatter with other grown-ups, Milly and Max sneak away.

There is one house left. Away from the street lamps. Away from the Mums and Dads. The end house is a small, funny looking cottage. It is much older than the other houses on the street and sits behind a dark gate and dark, iron fence. The roof is crooked and the trees behind the gate are twisted. Like all the other children, the twins have been told never to go to the house. But children often forget. The twins have forgotten they should always stay away.

A long pathway leads to the front door of the house. The gate is open. The twins have never been this close to the house before and Max doesn't want to get closer. "Look," cries Milly, pointing towards the front door. "A pumpkin," whispers Max.

"Doctor Brickleback must want to play the game," says Max. "Who is Doctor Brickleback?" asks Milly. But Max doesn't really know. He had just heard Dad call it Doctor Brickleback's house before. Nobody ever talks about DOCTOR BRICKLEBACK. Nobody ever talks about the house. "Mum said nobody lives here," says Milly. "So whose pumpkin is it?" Max asks. Milly pulls Max's sleeve. "Let's find out," she says.

Milly leads Max down the stony path. As they step closer to the house, they see their shadows in the glow from the pumpkin. The pumpkin has a thin smile and narrow eyes. The light flickers in the breeze. Now Milly would like to go back, but then her face leaps for joy. "WOW," gasps Max.

Next to the pumpkin is a very large red basket overflowing with every sweet treat a child could dream of. Jellies, bonbons, treacle toffee, cinder toffee, barley sugars, buttons, beans, humbugs, gingerbread men and gobstoppers the size of golf balls. Even sugared mice. Some sweets wrapped, some left sticky. So TEMPTING. Milly digs in and Max kneels down to read the sign. In front of the basket is an old green sign with words painted in red. Max is a good reader and says the words for Milly to hear. "TREATS FOR...THE CHILD...REN...YOU MUST... ONLY ...TAKE...ONE."

The words MUST and ONE are underlined in red paint which has dripped.

Milly is very excited to find two of her very favourites. Big fluffy PINK MARSHMALLOWS and also STRAWBERRY BOOTLACES. Max chooses a bright purple jelly worm. Milly looks at her handful of pink marshmallows and her handful of strawberry bootlaces. She can't choose. Milly looks at Max to check he is not watching her. But Doctor Brickleback is watching. He sees Milly from behind his dark curtain.

Doctor Brickleback is small and crooked and old. Just like his house. He wears a suit made up of cloth patches which are all different colours. The colours and the cloth look old too. Doctor Brickleback wears a funny little bow tie around his neck. He chews a long black liquorice cane, held in his small hand. His nails are yellow and pointed.

Doctor Brickleback watches Milly stuff her bag with pink marshmallows and then with strawberry bootlaces. He shakes his head.

"Tut... tut... tut," he whispers.

Milly takes two more handfuls. Doctor Brickleback looks at Milly with a mean stare. He licks his small pointy teeth with his liquorice black tongue. Black juices drip down his chin as he watches the twins run away. His smile is thin and his eyes are narrow.

"Tut… tut… tut," he whispers again.

Back at home the twins empty all their goodies onto the kitchen table. They each have their own big glass sweetie jar and count the treats as they drop them in. Max is upset when Milly counts more. Milly sticks out her blue tongue and so Max sticks out his yellow tongue. The twins giggle. They don't see Doctor Brickleback watching. His face is pressed to the window. Black liquorice juices drip down the glass. The wind howls around him.

"Time for bed," calls Mum.

The twins go to the bathroom. Dad watches Max brush his teeth as he combs Milly's hair. Dad always watches the twins brush their teeth after treats. "Who is Doctor Brickelback?" Milly asks. Dad stops combing and his face turns a funny colour. Max stops brushing, waiting for the answer. "Why do you ask?" says Dad. The twins look at each other. They don't want to share their secret about the house. "He was just the Doctor in the village when I was a boy," Dad explains. "Was he nice?" asks Milly. "Did he give you sweets?" asks Max. Dad does not answer. His face is now white. "Why can't we go to his house?" the twins both ask at the same time. Dad points his finger and SHOUTS…

"DOCTOR BRICKELBACK IS DEAD. HE'S BEEN DEAD FOR YEARS. NOBODY TALKS ABOUT HIM OR HIS HOUSE. THAT INCLUDES YOU TWO, YOU HEAR?!"

Dad is never cross and the twins are too upset to answer. Dad sees their worried faces and gives the twins a hug. "Sorry kids," Dad says gently. "Just don't ask about Doctor Brickleback again. Ok?" Dad asks, now smiling. The twins both nod, "We promise."

Dad sends Max down to kiss Mum before bed. "Be a good girl. Brush your teeth really well," Dad says to Milly. Milly grins and shows Dad how wide she can open her mouth. Just then, a blast of wind rocks the windows. All the lights go out. All is DARK.

Luckily, Dad still has his big torch and soon the bathroom is light. "What's happening," asks Milly, worried. Dad explains that the wind must have blown out the lights. He tells Milly not to worry. "You stay in the bathroom with the torch and brush your teeth," Dad says. "I'll brush my teeth really well," promises Milly. "I'll be right back," promises Dad.

Milly holds the torch in one hand, just below her chin. She brushes her teeth with the other and stands on tiptoes to see herself in the mirror. Her skin looks white and her lips and gums red. All around her is dark.

Milly brushes for longer than she has ever brushed before. The sound of the SCRUBBING and the WHOOSH of the wind outside hide the noises from downstairs. Dad has not returned quickly like he had promised. Milly then does hear something and stops brushing. The sound of the wind is now blowing through the house. Milly feels alone. Her heart begins to THUMP. "Mum... Dad?" calls Milly, but her voice is not quite loud enough.

Milly slowly steps down the stairs. Her eyes are wide and white. The torch light trembles because Milly can't hold it still.

The blowing wind rattles behind the kitchen door. Milly bravely opens it. The back window is open and moonlight gives the room a silvery glow. The white walls are dirty with small BLACK HAND-PRINTS. The air smells of liquorice.

Milly shines the torch at the kitchen table. The white table is dirty with small black handprints too. Sat around it are Mum, Dad and Max. They are slumped in their chairs. They look heavy and very still. "Mummy... Daddy... Max?" Milly says softly, her voice shaking. "Don't tickle me..." she says but Milly wishes that they do. Something familiar looks back from the table. From inside her sweetie jar on the table. Not the sweets she remembers. Gobstoppers, thinks Milly?

No, EYEBALLS! Six of them, or three pairs.

Milly's torch beam jumps to the frozen faces of her DEAD family. Mum, Dad and Max all stare back. Their eyes do not blink at the flash of light. Each of their eye sockets are stuffed with fluffy pink marshmallows. Below their marshmallow eyes, their lips have been sewn together with strawberry bootlaces. Pulled tight into SMILES. Not happy smiles.

Milly drops her torch and SCREAMS into the moonlight. And SCREAMS and SCREAMS and SCREAMS.

Milly does not live at home now. She lives in a hospital. She will always remember Mum, Dad and her twin brother Max. When she closes her eyes, she can still see their faces. She can hear her own screams. Milly can still smell fresh blood with liquorice. Milly does not like sweets now. She does not like the colour pink now.

As for Doctor Brickleback? Milly promised Dad she would never ask about him.

And she never does.

32

MUMMA SAYS

Hillier Townsend

I was afraid of the lady who lived in our bathtub.

She had too many things on her.

Mumma said, "Get used to it, wimpoid, we need the money."

But the lady had a row of ears going down her back and three baby noses on one of her shoulders and no hair at all. And it felt like her eyes shot knives when she turned her head to look at me.

So I peed and pooped in the hole in my little closet because I was afraid to see her in the bathtub.

Mumma said The Human Garden people were going to bring us a man, too. He would live in our cellar.

I said "I will never go down there! I said I will throw his food down the cellar stairs!

"The hell you will," Mumma said.

Mumma made me bring food to the lady. Once I closed my eyes so I didn't have to see her when I brought her soup. I bumped into the

sink and the hot soup spilled all over her baby noses.
The lady screamed, screamed, SCREAMED. The baby noses bled red.

Mumma yelled, "You little fuck, they're gonna take that out of our check!"

She hit me in a different place from last time so it wouldn't show.

I had very bad dreams that night.

The next morning the lady's eyes were closed.

"No," the lady said when she heard me put her food on the floor and push it over to her.

I saw lots of blood on her wrist. The one that had the cuff on it.

I thought maybe she had tried to escape. That would be silly. She couldn't run anywhere with no feet.

"Mumma says my job is to make you eat," I said.

That was the first time I ever talked to the lady in our bathtub.

"No more, Junie," she said. "No more of this living hell."

The lady knew my name!

I said, "Mumma says you have to eat because The Human Garden people will take you away if you don't and give you to somebody else, and Mumma will be *really mad* at me, and The Human Garden people are coming today for some of your ears, and if they are mad at her they won't give us a man and Mumma will…"

Then I started crying.

The lady opened her eyes and looked at me, but I didn't feel any knives this time.

"I know they're coming, Junie," the lady said. She smiled in a sad way and wiped her bloody wrist on one of the tongues behind her knees. "Here's what I need you to do…"

Mumma never knew why the lady in our bathtub got skinny and died. But I do.

The lady was smart. Every time I brought her food, she put tiny pieces of it in our bathtub so it looked like she'd eaten it. I hid the rest.

"This rathole stinks worse every day!" Mumma said every time she went past my little closet.

The next time The Human Garden people came they said that all the tongues and ears and other stuff on the lady were no good because they were all rotted like the lady. So Mumma threw Junie Two on the compost pile. That's what I named the lady in our bathtub, Junie Two.

I'm sorry that Junie Two went on the compost, but I'm glad she's gone.

And I'm really, really glad The Human Garden people wouldn't give us a man for our cellar.

There wouldn't be enough room down here for the both of us.

33

EXQUISITE

Phil Chard

Amber Andrews had been an easy target.

Too easy.

He learned from news bulletins that the girl he'd taken was fifteen, but her mental age had been much lower.

Amber was trusting.

Amber was easy prey.

Amber.

Am-ber

You couldn't pick a more suitable name.

It was the colour of hair which bonneted her youthful face.

Am-ber

Her eyes would light up in wonder at such simple things.

One day he bought her some replacement shoes which had Velcro straps instead of laces.

She played merrily with those Velcro straps for hours.

Am-ber...

Amber had been his favourite.

He'd kept her the longest.

They formed a bond.

He even became paternal.

Once he found her playing with a knife.

She liked the intricate chaos design carved into the blade and handle.

Don't play with knives, you can get hurt!

He hit her.

She cried.

He didn't like seeing her cry.

Am-ber...

An embroidered handkerchief dabbed away a tear.

Yes, before he killed her, he was like a surrogate father to her.

Cuckoo. Cuckoo. Cuckoo.

Three o'clock, time for tea.

He shook his head. Nostalgia was for the zombie masses. Amber was dead; someone else had taken her place.

Note to self: The cuckoo clock has seen better days. Consider replacing it.

As he filled the kettle, rain spat and slid down the kitchen window. Beyond it, his experiments rotted under the cover of dampening soil.

Note to self: would the experiments be easier to bury if I cut them into pieces?

The screams from the basement were more audible here. It was such a distraction.

Note to self: buy a radio for the kitchen to drown out their screams.

The kettle whistled, he poured the boiled water into his dead Mother's favourite china cup. A teabag was added, and the liquid was stirred seven times anticlockwise.

The screaming from the girl morphed into bad language. She was insulting him!

When he was a boy, girls used to say things like this to him.

His eyes narrowed. Mother was right about girls like that. Why were they always so late to learn respect for him?

Amber had understood.

That's why he let her live the longest.

She was treated well. She was fed healthy meals, three times a day, had her own bedroom in the house and could move around freely.

Mentally she was a young child. Her fragile state made her easy to manipulate.

He thought she was younger than fifteen because she carried a teddy bear around with her. He let her bring it to the house.

She was told she couldn't leave. She never tried to. He could leave her in the house alone and know she wouldn't try the door, wouldn't open it if there was a knock.

A smile had formed.

Nostalgia! What's wrong with you?

Amber was a fascinating experiment to study, but that was all. Her character was a fascinating mix of compliance, and child-like deception. Sometimes she would find things in the house which she knew she was only allowed in strict rations: sweets, chocolate, cans of fizzy drinks. Knowing she was often denied them, she would unstitch the arms and legs of her teddy bear, remove some of the stuffing and use the teddy bear to store her treats to eat when he was not around. He knew what she was doing, but was so entertained by the subterfuge that he let it continue. She could open up and sew the teddy bear back together with such expertise that it always looked perfectly normal.

The New Girl was shouting again.

The reverie faded.

Another day without food and water and she wouldn't have the strength to shout.

Nil by mouth.

That was his latest experiment.

It would be exquisite to see the New Girl broken!

Exquisite!

*

Shelby Collins returned from a dream world into the familiar delirium of darkness.

Pain registered in her ankle, where cold iron locked tight around bruised skin. She stretched out the leg; a metal chain snaked around the cement in pursuit. As her leg reached the semi-circle of chalk which surrounded her, the chain tightened, her ankle swam with pain again; she pulled it back and crawled back to the wall.

Why had God forsaken her?

Born to drug-addicted parents, she was in state care at a young age. Bullying and abuse followed. On her fourteenth birthday, a gift from a care assistant turned into a grope. She left him on the ground, holding his groin in agony. She ran until the landmarks were unfamiliar.

The exhilarating freedom lasted two hours. Aimless wandering had carried her along to an unfamiliar street. Arms grabbed her from behind, and a damp cloth was forced over her mouth and nose. A whiff of chemicals caused her legs to buckle. Consciousness deserted her.

She woke in the permanent shadows of the room she nicknamed the *Dusk Room*, and with so little light to decipher night and day, dreams were her only clue to how long she'd been there. She would count them. The valley, the forest, the beach, three dreams in which she was walking alone, sun-kissed and free, barefoot and smiling.

She had just returned from dream number four. In it, she was in the Dusk Room, where the dark outline of a human figure had watched her from the shadows. Fearing this was the end, she screamed repeatedly, but as the figure moved forward, no hook-handed madman appeared; instead it was a young girl who was carrying a teddy bear.

The girl did not respond when Shelby tried to talk to her, and her only movement came at the very end of the dream, when she dropped the bear onto the dusty cement.

Shelby slumped against the wall and inhaled stale air. Her eyes roamed the darkness, aimlessly. As dark thoughts swam around her head, the outline of an object caught her attention. Her eyes squinted to accommodate the new data and features emerged: furry foot, plump body, two fluffy arms.

The teddy bear lay where it had been dropped in the dream. Her eyes closed tightly. When they opened again the teddy bear was still visible. Shelby shuffled forward. The bear's features became more pronounced.

She scrambled onto her belly. The cold cement stung her skin as she crept forward with her arm extended. A peekaboo of pain registered in her ankle, blocking her progress. The teddy bear was an inch away from her fingers.

She gritted her teeth and extended her shoulder as far as she could, her fingers spreading as they prepared to grab. As her ankle chafed against iron, the pain accelerated, and a scream caught in her throat. Her hand appeared enormous as her arm continued to stretch and her fingers extended still further. As the pain reached a crescendo, her fingers snapped shut; she felt fur and pulled back inside the safety of the chalk circle, clutching the bear. Her heart was vibrating wildly and her breathing was rapid, but as the pain went down the gears, her body returned to order.

The teddy bear was examined, front and back. It fooled her eyes, but not her hands. There were two solid, cylindrical objects in the legs and something felt alien in the arms. She ripped the stitching in the legs apart to expose two cans of lemonade hidden beneath the fur. Her jaw dropped. Giddy hands snapped open the tab and the can was thrust to dry lips.

The dizziness was like the first cigarette after two days of abstinence. When the pleasure faded, her hands interrogated the stitching in the teddy bear's arms. Two chocolate bars emerged from the fur. She clawed at the wrappers.

*

A harlequin mask stared back at him in the mirror. With bad girls, he never showed his face. Let them die in wonder. Let them never know who'd taken them.

The experiment was over. The New Girl had been without food and water for six days. She was done. She would accept death in her condition. She would welcome it.

White gloves dusted his lapel and removed a crumb from his shoulder. That was better. The man in the mirror was ready to put a poor, wretched animal out of its misery now.

He picked up the rope and transformed it for death. White gloves caressed the noose. It was exquisite!

His excited heart raced as he walked to the basement. The excitement had affected his body. Shaking hands turned the key in the lock of the basement door. It opened with a theatrical creak, exposing a dozen ramshackle steps. A clip-clop of boots descended slowly.

The girl was in the corner. A hand shielded the light from her eyes. In her other hand was a teddy bear. He recognised it immediately. Amber's.

There were drinks cans in the corner, and food wrappers. The stitching in the legs and arms of the teddy bear was loose.

She had eaten! She had ruined the experiment! How disappointing this girl had proved to be! He was certain he had got rid of the teddy bear. How careless of him!

He let the anger subside before walking towards her. White gloves caressed the noose. At least he would enjoy the final act.

Polished black boots stopped at the chalk perimeter. She stared up at the mask with defeated eyes. She said nothing. He took two steps inside the chalk circle. She didn't try to claw at him, her reaction was panic. She stood up and backed against the wall. One hand was still shielding the light from her eyes. The other hand clung childlike to the teddy bear.

As he stepped forward again, she could do little but make whining noises from the back of her throat to signal her distress.

Excellent! A cornered animal! Squeal! Squeal! Squeal!

It was shaking. It knew what was coming. He could smell the animal's fear. The pleasure was intoxicating. He had to pause for breath before taking another step forward.

The wretched animal in front of him shuddered as it sobbed. It offered no resistance as he threaded the noose around its neck. He reached up, to pull the rope over the metal piping above the animal. It would easily hold the animal's weight, it had the others.

*

Time slowed as he crashed to the ground. The shock overpowered the pain. Instinctively his hands covered his throat. Crimson poured through the fingers. He spat blood as the pain overwhelmed him. It reached a violent crescendo.

The mask hid a confused expression. He looked in the direction of the girl.

The teddy bear she had held was now in two parts. The body of the teddy bear was on the ground. The Velcro straps from Amber's shoes were visible, sewn into the neck of the bear.

The Man in the Mask pictured Amber's tears when she was told she couldn't play with the knife. His imagination painted the scene of Amber's bear being ripped apart and sewn back together to circumvent his rules. He never noticed the missing Velcro on her shoes.

In the New Girl's hand was the head of the teddy bear, which had been hiding the handle of the knife. Another Velcro circle bordered the neck. The blade, previously hidden inside the body, was now exposed and stained with his blood.

*

Shelby Collins walked towards the Man in the Mask with the macabre weapon still in her hand. She fished in his pockets, pulled out a small key and unpicked the lock of the shackle around her ankle.

Hidden eyes stared up at her from the mask. His breath was wheezing and frenzied. Sensing he was near his end, she reached down and pulled the mask from his face. Shelby Collins wanted to see the man who had taken her captive. She wanted to see the light extinguished in his eyes. When she did... it was exquisite.

34

OVERLOOKED

Tom Nolan

I kill people. Not professionally. I'm self-taught and I do it because it's fun. I'm telling you this on doctor's advice.

I live twenty floors up a tower block that's surrounded by houses. The world is my Xbox – with less impressive graphics. I see when people's homes are unprotected and there's an opportunity to get interactive. If your place is overlooked, someone like me is watching, stroking an erection over you and your loved ones. Guaranteed. What you get from scary films, we get from you – as an appetiser.

Winter is best because I'm a morning person and it stays dark till late. I peel back the crusty sheets, pop a pod in the coffee machine and take up my position. Wannabe victims have their lights on and their curtains open, asking for it. The rest of the year I live inside my head.

Two young professionals live in number 48. Wifey runs three times a week. She's short and delicate. Hubby is corporate bland. I don't care about him.

Number 46 next door is divided into flats. The owner, four students and two musicians live there. You can tell what they sound and smell like by looking at them.

One of the students has an old piece-of-shit Honda with a broken handbrake and the kind of rust that needs cold-sore lotion instead of turtle wax. I know about the handbrake after watching his three comic genius buddies push the car across number 48's drive so Wifey and Hubby couldn't get their BMWs out in the morning.

Imagining Wifey's irritation gave me the sort of hard-on that always summons Mr Headache. He's been with me since I was twelve. Some people get first-night butterflies; I get an intra-cranial chainsaw, but it goes away when the action starts.

They don't use the front door at the student house. There's probably a bed jammed against it, maximising the landlord's income.

But essential as surveillance is, you have to walk the ground. It's noisy, immerses you in traffic stink and you're stepping over dog shit, cigarette ends and phlegm balls – but if you don't walk, you can't dance.

Michael, the students' landlord drinks in The Coach House. I engaged in conversation with him and learned the students are going home at the weekend for the Christmas holidays. The musicians have a gig up north on Monday and will be gone for a couple of days. With Michael being picked up at 6:15 every morning to work on the buildings, that's an inviting window of empty house opportunity.

I stayed up all night, planning.

Bullet points:

- Number 46 unoccupied.
- The Honda would fall apart on any journey longer than a downhill mile so the owner leaves it parked on the road and goes home by rail.
- Hubby's job gets him out early and sends him home late.
- Wifey is a surgeon at the Children's Hospital – Oh the irony!
- Side door of 46 not overlooked.
- Houses divided into bedsits are easy access because, apart from their own room, nobody worries about security. No alarm and cheap locks.

The planning made my wrist hurt so much I had to take an hour off. If I'm ever caught they won't need the CSI dark light; they'll trip over the deposits.

Next day, I went to four charity shops and bought sufficient clothes to go to town as myself, come back as someone else, do the job, go out as a different someone else and return as myself. Inconvenient but effective.

By Saturday tea time, 46's paying tenants had all gone.

Monday morning, the van collected Michael for work at the usual time.

Hubby drove off half an hour later.

Mr Headache settled in behind my eyes but was in a relatively gentle mood.

Game on.

I push the Honda across Wifey's drive.

The side door of number 46 has an old latch lock that barely engages the frame. I'm inside in two seconds. It stinks. Mildew, curly lino, nicotined ceilings and damp-bubbly wallpaper. Shithole. Cheap locks but nothing worth stealing.

Rule one: always bring a weapon for emergencies but where possible use only what you find on site, so nothing can be traced back to you. I find a roasting fork, a selection of knives and a ball of string. The kitchen also has enough filth and mouse shit for a health inspectors' convention. It would take more than that to dampen my excitement.

Soon I'll savour the moment that Wifey's life departs. I'll strip her and lie very still, feeling her body go cold against me. Then I'll start to move. We'll get acquainted in the musicians' room, beneath posters of leather-clad babes draped around phallic guitars and motorbikes. I want them to *watch* me, these women who wouldn't even *see* me in the street, who would turn away if I approached them in a bar.

I need urgent release but I know from experience that at the first hint of auto-relief, Mr Headache will invite Mr Unbearable Agony to chop at my optic nerves until I have to double up screaming.

The doorbell rings, followed by a drum solo on the knocker. My heart joins in the musical motif by trying to hammer its way out of my chest and I come in my pants. Mr Headache allows this without reprisal because I couldn't help it and by the time Wifey is tied up and I've savoured the aromas of femininity and fear, I'll be ready again.

I open the door. She's yelling: "My drive is obstructed. I am a doctor. I could be called to an emergency at any time. Do you want a death on your conscience?"

She has a 'power dressing' voice that carries irony well. But she isn't wearing a business suit; she's in white coat and scrubs – and surgical gloves. At first, I see only one glove because her right hand is behind her back. Then it isn't and it's swinging a tyre lever. I hear my cheekbone and lots of teeth shatter and the floor sucker-punches me from behind. The ceiling fades to black.

I'm lying on my back with my arms stretched out. My lips feel as if I've spent an hour with a blind, forceps-happy dentist and the rest of my head is throbbing. But I've had worse from Mr Headache.

The carpet smells mouldy-damp. Can't be healthy to lie on.

What's that hammering noise? I hope it isn't someone at the door. I don't want to be rescued before I get to hurt Wifey – big time for a long time.

She's kneeling beside me. Making conversation, I question the ethics of her impromptu dental treatment. She smiles. I follow her gaze and see that the noise is caused by her nailing my left wrist to the floor. My right arm is already secured. Why doesn't it hurt? I suppose that'll come later.

She stands to admire her work.

I try to swallow but have no spit. The world swirls and goes white for a second. Is this what people call panic? It doesn't feel the way it looks from the other side. Interesting.

The bitch squats to adjust something. I try to kick her in the tits. Nothing.

"I divided your spinal cord," she says. "Keeps you still but unfortunately provides excellent anaesthesia. Consequently, I didn't *need* to nail your arms down but it's the aesthetics of the thing. Speaking of which…" She dangles a lump of meat in my face. It's the size of a clenched fist and its lower half is covered in wrinkled, hairy skin. She tosses the meat away. I presume it was part of me. Must remember where it went. Maybe it can be reattached – if the mice leave it alone. "You had the sticky remains of an erection," she says. "I found that offensive in the circumstances, so I cut your balls off. Not my neatest work and not a sterile operating environment but you won't live long enough for infection to set in."

I scream but stop when she moves a microphone.

"A record for posterity." She trickles water into my dry mouth, clearly anxious about sound quality.

"You're 'ucking crazy," I say, as if this is news. The lack of 'F' reminds me of my missing front teeth. "Honestly, I wasn't going to…" I don't bother to finish. I know all about entreaties and deaf ears.

Wifey tells me she sees many interesting things from her bedroom window – "But few as fascinating as you blocking my drive."

She stands and dusts her knees with her hands. "Going to work now. I'll pop back later to finish you off. You'll be fresher when Michael gets home. He's a nice guy and this place is smelly enough already. Sorry to be blunt but I find it best to be straight with patients."

She places the microphone on an upturned plastic bucket beside my head. "Voice activated. Speak whenever you want."

"Why the 'uck would I want to?"

"Because someone might find the recording. A chance to get even." She smiles and points to herself. "Healthcare professional – kindness is my thing."

"You won't get away wi' 'is!" I scream. Avoiding clichés has never seemed less important. Ditto the lack of a 'th' sound.

"That's probably incorrect," she says. "Nobody will see me pass through the hedge. The white coat will go to central laundry at the hospital and I'll dump the gloves in a clinical waste bin, which will soon fill up with other bloody odds and ends. Make the tape."

I'm alone in the mouldering house. Can't judge the passage of time.

Always thought I'd do more with my spell on the planet. If there's a God, my life will take some explaining. Maybe He'll see the funny side? The evidence suggests He has a sick sense of humour.

I scream for help. Going through the motions.

The skin on the left side of my neck itches. I try to think of something else but there are only worse things. So I dictate this account, partly to distract me from the itching, partly for the reasons she suggested, but mainly to take my mind off the fact that I'm waiting for her to come back and kill me in what is unlikely to be an award-winningly humanitarian manner. I have no feeling below the neck but that leaves plenty of places to hurt – and hurt them, she will. I know the look in her eyes, having seen it in the shaving mirror.

I thought I had covered all the angles but it never occurred to me as I was watching people, that someone might be watching me.

God, the itching!

I turn my head to scratch my neck against the carpet – and I see why she raised the microphone off the floor. To my left, the blood running from the tube in my neck has reached the sideboard. She lied about finishing me off on her return. *Respect!*

Now that there is no pain in my future, I'm slightly disappointed. I always like to maximise my experiences and so few remain.

A sponge is swelling in my head and my pulse must be topping two fifty as my heart fights to compensate for the dropping blood volume. I can feel it in my neck.

It's intense.

See-through figures crowd into the room. They're all people I last saw in circumstances not dissimilar to this – except I was the one moving around. There's a lot of bad attitude in here, so if it's not an hallucination caused by oxygen deprivation, things are going to get very interesting very soon. *Result!*

35

POT HOLING

Rachael Howard

Sarah slumped on an outcrop. "How much further?"

Jan turned, her torchlight blinding Sarah. "Nearly there."

Jan hitched up her trousers. "Come on you wimp."

"I am not moving until you tell me EXACTLY how much further." Sarah rubbed at her bandaged ankle. It was getting tight.

"Just one more tunnel. Better than squatting in that dingy cave waiting for rescue." She patted Sarah on the shoulder. "Come on, Chuck. This route is real easy. Why nobody bothers with it much."

Sarah struggled up with Jan's help. "Just one more tunnel?"

Jan gave a jolly hockey-sticks smile. "That's the spirit." Then hurried on.

Limping, Sarah slowly followed her into a small cave.

"A dead end." Sarah grimaced.

"Nope." Jan pointed down.

"Fucking hell! You are kidding!" At ground level was the entrance to a small tunnel. Not even high enough to crawl through. "I can't get through that!"

"Of course you can. It's only twelve feet. Look, I'll tie a rope around you so I can pull you through if you need it."

"Are you sure it's safe?"

"It's fine. You can see the scrape marks from other people's boots."

"I'm more worried about them still being in there. All juicy and ripe."

Jan took a deep sniff. "Nope. Lovely fresh air. Off we go."

Sarah didn't feel any safer with her harness tethered to Jan's. "How long have you had this rope?" she asked Jan's disappearing boots.

"Stop moaning and come on."

A tinkle of stones behind Sarah made her spin, her head torch causing a dizzying sweep of visibility. Nothing. "I'm getting spooked down here."

"What was that?"

"Coming," called Sarah as she lay on her belly and inched into the tunnel.

It was better than she thought. Though she could not get on her hands and knees, the tunnel was wide enough that her arms could move freely to drag herself forward. The rock had regular grooves in it like someone had gone ahead with a small chisel and left handy ridges for her fingertips to grip. It was slow but at least she didn't need to use her ankle much.

"I'm out," called Jan. "I can see light. Just."

The promise of an exit caused Sarah to wriggle and claw more violently, desperate to be in the sunlight.

"Take it easy. I've got you." The rope pulled taut and she moved forward more easily.

Sarah turned her torch off as the faint glow ahead indicated the exit. "I can see light! We're at the entrance!"

"Well, no. It's just a hole in the cave's roof. But we can't be far."

"What? You told me…" Sarah lurched forward, slamming her back against the roof of the tunnel.

"Hey. Take it easy. That's not solid rock you know."

A skitter of pebbles fell past Sarah's head. She froze.

Jan's voice was slow, laboured. "Calm down. You're OK. Just let me pull you clear."

Another scattering of pebbles from above.

"Fuck that. I'm not staying here." Sarah thrashed with her legs, squeaked at her ankle's protest, and heaved herself forward. She bashed the roof again.

A grumble of earth and stone broke free and enveloped her. "Jan!" She felt the rope tug but she couldn't move, the weight on her back holding her still.

"Don't move. Just let it settle a minute." Jan's calm voice reassured her. "It isn't going to be as bad as it sounds."

After a wait of forever Sarah heard a scrabbling ahead, then Jan's fingers entwined with hers. "See kid? I'm here. Now let me take a look."

She could hear Jan's laboured breaths while bits of earth fell around her head. "How bad?"

"Well I've seen worse. There's been a bit dislodged but it's just soil and stones, easy to shift. The rest of the roof looks secure. How much of your body is pinned down?"

Carefully Sarah wriggled her limbs and body. "I can move everything below my waist."

"Great. Just your chest then. Can you breathe OK?"

"Feel a bit dizzy but yeah."

"Good. Stay put, ha ha, and I'll be back in a mo."

Sarah felt desperately alone as Jan and her light disappeared. She strained to hear her. Finally, a very slow scraping. "Hurry up. I'm getting cold here." Another slow scrape. "Jan!"

"What?" The reply came from ahead and echoed off cave walls.

"Where are you?"

"Looking for something to dig with. Just hold on. I'm coming."

And another scrape.

"Jan! There's someone here."

"What do you mean?"

"There's someone in the tunnel, behind me!"

"Great. Give them a shout. They can start clearing from that end."

Scrape. "Hey. Hello. The tunnel's blocked." Scrape. "Hello. Can you help?" Scrape. "Come on you bastard, help!" Scrape.

Sarah clawed at the walls. Tried to pull free. But the earthfall held.

Jan was suddenly ahead of her. "Stop panicking. What did they say?"

"Nothing. They aren't saying anything."

"Well they'll just have to bloody wait. Won't they."

Sarah gripped Jan's hand. "I'm scared."

"You're allowed to be. But you're fine. Just wish those pricks behind you would help. But there you go. OK. I'm going to clear a bit at a time then test if I can pull you out. It's going to take a while though. Ready?"

"Yeah."

Sarah covered her face as mud and stones slid over her. Jan dug so slowly. The grit trickled around her neck and made it itch. Something brushed against her damaged ankle, soft and bristly. It pushed her ankle hard against the wall and she gagged with the pain. "Jan!"

Sarah kicked out with her good foot. It contacted with more softness. A firm cushion that swelled and hardened, pushing her foot against the opposite wall. Now her legs were spread wide and pinned fast. "Jan! They're doing something."

"Great. You back there? Try to clear some of the soil your end. We'll meet in the middle."

The pressure moved up her legs, forcing them outwards. "Oh God. No! Jan, they're… they're…" She lashed around frantically.

"Stay still. There's still too much soil."

"No" Sarah clawed at Jan's arms. "Stop it. You bloody perverts! I'll fucking…"

Another inch forward on her legs and pain shot upwards from her hips. She screamed.

"You bastards, leave her alone!" Jan shouted, scrabbling at the soil, throwing handfuls behind her. "I'll get you out. Just hold on. I'll kill the bastard! You hear that back there? I'll fucking kill you!"

Another shift and Sarah felt a hard pressure against her crotch. "Jan. Please!" A sob squeezed out of her as the pressure pushed up. Something sharp scraped across her pubic bone and buttocks, ripping her trousers. "Jan. Please. Don't let this happen!"

Jan gripped Sarah's wrists and pulled with no success. She growled and dived back at the pile of rubble. "Get off her, you shits! You won't get away with this!"

The soil moved more easily, handfuls thrown into the darkness. "Nearly through. I'll see them in a second. Don't worry. Cowards! You hear me? I'll cut your fucking throats!"

There was now a fiery band across Sarah's back and belly. "What are they doing to me? Jan? It hurts."

"Get off her. You hear me? Nearly through, baby. Nearly there."

Sarah moaned. Her energy drained by that fire around her body. Her vision blurred.

Jan scrambled out to grab a torch. "Hang in there!" She dived back over Sarah.

A grunt and the last of the soil slid off. A miasma of rotting air flooded her lungs. She tried to retch but it made her waist burn even deeper. Her energy was draining into the pain.

"Right you bastards…" Jan turned the light on. She gasped. Sarah felt her shift off her and wriggle backwards out of the tunnel.

"Help me." Sarah gasped.

"I… oh God…" Jan looked back, her face contorted with terror.

Sarah looked deep into her friend's eyes. Saw the reflection in them. A huge, glistening-white grub-like mass lit up by torchlight. Her body half in it.

The creature nearly filled the tunnel, ooze clinging to the walls. The bristles smothering its body scraped against the walls as the body pulsated. Empty eye sockets squeezed closed as its pointed beak opened wide.

"I'm sorry," Jan whispered.

Sarah saw the reflection of the beak snap shut on her body before Jan turned and fled.

"God help me!" Sarah screamed as the fire burned deep and the light faded with her life.

36

ICE CREAM VAN

Jessica Brown

She was screaming. She had barely stopped since she'd broken her leg three weeks ago, and stoicism clearly did not run in the family. Is it wrong to want to smother your child? To lock them in a sound-proof cell and swallow the key? Richard was usually the patient father, the good cop to his wife's bad cop. But now he was lost. How do you shut up a six-year-old without getting arrested? Sarah had gone out with her 'girlfriends' (to bitch about him no doubt), leaving him with the racket. He loved his daughter, he really did, like any parent does; it had broken his heart watching her fall off that pony. The moment of silence before the ear-piercing screams ricocheted around had been the longest of his life.

Silence? Oh wouldn't that be lovely...

"Amelia, what can I do?" he pleaded, tempted to get down on his knees and grovel.

Amelia stared at him through tear-pooled eyes; he swore he saw a fleeting look of pleasure at his desperation. Her room looked like the latest Toys R Us catalogue: pristine soft toys, puzzles, dolls, all surrounding her, purchased first out of guilt before an attempt at bribery. But nothing had sated her.

"I-ice cr-cream," she blubbed.

"Ice cream?" he asked, tentatively.

"Mu-mummy said n-no more ice cream!" she sniffed.

Of course she did, she wanted daddy to deal with the consequences.

"Sure, honey! Ice cream! I'll go get some!"

"S-s-strawberry n-NOW!" The threat was laced through each sob.

Richard raced to the kitchen. He had hidden half a tub of Neapolitan in the back of the freezer. His smugness slowed him and he thought of Sarah returning, brimming with the afterglow of her bitchfest, waiting to bask in his disorganised, dishevelled stress. Screw her, he had this.

He rummaged through the freezer, through the stack of ready meals he hoarded for his nights alone, which was more often than not. But there was no ice cream. His eyes flitted to the recycling box just visible through the back door–

–She'd fucking eaten it.

It was time to think outside the box: biscuits. The tin was full of those gopping pink wafers. Surely a fair trade for gopping pink ice cream?

Richard trudged back towards the screeching, biscuit tin head-locked under his arm.

Amelia paused for breath, looking hopeful. "I-I scream?"

Too right you do, he thought. "How about biscs?" He rattled the tin.

The racket promptly resumed.

Richard went back to the kitchen, shutting all doors firmly behind him. He sat, head in hands, in thought. It was Sunday, 4:30pm. The Supermarket would be closed and the corner shop was too far to walk and leave Amelia alone.

Just as he was considering perforating his eardrums, the chime of *Greensleeves* echoed into Richard's consciousness. He shook off the randomness of the tune in his head, before he realised it was really playing. Outside.

The Ice Cream Van!

If there really was a God he'd answered Richard's prayers. Either that or it was bloody perfect luck – whatever it was he'd take it, he'd even take a deal with the Devil right now. He leapt to the window and peered outside but it was too misty to see further than the houses opposite. The timeless tune was getting louder; it would be outside the house in a moment!

Richard hastily grabbed his shoes, crushing down the heels, and shouted up the stairs, "Daddy's gonna get you ice cream!" He stuffed his keys in his pockets and shot a brief glance at his coat as he ran out the door, letting it swing behind him on the latch. It was cold but he'd only be a second.

Greensleeves engulfed the isolated street in nostalgic tones as he stood by the curb, rooting for change in his pocket. Come on, it was bloody freezing.

What? The folk music was diminishing, slipping away like Richard's sanity. No, it must have gone down the street behind, he could still catch it!

He started to jog, tripping over his half-on shoes, kicking his heels up to his hands and hopping to pull them up. The mist was thicker now and the streetlights were starting to switch on, polluting the twilight and hindering any remaining sunlight with a woolly haze. He followed the music, growing quieter but still definitely local, round to the next cul-de-sac.

It struck Richard that it was odd that there would be an Ice Cream Van visiting in the middle of winter; but then, he had heard it several times since moving there, and often at strange times. However, he had never actually seen the vehicle itself. Come to think of it, he hadn't even seen a child skipping along with an ice cream.

He saw a flash of white between two buildings, the shiny pink tip of a giant plastic ice cream unmistakeable. Fuck this, he wasn't gonna let Sarah win. All doubt faded and Richard legged it, beelining for the end of the street. It was one-way, he had it now!

Richard got to the curb, panting. Maybe he should visit the gym more. Sarah often suggested it, spitefully, which just made him all the more reluctant to go.

He looked down the road, *Greensleeves* amplifying once again. The fog was thick now, visibility down to just a few metres, permeating him with claustrophobia. He looked around at his surroundings, his vision grasping for the prosaic neighbourhood he should have been standing in, or at least another person. He was waiting for something, he knew that… he was waiting for something for his daughter. She needed him. Wait, he had left her alone! He looked at his watch instinctively but the hands pointed at numbers he couldn't decipher. How long had he been gone?

He turned to go back the way he came but, as he did so, reality shifted and he found himself standing at the edge of the road he'd just come from. He turned again abruptly, tripping off the curb onto the looming road. He could feel the glare of the streetlight above him and looked up. The light was floating like a glowing orb, suspended in the air, absent of its metal stem.

He crossed the road, mounting the pavement on the other side, looking for an escape, but just toppled back onto the same tarmac, stepping through an invisible door to arrive where he'd begun. The street was no longer familiar, no longer framing the friendly middle class homes, abundant with fluorescent joggers and dog walkers. Instead, the road ran straight, undeviating, unworldly, yet somehow inviting.

Who was he? Where was he? He could hear a girl crying, the sound echoing and colliding with a familiar harmony that caressed his nerves. Where was the music coming from, and why did it sound so familiar? He racked his brain for answers, but even the questions kept slipping out of reach. There was one thing he was sure of: he needed to follow the road. Somehow, he knew what awaited him at the end of this highway to hell, but he had to finish what he'd started.

He started to run blindly down the street, the need for cardio skills negated by adrenaline. His footfalls fell silent on the street, running through the cloudlike fog, the sound swallowed by the eerie score.

Richard stopped. The broken headlight of a derelict van was visible through the trees. He approached it, extending his arm to smooth his hand over the rusted bonnet, studying the pink paint peeling off the plastic popsicle. A sour tinge tainted his nostrils. He wrinkled his nose involuntarily, before twitching the corner of his mouth; distaste replaced with desire. He reached the shutter, the aura of the imperial salesman handing wafers and wrappers lingering beneath the green velvet that now covered the glass.

Richard pushed past the brambles, hooking at his goose-pimpled skin, to the back of the van. One of the double doors was ajar, but as he leant on a supporting branch, gravity swung it open enticingly. He squeezed in without hesitation, the compulsion to seek what he sought overwhelming. He was hit with the stench of rotted milk, curdling in his lungs, engulfing his airways. He inhaled deeply.

A drip of thick, yellow, sludge clotted on his forearm, and another, and another. Richard looked up, the ceiling a chasm, a thousand slippery stalactites suspended, exuding creamy ooze. He squelched through the cave purposefully, towards a soft amber glow glistening off the wet milieu.

He turned around a corner and saw the Emperor of Ice Cream moulded into its viscous throne, beckoning him. The Emperor chuckled, its dark chocolate button eyes sliding asymmetrically down its face. Milky spatter flew from its gelatinous grin, as it held up a strawberry ice cream.

Richard continued his approach but began to sink, leg by leg, up to his waist, in mucilaginous liquid, freezing him to his core. The Emperor's laugh boomed, causing the melting spikes above to rain down more sticky liquid, whitewashing Richard.

Richard stopped, his trance fading. Panic swept over him as he struggled to release himself from the bog to no avail. He grabbed something solid, pulling it out of the sucking swamp. It was a skull, a small one, the cratered eye sockets revealed as the slop ran away. He dropped it sharply, but could feel more all around him as he floundered in the graveyard swill.

Soon he was up to his neck, melted ice cream in every crevice. The skulls were clustered around, bumping into him. They began to rise out of the mire, bobbing around him, the heads of a hundred children.

"What would you give to go back home, Richard? To take this ice cream for your precious daughter and be free from this place?" its voice rasped and burbled.

"Anything, anything!"

"As you wish," rumbled the Emperor.

Richard clutched onto his melting surroundings uncertainly, writhing until his legs were free. Finally, he reached his feet, his breath bubbling through the torrent pouring down his face. He looked at the Emperor, flinching, tentatively reaching out his hand for the cone.

"She will have it, don't you worry!" it said, its gaping mouth a swirling, expanding black hole. "Now, be gone!"

Richard bolted, slipping and skidding toward the exit now plunged in darkness, not daring to look back. He barged out of the van, the brambles tearing his sopping shirt as he fought his way through them. Kicking away from the final branch, he ran, the fog now fading. The streetlights, released of their misty smother, began to reveal his familiar town. Richard slowed slightly, spluttering foul fluid from his lungs, his arms tacky as the air dried them.

He put on a spurt as he remembered Amelia, waiting for him, alone and vulnerable, but at least safe from his nightmare. Jogging up his drive, he was thankful for the cover of night, making it hard for neighbours to see the state he was in. The smell of sour milk was overwhelming, making him gag as he opened the front door. He paused, the soft chimes of the song that would now haunt him forever echoing in his ears. But the air was still and silent. He shook his head, he had to pull himself together.

"Amelia?" he called up the stairs, tentatively. "Sarah?" Nothing.

He darted up the stairs, leaving a slimy trail up the banister, bursting into his daughter's room.

The door collided into something with a dull thud. Richard gave it a shove, the dead weight on the other side grating along the carpet.

Richard pushed through, traipsing on something with a squelch. He looked down. His wife's brain was trodden through the carpet like red jelly, splinters of skull protruding like white chocolate shards, blood drizzled as if it was a sweet berry compote.

Amelia's slight body sat on the bed, propped against the wall. In place of her head, a neon pink globe of ice cream was starting to melt, seeping down her neck. A slash of red sauce defined a mouth but instead of chocolate buttons, Amelia's bright blue eyes protruded and sagged from the sticky face.

37

TEDDY

Paul Shearer

"Sleep tight, honey, and don't let the bed bugs bite." Daddy knows it's not the bugs I'm worried about, it's the monster. That's why I have Teddy to protect me. I can hear them fighting sometimes, like when I wake up from a bad dream or 'cause I need to wee. It's almost like they're whispering but I can still hear it hissing as it tries to get to me, but Teddy saves me, he always saves me.

Eventually she closed her eyes and he took his place at the end of the bed, waiting for the inevitable moment when it wakes up. The growls are starting to creep from the shadows as he stared out the window and, for what felt like the billionth time, contemplated a life away from this. There's no frame of reference for him to discover if any of the others thought like this. Did they ever question their existence or dare to dream of something more than the constant battle? This warrior-protector instinct was as ingrained into his psyche as the need to eat was for the girl or the need for teeth from the tooth fairy (he hoped it had been the last he'd seen of that irritating, pious little cunt).

The growling's getting louder now, smoke escaping from under the bed and he draws the small, illuminated blade from within his fur. Whether from under the bed or inside the drawers or wardrobes, whenever they came, one of his kind would be there to protect all the little boys and girls. He assumed that this had always been the way, but as he had no history books or lore to tell him, there was no way to know for sure.

The tentacles had started to appear, snaking out through the air and slowly ascending towards the edge of the bed, and soon they would be followed by teeth. But tonight felt different. There was an element of uncertainty that he had never felt before. He had never seen all of the creature but he guessed it wasn't pleasant, at least if the tentacles, teeth and glowing eyes were anything to go by. Those eyes, the way they burned in the darkness that seemed to envelop the creature, always seeming to be on him whilst also on its prey. It was the eyes that scared him the most (not that he'd ever show it). Fear was not an emotion shown by teddy bears, fixed as they were with an uncompromising stare, one commonly associated with any soldier having spent this long in the trenches.

And this was the best part of his day. Most of the time he was being tossed around, or crushed into some space, sat on, or forgotten, only to be retrieved several hours later. It was days of abuse, physical and emotional, and this was a welcome release. A battle worthy of being the final fight in some videogame or movie every single night. He'd often wondered what would happen if it ended. He'd never lost and every night the creature came back again, fresh for the fight.

The eyes appeared and darkness seemed to spread out from under the bed and creep across the floor. Those same eyes now stared up at the small bear and he felt every tiny bead of stuffing cry out, compelling him to raise his sword and prepare to fight. But he fought against it. If he was ever to have answers, he would have to be strong, he'd have to resist the urges, fight every inch of his basic programming. He'd have to walk away.

The creature had sensed that something was different and became wary to leave the sanctuary of its lair. Was this some sort of trick? Some new tactic his kind had never seen before? Or was this what victory felt like?

The bear locked eyes with the creature, made it aware of the situation and, when he was convinced they were on the same page, he stepped away and lowered his sword. He moved across to the far corner of the bed and turned his back on the sleeping girl. He knew in that moment he was finished, that his life had ended. The urges had gone from his body and the glow from his sword dulled.

He turned his head to watch as the world faded away from him, the final images registering in his blank, uncompromising eyes being that of the creature, still enveloped by darkness, crushing the little girl as she woke from her sleep, her eyes crying out to him in disbelief at his betrayal.

38

A NIGHT WITH LUCILLE HOGWEED

Milethia Thomas

You've moved, haven't you? All of you. One whole foot – in three months! Clever. You can't out-wit your master, though. I put down the string, and the string never lies! But still, you're clever things. And naughty! Exceedingly, naughty children.

If people knew about your capabilities, they'd run. Ha! Maybe it's the cocktail – my piss and comfrey – that has given you your evolutionary leap. Who'd've thought? Should patent it.

Mind you, if you don't stop moving, children, I'll have to kill more of you.

You have been warned.

Ahhhh! My beauty. You're cramped. Your babies are fast developers – aren't they? I turn my back... Tsk! Welding gloves on. Jeez! You're all as tough as my mum's Sunday beef joint. Little blighters! Don't want to come up, do they, beauty? I wonder what they'd sound like if they could talk? "Don't hurt widdle me!"

Done it!

The sight of you re-ignites an urge. I had that yucky fumble with Doreen Minging Fitzwilliams forty years ago, but she ignited nowt. She was an eyesore – but you're a goddess. Touch me now, won't you? You must lean into me. It'd be too forward of me to make the first move. The wind will help you. That's it. Lean...

Harold unbuttoned his shirt and flesh flopped out that was streaked with keloid scars and fresher welts.

Come on! Come on!

Car headlights punctured the darkness, wrenching him from his intimate thoughts.

*

"It's not my problem that a stuffin', stupid, little rugrat decided to tramp all over my land and plants." Harold, fumbling over the last few buttons of his shirt, sniffed his annoyance up his nose and wiped the sweat off his face with his shirt sleeve.

The policewoman cringed, crossing her arms. "That 'stuffin', stupid, little rugrat' is a five-year-old who is now in hospital with burns caused by your plants, and there is a traumatised ten-year-old neighbour who witnessed what happened."

Traumatised, my arse! Harold leant forward. "Yeah? Well, that ten-year-old has plagued me ever since she moved here. She stands in my garden staring. Bloody, little freak." *Special needs – must be.*

"Watch your language, sir."

I know you, missy policewoman. Came before. Some idiot complained about me firing water pistols at cats. Hate the little shits – defecating in my garden. Luckily, they disappeared. Tried to blame me for that. "As I said … um …" *Interfering bitch.* He clicked his fingers.

"PC Reynolds…"

Nowt PC about you, is there? "It wasn't my fault that he decided to run from his house, down the road to my private property, and then through my Hogweed wearing nothing but his swimming trunks because he thought he was Mowgli. You should be prosecuting his mam for not keeping a bleeding eye on him. She told him stories about it being a jungle! What mam tells their five-year-old that Giant Hogweed is a bleeding jungle."

"Remove the plants, sir. The local authority is aware and will visit you about this."

*

Seething, Harold looked up at the three-quarters of an acre of six-foot Giant Hogweed. *Magnificent. And I am the architect.* His most precious was Lucille. Eight feet, eight inches of gorgeousness standing majestically in the centre; a perfectly formed stem – leggy – with a satellite-dish sized flower head that dwarfed the others around her. She was mam to all the lesser Hogweed that surrounded her.

No time for sentimentality. Your babies are blocking my path to you. Time is of the essence. Need to move you, Lucille, before people dig you up.

He ripped at her babies, snapping them and tossing them away. Hogweed foliage quivered, bending towards him. Harold looked up; Lucille's gargantuan head shook. *No wind. Queer!* He returned to his task.

*

His obsession with Giant Hogweed had begun as a teenager at the time he had tried to drown Gran's cat in a stream. As Pusskins squirmed and clawed, lacerating his arms, he'd slipped on a stone, and his arm brushed against Lucille. His groin tingled at the memory, and he reached down to further savour the sensation. Lucille's touch had all the intensity of a first kiss. Admittedly, the initial pain was the worst he'd ever experienced, but then a blissful surge of warmth enveloped him; like an addict, once it wore off he craved more. Craved Lucille. It wasn't until later he realised that not all Giant Hogweed possessed the ability to cause instantaneous blistering and pleasure like Lucille's touch. She was special.

Afterwards, his sun sensitive skin would blister. *Phytophotodermatitis.* He relished this word, believing that it gave him an individual identity. At every opportunity, he exposed the area to the sun and would pop the blisters – excruciation melting into bliss as the release of endorphins after the pop became nectar to him.

*

Feet crunched down on the pebbled path alongside the Hogweed. Harold froze. *Someone's skulking. Trespasser!* Spitting on his hand, he slapped it on the stray toupee hair that masked his vision, sweeping it to one side, and tip-toed to the end, peering around the corner.

The bloody boy's father! Harold watched him pull his hooded top around his face. In his free hand he carried a can of petrol that he poured around the base of the plants. Harold's tense grip on the axe sent pain coursing up into his neck. *Doesn't matter about the little ones, but it'll burn a path to Lucille. Steady yourself, Harold. He's a muscly bugger and mustn't be given the upper hand.*

"Could you move away from my plants?"

The father flinched, then turned to face him, contempt on his face.

"Please."

"My little lad's in hospital because of your plants, and you want me to stop what I'm doing?"

Harold nodded.

"Piss off!"

Harold could not tolerate rudeness – it wasn't part of his well-adjusted nature – so he didn't expect this from other folk. He bit his lip, hard, injecting an endorphin-rush into himself, then gouged a nail into a blistered Lucille love mark for good measure – *Jesus!* – and moved towards the man.

"I said – very politely I might add – move away from my plants."

The Father took a lighter out of his trouser pocket and bent down. Click.

"Don't do that."

Click. Nothing. He shook the lighter. "Come on!"

"I've asked you not to do that."

Click. The flame danced.

Anger fogged reason. Harold charged, embedding the axe in the back of the father's head. Flame extinguished, the lighter fell to the ground.

Panting, he marvelled at the father's expression as his hand came up to feel the axe head, before he fell forwards like a cut tree. As blood drained out, eagerly drunk by the earth around the Hogweed, panic replaced Harold's rage.

Got to get rid of the body.

The skull levered open as Harold rocked the axe to remove it. Hurriedly, he dug a hole in his potato plot and buried the axe. Then he took the man's arms and dragged him. W*here? The Shed. Jesus! You're a hefty* bastard!

And that's when he saw it. As he thought it – *Lizard?* – he knew that he must be off his rocker. *A lizard? A walking lizard? What the hell?!* "Oy!"

The lizard disappeared, leaving behind trails of its shimmering self.

No time to waste. Harold resumed pulling the man by the arms to his shed. As he backed into the shed, he couldn't lift the shoulders free of the ground with the weight of the father's *stupid fat head.*

Screeeeeeek!

"What?" Harold looked back into the shed. Fingers trailed down the glass, leaving a filthy smudge on his usually pristine window. Outside, a shadow hastily disappeared.

"I'm not having that!"

He paid no mind to the head he stepped on when leaving the shed or the leg he crunched down on, before stumbling and falling to his knees.

As he raised himself off the ground, the lizard sprinted past him. "I'm going to tell on you."

Harold heaved himself to his feet and bumbled after the lizard, throat burning as he mouth-breathed.

Now I've got you.

The lizard pushed back into the Giant Hogweed, beckoning him with a finger. Harold's stomach lurched, bile rushing to his throat, and he charged, imagining the pain he would inflict on the *bastard lizard*, squashing it and grinding its bones into the earth; but as he neared, lizard pressed against Lucille. Harold's charge faltered. Her gorgeous stem was – *Bending! Bouncing!*

"Nooooooo!"

As he reached out, about to make contact, lizard side-stepped him, and – *Can't be!* – he was enveloped by the Hogweed.

Harold's foot snagged on something, and he fell onto his beloved Lucille. He was twanged off her, face-planting the ground, and tried to lift himself up, but an arm was restrained by…*Rope?* Violently he was flipped over, and a rib painfully displaced.

"Get this off me!"

"We have you now," a young voice said.

We? Jeez! My arm…burning!

Harold managed to raise his head. He could now see that the lizard – *The girl neighbour!* – was dressed in what appeared to be a fluorescent wetsuit and gloves.

"Lucille doesn't like you killing! Lucille doesn't like you killing!" she said, in a sing-songy voice.

"H – how do you know about Lucille?"

"She talks to me, in my head, says that she's sorry about the little boy, but her babies were defending themselves because…The girl's eyes narrowed, and she got down on her haunches to whisper harshly – "Murderer! You've been killing her babies!"

Lucille quivered, and her foliage closed in.

A pained laugh. "Absolute twaddle. Stupid, little bugger!" The roots that held him tightened, searing into his skin.

"God! No!"

"Lucille says this isn't for my young eyes… See ya! Wouldn't want to be ya!" The girl skipped away.

Harold looked up at Lucille as her – *Beatific!* – flowerhead hung over him. "I love you. Lucille. My true love." The restraining roots relaxed. "We'll go away together, Lucille. Start over."

Her head bounced gently.

You're nodding, my beauty.

She coyly looked away, and all quivering ceased.

"My beauty?"

When her flowerhead gazed upon Harold one more, projectile-sap spattered onto his face, melting skin and muscle.

Harold's skin began to rip, in the same measured way in which he would delicately slice into a salmon to obtain slivers. Corrosive sap was drip-fed into the wounds.

He tried to scream, but Lucille's long, keen roots undulated their way through his mouth, wrapping themselves around his uvula and slowly began to slice; before trailing down his throat, seeking a moist area to settle in for the duration.

Please! Lucille. Hear me! I love you. Stop! Stoooooop!

He managed to turn over, his face grating against bony cat remains.

No one heard Harold's silent screams.

*

By Harold's childhood river, a spirited, smiling girl in a fluorescent wetsuit pointed to the ground. Lucille Hogweed slithered towards her, roots positioning themselves in the prepared hole. Familiarity soothed her, somewhat, after the trauma of losing all her babies to environmental health at Harold's house, and she briefly reminisced about the strange and violent boy called Harold who had at first obeyed her will but then became possessive and disloyal.

She liked this quirky girl, who, unlike Harold, was compliant and intelligent – enough that she thought to wear a wetsuit to protect herself as she ran through the Hogweed, and then washed the toxins off in the river. A girl who simply found Giant Hogweed beautiful and would spend hours communicating telepathically – a talent that Lucille would use to her advantage.

With her entire family exterminated, Lucille would send messages via the 'root-wide' network. And others *would* come.

The girl skipped towards her. "I love you, Lucille!"

When the purge began, Lucille would probably let this one live.

"You're mine." Cautiously the girl wrapped her rubber arms around Lucille.

Lucille shuddered.

I'll let her live. For a little while longer.

39

DISTANT PERCUSSION

Freya Eden-Ellis

'Let storms be mere distant percussion, in a world of music to which you dance. Let love and joy leave your cheek blushing. Let me give you every chance.' My dad's old rhyme: to comfort me to sleep. I recited it then, a private moment between us, even though only I was there.

His death was the first sleep that I'd comforted him into, one hand on the polished wood where I thought his still heart might lie. It was hawthorn at his request. I knew there was a reason, it snagged in my brain like litter flapping on a tree branch, but I couldn't quite pick it out. I couldn't remember the significance.

Every night until I left home he had sat beside my bed and spoken those words. He smiled so they seemed like wishes made of love. They weren't. It was a strained smile and they were sweet words to disguise a bitter ending. I remembered that ending quietly, with my hand on his coffin, and wondered how the rest had slipped so easily from my mind:

'This room is locked, it is sealed tight, the entrance blocked to imp or sprite. My daughter will be safe from harm, impervious to spell or charm. Remember well the deal we struck. Risk our anger, end your luck.'

I thought he was trying to make me feel safe, but he was talking to things I couldn't see.

Odd folk, that's what others call us. I may have been away and lived in the world of clean-shaven suit-wearers, of friends who meet for lunch and tap at laptops on trains, but it was a charade. I'm a woman whose 'r's come out with a curl in them. I snort at sensationalised news alerts, yet follow word-of-mouth folk wisdom passed down to me with a faithful dedication I've never managed while sitting in a pew.

Down here we don't just hear stories, we inherit memories. When you're born in this landscape, you're as much a part of it as the bouncing, white umbels of cow parsley that froth at the verge each spring. It was comforting to know I was returning Dad into its sweeping green folds.

After the wake, a silver-scythe moon cleaved apart clouds with a meager light. Stars shine brighter the greater the darkness, but the rural night was shrouded in sea mist. The comforting constellations – familiar, regular, sublime – were obscured by thick blackness highlighted with billowing wisps of white.

I paid no attention to the unfriendly night; I'd been away too long in the perpetual electric glare of the 24-hour world. The pub where we'd thrown Dad's final party, all warped wood lit by a gentle copper glow, made the path home seem short. I'd walked further in areas where women carry car keys between their fingers at night like daggers.

I was stoic as hands grasped, hugged and patted at me. Faces wreathed in misery, alcohol-laced words whispered in my ear. Embraces, kisses, sobs. I left with relief.

It would be my first night alone at home. I had found him lying at an unnatural angle by the door, beneath the landline. There was no phone signal here. Had he been trying to call? 'Help!' 'Goodbye.' 'Watch out.' His final moments had not been peaceful. Whatever had possessed him before his heart ceased to pulse had mangled his mind. His mouth gaped. His fingernails were full of flesh and blood where he had scratched his eyes blind.

I was afraid of going back there, not because of ghosts or anything so insubstantial, but because the memory of finding him like that was a hidden banshee, wailing whenever I was near the house. But my flat was hours away, and I had several more hours' whiskey in my blood. Besides, it was our home.

Before the ambulance had taken him, I'd taken something of his. It was a hawthorn ring. I grasped it where it hung around my neck and flinched. In the cold outside, my skin was as icy as his had been. It is dreadful to touch a once living body that you love and feel only cold, stiff death. It lingers. Any human touch reminds me of it.

The noise of the pub rang in my ears. The wind made my cheeks sting. The trees made a mass of black, crooked shapes across the landscape, crowding at the edge of the road – skeletal mourners at a graveside. Their branches leapt with thunderous zigzagging into the sky so that it looked cracked, a broken mirror. On the banks of the road, they formed the hunched back of a crouching man, a snarling dog, waiting, watchful, shrouded Death.

I looked through them. Far below, the hill tumbled into the sea and the Isle of Portland rose, shimmering through the haze. Beads of light traced the line of a road. Portland has only one road in and out and there are some on the Isle who have never travelled its full length once. Even us odd folk here whisper about those people. That was where my dad grew up, though he denied it to anyone who asked.

In the breeze stirred a new note. Its sound was wind, blown through wood or bone. It floated above an unnatural percussive beat that could have been the patter of heavy raindrops on hollow trunks had they not been so sonorous and regular.

On top of the ridge, five mounds lay against a fog-addled sky. Bronze-age barrows, long looted, but not empty. Music seeps from them when their inhabitants are abroad. I had heard it once before. Below the mounds crouches a spiny hawthorn tree traced with whorls and fissures.

When I saw it, a memory wormed its way back in – part of the oddness I'd shed these past years. A menacing beat, an executioner's drum, booming ever closer. Dad placing me in the hawthorn tree, telling me to close my eyes. *'They respect the hawthorn; it's thorns will not prick you and it will keep you safe while we obey their rules.'* A fear

I couldn't comprehend compelled me to do what I was told without question. When the music faded, Dad took me home and burnt a contract leasing land for a smallholding. He kept the fire alight all night until the ashes were thicker than the flames.

A chord struck as I paired the memory with a new one: Dad telling me last month he had a secret buyer for the house. No one must know, he had said. I thought it was just his Portland oddness. I had told my old friend, and in villages without phone signal news travels faster than waves down a wire.

The sound grew until it was unmistakably rhythmic, instrumental. The distance back equaled the distance forward. I looked over my shoulder as the pub lights extinguished. I could run and hammer the door, but why? Because in my grief I had heard fairy music from ancient graves? I forced myself on. We were odd folk and we believed things; but I was modern. I'd outgrown folk hokum, surely? I clutched the hawthorn ring.

The creaking of dry branches bending was not solely the wind's doing. There were things in them, feet on them, hands that snagged the top of my head as I tried not to see. I closed my eyes; a child shaking away fear under bed covers. The skittering of dead leaves was the chattering and snickering of hidden forms. In the tangled undergrowth, their bodies reared and bent into the cracking, fractal shape of jagged trees.

A teasing voice began a malicious distortion of Dad's rhyme. I heard it through the wind-blown dark and shrank inside my body. I think I stood still, think I ceased to breathe. My heart echoed Dad's.

'Storms will be your life's percussion; we make the music, lead the dance. All love and joy will fade to nothing, against us you don't have a chance.'

And then:

'His house was locked, it was sealed tight, but locks are nothing to our might. Dreadful how he came to harm, falling under spell and charm. Shame he broke the deal we struck, by our anger, ends his luck.'

The voice was playful and sharp, a kettle singing. Then another voice: rattling pipes, breath forced, but I recognised it. They were playing my father's vocal chords like a flute. They were clicking his teeth like a ventriloquist's dummy. I could hear the snapping back and forth of his jaw.

Terror made me want to run, but I couldn't run from him when I missed him so deeply. As I stood dumb, a force shoved me hard in the back and I fell scrabbling into the earth, grasping at dirt that rumbled and tipped, lifting me up and pushing me on.

From out of the blackness a shape emerged. It stepped with the jerking dance of a hanged man. A deeper mass of dark in the night ahead, it leapt with inhuman strides. The arms flung about like a marionette, the head hung loose at an angle. His knees bent acutely – a doll being marched. The clouds parted and that thin slice of moon laced the blood-drained features of my father's face with silver. His eyes did not glint; they stared at nothing with cloudy apathy. His face was a pale mask. His body was strung up by invisible magic and his head snapped back and laughed the hollow, barking ring of wind through a fallen log.

In that moment of light, I saw that the banks and ditches, fields and verge were full of crouching, creeping shapes. They were people in another form, as allied with nature as humanity has made an enemy of it. They did not need camouflage; they were made for blending into shadows and bending to the landscape. Odd-folk: truer than we ever were.

They were delighted that I saw them and mocked the jig they forced my father to perform, as they propelled us all in a procession down the road. They were ensuring that on my journey home, I understood what had haunted him had been bequeathed to me, that what I thought we owned was theirs.

When I looked away, my father's vacant, lifeless body skipped closer as though to shake me awake. When I paid him attention he receded, calling me on. My shaking felt like the world trembling, my guttural heaving the howl of a doomed earth. I dared not look behind. I could hear the thickening crowd of them, preparing to leap upon me; bury me under their mass; tugging, scratching biting.

I was found the next morning, propped and jabbering outside the house. My father's corpse, his scratched and clouded eyes rotting, lay cradled in my arms. There was dirt under my nails, on my hands. They wondered how I'd managed it, to break open the earth and rip the hawthorn coffin to pieces. They whispered 'how tragic.' I couldn't tell them the truth. The only words that I could muster were the ones the odd-folk had sung to me:

'You could never own the power of our sacred tree.

You were safe at our discretion; even death won't set you free.

And once you're gone, no hawthorn box can tidy you away.

Or keep you in the earth for worms and rot to take their prey.

We own your land, you cannot sell, or we will take your skin.

We'll seize your soul and evermore we'll haunt your curs-ed kin.'

The unfathomable fear I'd felt in the hawthorn tree was instinctive. Distant percussion was a warning from the barrows: 'you live on our land, by our rules.' Dad risked tricking them to free us both, but he is dead and now the deal is mine.

40

THE REMAINS

S.V. Macdonald

The stench hits her first. And then an instant clenching of the bowels, a fist that tries to force her insides out onto the sand. She covers her mouth, fighting the heaving and retching sick in her throat, forcing it back. After all, she has seen death before.

But not like this. The smell intensifies as she rounds the shallow, sandy shelf that leads to the beach. Then she sees it, stranded on the striated fossil rock. An offering sent back bloated and battered by the sea; headless, hairless. Hind legs stretching out. The length of claw scoring the soft rock. Shock of white bone at the neck. The black gaping hole at the stomach.

Again, her gorge rises and the world is suddenly bound by grey. Her hand goes to her throat, needing the reassurance of her own whole skin, her pulse, the continued beating of her heart. And then –

'Are you all right?'

The touch on her arm. The shock of contact – confusing when her mind is full of the dead thing on the rock. She turns her head. Nods automatically.

'Just got a fright.'

He smiles sympathetically. Guides her a step or two upwind. Takes a step back. Looks away. Somehow the gesture is familiar. His face, too. Someone she has seen around, out walking maybe. Her mind scrabbles to place him, to know what to say next. A sudden flash of memory, just as suddenly gone.

'That thing – what is it?'

'You can see it?' His eyes widen in surprise.

'What do you mean?'

He shrugs. Pauses. Looks away. 'Could be a badger? Maybe a seal.'

Maybe a dog. She glances around the beach. Her own little dog is ignoring her, barking at gulls near the edge of the waves.

For a while they watch the dog, as if there is nothing else to say. But all the time it lies between them. Waiting.

Finally, 'Should we do something…?' She gestures to the lump of bone and putrefying flesh rejected by the sea.

He almost smiles. For a moment, she thinks he is laughing at her and her weakened stomach curls. His eyes are unfathomable.

'Nothing we can do. Leave it for the tide.'

She nods. Obviously. The sea will reclaim it in a matter of hours. With a final shrewd and searching look he turns to go. The tangled scrub swallows him up as if he has never been, and her little dog comes running back, puzzled and impatient, ready to go home.

For the rest of the day the image of the swollen dead thing haunts her thoughts. Concentration is fleeting and nothing sticks. She tries to read but loses herself in mid-sentence, the words wandering half-finished across the page. Finally, she tosses away the book with a sense of need unfulfilled, choosing the view from her window instead. Fog creeps up as the day grows short and at the back of her mind she is counting the hours until the tide turns.

As the early evening dusk begins to settle she finds that she is stiff with sitting; some exercise would be welcome. She calls the dog. The prospect of a late walk excites him and she is glad to let him off the lead.

All the way through the muddy wood she tells herself that the beach will be empty, washed clean. There is no wind and the very stillness of the leaves and the silence of the birds heighten her sense of unreality. Perhaps she is only dreaming this walk – in a moment she will open her eyes and be curled up in her armchair next to the fire.

It is almost dark when she reaches the beach. Foolish not to have brought a torch. The mist is unearthly. Everything is hidden. Not even the pale curl of waves is visible against the dark mass of the sea, and her only guides along the grey and murky sand are the faintly luminous shells that crunch underfoot. The foggy air is thick with the stench of seaweed – nothing more – and all at once her shoulders relax and drop. Only then does she realise how tight and tense she must have been. She almost smiles. But then the dog barks, and the lightest of breezes picks up, stirring the fog into clammy fingers that chill her exposed skin. And the foulness of death fills her lungs again.

Spurned by the tide, the little corpse is a huddled mass of darkness against the slightly lighter rocks. And in the deepening gloom, she begins to imagine that it moves. Just the tiniest jerk of a fleshless paw. She freezes. The fog swirls and swallows it up and she is suddenly very alone. Panic rises, metallic in her mouth. She calls for the dog. Her voice is small and thin, swallowed up by the murk. There might have been a bark – no, a yelp… and then nothing. Nothing but a kind of slither…

It is enough. She throws herself backwards, towards where the path should be. The rock is wet and her boots fail to grip. She hits the sand hard and her jeans are instantly soaked through; her hands burning with sharp, gritty scrapes. She scrambles to her feet. Green slime as slick as ice underfoot sends her back to the ground; and still the slithering sound persists.

White bones reach out from the darkness. She snatches her hands to her chest, curling herself around them. The bones, no, the skeletal paws grope blindly on the sand, tearing at the green rocks, creeping ever closer, dragging the headless rotting flesh towards her.

Her throat constricts like in a nightmare or lucid dream where a scream would wake her to soft clean sheets and the warmth of her bedroom, the safety of a light switch to chase away the darkness. And for a moment she closes her eyes, absurdly hoping that this too is a dream. But then foetid breath gasps in her face, so close she can taste it. Her eyes fly open. Inches away, the severed neck gapes like a yawning mouth seeking hers.

With strength beyond their size, little bones lock lovingly around her neck. The foulness fills her head, chokingly strong. Her vision turns grey. Her mind reels with the horror, seeking darkness and oblivion. But something in her refuses to surrender. Blindly she punches out, the flesh giving way with soft squelching sounds that make her retch, reminding her that she is not dead yet. She finds something hard – the spine, perhaps, or a shoulder, or *something*... She grips and twists, feeling the joints split apart like cooked ribs. Suddenly the grip around her neck loosens and falls away and she is up and stumbling back across the rocks, falling at every other step but forcing herself up and on, ignoring the searing pain as the rocks gash her knees and twist her ankles almost unbearably.

She limps through the woods, almost on safe ground, the darkness like a living force trying to draw her back to the beach. Tears sting and blur her eyes and she fails to see the hooded shape on the path until she has pitched into him, sending them both sprawling on the muddy ground.

Hands clutch at her and this time she does scream. Something clamps over her mouth, cutting off her breath for one endless panicky moment before she is released.

As she draws breath to scream again he rasps, '*No!* They'll hear you!'

She twists round to see his face. The man from the beach. Of course.

'W-what do you mean?' She pulls back, wary, trying to get up on her battered knees.

'*Them.*' His eyes roll wildly towards the scrubby undergrowth. And now she can hear it. The rustling in the bushes. The all-too-familiar slither of cold flesh on wet ground.

Somehow he is upright and pulls her to her feet. 'We have to run. *Run!*'

He drags her along the path. The rustling in the bushes keeps pace, even begins to pull ahead as the woods thicken. This part is familiar, the part she always dreads, where the path is constricted by massive chestnut trees and almost disappears before it opens out again and edges the field. The perfect place for...

'*Ambush!*' He points upwards, as if he can see through the eerie fog. The trunks of the trees appear and the path narrows. He jerks to a halt.

'One at a time.' He takes a deep, ragged breath. 'You first. And keep running. Stop for nothing. Understand? Beyond the trees. There will be help.'

She nods, not really understanding but too frightened to disagree. Red eyes flicker momentarily above them and go out, so quickly it could have been her imagination if not for the chittering rising from the scrub around them. Before she has time to think at all he pushes her forward, keeping close, warm hands on her cold shoulders. Instantly there is a change in the air and a smell like an open grave. Something very big crashes down and suddenly she is propelled forward and she runs like she has never run before. Away from breaking branches and the harsh scream that suddenly cuts off – away from the claws and teeth that tear her coat and the nightmare sounds of blood and death that call to her every instinct to run, get help... and suddenly, overwhelmingly, to *fight*.

She crashes through undergrowth and all at once it breaks and she is in the open field. Strange hands grab her and blindly she strikes out. Fighting to get away, deafened by the sudden yells that fill the air. Her legs are swiped from under her and the strange words she hears as she goes down are, '*Check her for bites...*'

*

Her head aches. Something is pushing at her arm. Snuffling. Whimpering... Her eyes snap open and she throws out an arm to ward it off – but it's just the dog. And she is cool but not chilled. Somewhere warm...

Puzzled, she looks around. She is half-lying in her armchair, safe at home. Just a dream, then? But her head really aches. She glances at the dog and all at once realises she is wearing her coat and boots. And she is muddy – worse, there are splashes of blood all down one side. And there is a kitchen knife in her hand. She struggles to her feet. Every part of her aches now. Her knees sting as clotted blood is torn from newly-formed scabs. Her hands, too. And her neck...

She glances in the mirror, prepared for – what? The muddy face, certainly. The tangled hair. The blood. But not the thick, short gash just below her jawline. Livid and angry, it pulses with every beat of her heart.

And she is not prepared for the words scrawled in red marker that she must strain to make out:

The infected turn at midnight.

She examines the tiny trails of green forming around the wound. She checks the clock. Lifts the knife. Runs the point along the painfully raised, corrupted skin.

And pushes it in.

41

THE FOUR

N.W. Twyford

They're Horsemen, the Survivor thought, with all the certainty of a man who had witnessed a true, logic-shattering atrocity.

They're Horsemen and they're all our fault.

He had staggered out of the burning remnants of the compound and towards the shore, where waves lapped at the coast, ignorant to the horror that had occurred only several hundred metres away. He did not know if any of the others had made it out alive. All he knew was that things had gone very, very wrong.

They *had* to be Horsemen, he thought, suspecting that his sanity was cracked, perhaps broken. Only Horsemen could bring the end of the world in such a way.

The yellow one was Famine, the colour of wilted crops. The green was Pestilence, the shade of infection. The red was War for the blood that flows. And the last, a purple so dark it was almost black.

That one was Death.

They didn't exactly... look *like Horsemen though*, he thought briefly, before the observation passed with a bitter choke of a laugh. It didn't matter. They brought ruin: that was all that mattered.

The Survivor still carried the hypodermic loaded with the sedative, just in case he had to use it. The gesture was, of course, futile. There would be no way he could use it.

Not on them, but it had other purposes.

Loading up his pockets with as many stones as they would bear, he waded in as far up to his waist. The water was shockingly cold.

He removed the cap on the syringe and pressed the needle's tip to his wrist. He did not struggle to find the vein; his pulse was racing, the veins surging with blood craving oxygen.

Depressing the stopper, he continued walking forwards before the drug took hold.

His last thought, as the waters rose around him and the feeling of utter and absolute numbness took hold was surprisingly abstract.

What would others think of them?

*

They were monsters, the Scientist thought. That's what he was there to study, and to assess, in a remote location that didn't technically exist. Proper, dyed in the wool aberrations. Part machine, so they said – although you wouldn't know it to look at them – part... something else. Flesh, of a type, but what flesh; who could say? They were ungodly. Unnatural.

He'd come to the project late, had been assigned to it because no one else could be.

There was no one left. The original team had all gone mad.

Mad might be oversimplifying it somewhat, he thought, ever rational. Certainly they were beyond use. Some were struck off, retired to quiet places in the country to live lives without consequence or stress. They would certainly contribute nothing further to science. Perhaps that was for the best, given what they had created.

One member of the team had been institutionalised, possibly never to return. His language was similar to that of the subjects; uh oh, uh oh, uh oh, over and over again, accompanied with lurches or head butts against padded walls, the movements following the same rhythm of the idiot speak. Sometimes he wouldn't stop until forcibly restrained, hair matted with his blood.

Another had opened his wrists.

And another, believing his colleagues dead, had taken a walk into the sea and never came out again.

The creatures did not know this, did not know anything, as far as the Scientist could tell. They were idiots; actual simpletons, tumbling around on their faux landscape; unawares that they were being watched, that they basked under a painted sky, a faux ceiling of Truman Show-like ingenuity. The sun was fake, and laughed at them, and they did not question that. The plants were phony, and issued orders, and they did not question that either. As far as they knew, the whole world existed for them.

It made no sense. The whole thing was naive and coddling and utterly mad.

The Scientist did not know how they had come to be; the previous team had destroyed most of their notes in a delirious haste, the fire ravaging their office, burning at least one of their number severely. Were they once apes? Some sort of bear? Surely (and this was where reason reached its end) not once man? He supposed it was best to act like it didn't matter, in terms of his studies, although that logic only sat right when accompanied by two fingers of whisky, applied on repeat.

He never used to be much of a drinker. It came easier now.

The question he'd been asked, the wrong question, but the one they were paying him for was at least one he could explore without his ethics crippling him.

What can we use them for?

*

They were fucking useless, thought the General. Who ever thought they would be a good idea was clearly out of their minds, he concluded, and he knew he was right, given what had happened to the first team. The new project leader, a man who seemed permanently tired and who tried to give an objective, almost disinterested air seemed to smell more of drink and smoke the longer he was on the project for. He didn't have any answers. It was stupid to assume he would.

Their purpose eluded him, and who could blame him for failing? They were completely untrainable, even simple conditioning escaped their idiot brains; their grins fixed like skeletons. The most one could manage was getting them to go to bed, which was achieved by monotonously repeating the same, simple command, over and over again. They resisted everything else.

If they couldn't be used and they couldn't tell the public (which they couldn't, not without the most damning of inquiries) then perhaps termination was best.

Or it would be, but the damn things were indestructible. They were bullet proof, flame retardant (flame retarded, the General joked to no one), you name it. They did not require sustenance, so God knows how they were alive. Maybe they weren't, and that was the point.

All he knew was they could trample a man to death while laughing, tear his arms off like a child pulling legs off a spider – sometimes cooing for good measure – and hug him to the point where his skull split, all the while doing a little dance. The smile never dropped once.

In all the horrors of man, war, and science, he'd never seen anything like them before.

*

They were certainly original, thought the Politician. He'd never seen anything like them before either.

He still wasn't entirely sure how this had come his way; a contact of a friend of a former colleague looking for a favour led its way to him, and he had a reputation for solving the sort of problems that had no right to be fixed.

He knew spin. There was no story he couldn't turn good – he prided himself on that – the trick was knowing when to start and end it, where to point the cameras, how selective you were with the facts.

Every story is a snippet of reality. The trick is showing what reality you want.

An idea came to him; one so blackly funny he wanted to laugh but he didn't want to risk a thing. A way to make these abominations profitable, a way to put them to work, even if they didn't know it. They would not be engines of war, but entertainment. And entertainment was *far* more profitable than war.

You'd need to omit any human interaction whatsoever, he thought. The fear was palpable from the security tapes, even at a distance. Isolation and a cheery soundtrack should remedy it.

No kids. They'd crush them in a second, in a wave of enthusiasm. There were rumours, from the contact that something like this had happened before, had led to the team that developed them all leaving under shady and hasty circumstances. It didn't bear thinking about; the pulped remains of the infants, dragged and spread like bloody rags, used to add the missing red to a landscape of greens, blues and yellows.

He would have to make sure there was literally nothing they could destroy, because boy, could they destroy a lot. Their enclosure was reinforced titanium behind the fake scenery and bright colours, tested and replaced monthly. Perhaps they didn't really want to get out; they only wanted to amble wherever their imaginations took them, and their imaginations were as limited as their intelligence.

He started to make arrangements.

*

I don't know what the fuck they are, the Producer thought, *but they've got potential.*

He liked the format – the four of them, each with a different colour, different shaped accessories. They were distinctive, marketable.

The Studio Head had gotten the footage from... somewhere. He wouldn't say, and the Producer was smart enough to know not to ask.

The conditions were simple and mysterious. The studio would receive the rushes, unmarked, with no correspondence or paperwork, and they could do whatever they liked with it; in fact they were encouraged to edit it, add sound, effects, narration, you name it. Anything to make it seem less real. Anything to stop people suspecting.

As far as anyone outside the studio knew, this was their latest hit programme. All that the supplier asked for was their fifty percent share of profits. They were a silent partner in this particular co-production.

When you took design, costumes, actors, props, camera crews, sound and everything else out of the equation, it was quite a bargain.

*

They were magical, thought Timmy, two and a half, and who took a few attempts to say the word. Magical.

The characters danced, played, sang, hugged, all under a smiling sun, with blue skies and fluffy clouds and even fluffier bunnies. He sang their songs and recited their broken English. He loved them.

*

They were weird, thought Timmy's Mum, who didn't like them. They were repetitive and monotonous and their songs were gibberish, but hey, Timmy liked them and they kept him quiet which let her have some time to herself.

The one thought that stuck in her mind as she left Timmy in the living room, that passed by, a flicker in her consciousness, was one most parents ask from time to time.

Where do they come up with these ideas?

42

KNUCKLEBONE BLUES

Matt George Lovett

It was a steal for ten bucks. The pitch was still perfect, the reed-board was solid. It was in D, too. The Mississippi key. And when Dwight kissed it, it made a sound like the wails of a thousand broken-backed cotton-pickers. All things considered, Dwight was pretty pleased with his new harmonica.

Ten bucks meant he'd have to go without take-out. But if that little harp could help him break through the wall, it'd be worth every hunger pang. He'd been off his game ever since Alisha left him for upstate and he'd had to go solo. New Orleans was a jazz town; guitar music was always gonna take second fiddle. At least with a harp he could give it a blues twist. Snare some of the old boys who still listened to Muddy Waters.

Dwight returned to his run-down flat, eager to try out the mouth organ. In lieu of take-out he poured a few quick ones, and waited until their fuzz had stolen any thoughts of food. As the sun slid beneath the Mississippi Dwight felt the muses tugging at his sleeve.

He plucked the harp from its case and held it up to the window.

Moonlight danced in the engravings, showing a skeleton in a Stetson brandishing a guitar. Dwight liked that.

A necromantic bluesman.

Dwight snatched up his old acoustic and snapped the harp into his neck-rack, Dylan style. He strummed out an old twelve-bar sequence. His lips inched to the harp and Dwight blew. Gentle at first, virgin nervous, before he found his courage and fell into step.

The melody was slow. Succulent, easing along like a strolling mama. The harp didn't taste metallic. It was sweet, warm, somehow inviting. Strangely familiar, but he couldn't put a finger on how.

Dwight's mind swam with words, and those words needed voice. He broke away from the harp and sang soft and seductive.

The Devil danced in Delaware, the angel fell in Maine

Break me down in Chinatown and take me as your thane

I'm the ragged vagabond with heaven in my veins

So seek the truth in knucklebones and lay me in my grave.

By the time the clock hit two, Dwight had wrestled out the rest. He couldn't remember the last time he'd written a song so fast. Not since Alisha left. And those lyrics. They were good. Real good. Important-sounding nonsense. Weighty, poetic, like Dylan or The Dead. It was the harmonica that brought it all together. That luscious main line. It was the kind that stuck in your head and just wouldn't quit. Dwight went to bed with it still running, and woke with it the next morning.

It was only then, lying sweat-slick on the bed, that Dwight put his finger on why the harp tasted so familiar. It tasted like Alisha.

Dwight's next gig was at Mason's on 42nd Street. Ten o'clock Tuesday in the back-bar to give the regulars something to get drunk to. If he was lucky, he might earn enough to pay for the streetcar home. But he had 'Knucklebone Blues' to play and his new harp in hand. That was something.

Dwight's routine Stones, Dead, and Stripes covers were as flat as usual. A drizzle of applause. A slight lull in the chatter. When he slipped on the harp-rack he got a few rolled eyes, and one shout for "All Along The Watchtower!"

But when he started to play, the chatter stuttered into silence. He kissed the harp, it howled like a widow, and all eyes fell to Dwight as he began singing them cryptic lyrics. By the final chorus, more than a few were mouthing along. When his last chord rang out, it did to applause like leaves in a hurricane. Every soul from the blonde at the bar to the brunette sampling the crayfish was cheering.

"Damn son you can play!"

"Your voice is so steamy!"

"Where you playing next dude? That was hardcore!"

"You free next Saturday? We want you to play a set out front."

Saturday crowds were always larger, and expected a high standard. Dwight hadn't played a Saturday since Alisha left, and even then only as warm-up for some out-of-state touring act. That Saturday, to Dwight's surprise, the bill was empty. 'A Night With Dwight Living' said the flyer. No qualifiers, nobody else. Just his name, and the Stetson-wearing skeleton he'd sketched for the PR people.

The crowd was larger, and spiced with folks from last Tuesday; the blonde, the brunette, and more, they pushed their way to the front. They stared up at Dwight like starving street-dogs, aching for his first song. Which, of course, was 'Knucklebone Blues'. It sent the crowd into fits from the first harmonica blast, mouthing along like cultists at a sacrifice. Dwight filled the rest of his set with old material from his and Alisha's sets, making sure to inject each with harmonica. Like whiskey to a drink-dog, each harp-note gave the crowd new life, and kept them sweet until his finale – a reprise of 'Knucklebone Blues' with a faster tempo.

"I ain't never seen anyone like you!"

"I feel like you can see inside me. You know?"

"It's like you're dancing with my soul."

Dwight didn't take the streetcar home that night. His fans got him good-old-days drunk, and he rode a cab home with the brunette. He tipped generously.

The next few months Dwight earned gig after gig with the coming of the sweltering summer. He'd always known he was a genius, but he'd never had proof until now. It was like once people listened to 'Knucklebone Blues', they couldn't listen to anything else. It was the hit he'd been trying to write since he was fourteen. Now he was finally claiming his dues.

He had his loyal followers who'd watch every gig, their ranks swelling week by week. The brunette, Kayla, and blonde Katrina, they were the ringleaders. Singing along at every word and going hysterical for the harp. Dwight used some of the pay to have T-shirts made, and each of them bought one. But they wouldn't buy recordings. They said there was no point.

Dwight got his first shiver in mid-June, with the Louisiana sun slow-roasting the whole city. He played a show at The Maple Leaf, his largest yet. He saw Kayla at the bar when the crowds filed in. As she snatched for her beer, Dwight caught sight of her hand. It hadn't been bandaged, and Kayla didn't look to be in pain. But somehow, all the skin had been torn from her knuckles. Even from the stage Dwight could see the enflamed flesh, and even a few hints of white bone beneath. He asked her about it afterwards but she just laughed it off. She said she'd had an accident opening a tin.

At Dwight's next gig Kayla wasn't alone. Most of the front row had the same mark, flesh crudely carved from the knuckles of their left hands. They held them up during the set like badges of honour. Dwight started to spot tattoos too, now he was looking for them. One girl had 'The Devil Danced in Delaware' etched onto her arm, another had 'The Truth in Knucklebones' spiralled round her thigh. By July, Katrina had braided suspicious-looking bones into her buttery locks.

Rather than ignore it, Dwight embraced his followers' kinks. He grew his hair long and hung himself with talismans. He swapped his singer-songwriter stage-talk for an invented cult-leader persona, inciting the crowd to "Bear witness my brethren!" and "Praise the spirits!" He began calling himself 'Ragged Vagabond,' and claimed that the harmonica contained the spirit of a long-dead witch. It was all trash talk, of course. But the fans loved it, and their ranks swelled beyond Dwight's dreams.

In August Dwight played Riverside in Chinatown to a crowd of four-thousand. He played after a trio of support acts, and the crowd were almost frenzied. Kayla, Katrina, all his followers were there. Dwight played the best set of his life. The harmonica was eager in his mouth, almost intoxicating. He gave in to the wiles, and let it lead him places he'd never gone before. The crowd went with him, and spent two hours in a blazing reverie.

Dwight left Riverside through the stage door to a back alley, his pockets stuffed with the night's takings. He touched his heart pocket, where he kept the harmonica, and sure it was safe he moved to find a cab.

"I heard you on the radio, sugar."

He turned to find a ghost leaning against the Riverside wall. Dreadlocks hanging like willow-tails, leg cocked flirtatiously. A 'Ragged Vagabond' T-shirt pulled tight across her, and a Stetson-wearing skeleton inked fresh across her face.

"Alisha?" Dwight stared, "What are you doing…Jesus, is that a tattoo?!"

In response, Alisha sang softly. She had the voice of a jazz singer, smooth as sweet molasses, *"Break me down in Chinatown and take me as your thane."*

A lead pipe swung into Dwight's knee and he buckled to the ground. Dwight heard the snap before he felt it. The pain rushed up from his leg like a furious red wave. He tried to scream, but someone hooked a rag into his mouth. The last thing he saw was Alisha, smiling like a proud mother, before someone threw a sack over his head.

When his vision returned, Dwight was in an open coffin. He'd been laid down in a pit, with the stars snooping above. Between him and the galaxy, staring down in reverence, were his fans. Kayla, Katrina, dozens of them all peering down. With Alisha presiding over it all. Some had even brought guitars with them.

Dwight tried to rise and the pain in his knee spiked. He screamed, and Alisha bent down to stroke his hair.

"Hush," she breathed. Her face-tattoo danced as she spoke, "Hush now, ragged thane. We are here for you."

"Alisha, what is this?!" Dwight asked through gritted teeth, "Fuck off you weirdos, take me to a fucking hospital!"

Alisha stood, and nodded to Kayla. Kayla bent down, smiling pleasantly, and holding a carving knife. She snatched up Dwight's hand. He screamed his protests, but they were drowned out by the voices of the followers all singing in unison.

"Hail the ragged vagabond with heaven in his veins. Seek the truth in knucklebones and lay him in his grave."

Kayla stripped the flesh from Dwight's knuckles in one practiced cut. Blood flowed down his arm as Kayla offered it up to Alisha. She took Dwight's hand tender as a lover and began to suck on the wound. Drinking in the blood with heaven in it.

Dwight was dizzy with the pain, "Wha…why?"

Alisha smiled, blood seeping through her perfect teeth, "Rest now, ragged thane. You have shown me the truth."

Alisha stood, fishing the harmonica from Dwight's top pocket. He tried to claw it back with his good hand, but it was pointless. Alisha stood up tall, put the harmonica to her lips, and began to play. That husky haunting melody as crisp as ever in the evening air, like the wails of a broken heart.

"No! Let me go!"

Kayla and Katrina slid the lid across Dwight's coffin. He tried to squirm away but it was no good. His followers jammed the lid in place, plunging him into gloom, and he heard the soft thuds of dirt being heaped over the top

"Let me out!" Dwight screamed, "Jesus Christ! I wrote that song! I'm your goddamn idol! Let me out!"

But nobody heard him. All they heard was the sound of the ragged harmonica, a dozen guitars, and every voice on the hillside singing in blissful union.

The Devil danced in Delaware, the angel fell in Maine

We broke him down in Chinatown and took him as our thane

He's the ragged vagabond with heaven in his veins

We found the truth in knucklebones and lay him in his grave.

43

THE ART IS ABSENT

Leo X. Robertson

She asked to put me in a room with other pieces. We both knew I had nowhere else to go.

It can't be that the curator observes artistic symmetry between my statement and that of Gary Lynch's *Bed and Breakfast*—by the end of the week I'll know every contour of dried blood upon that four-poster's sheets. There's no parallel between me and Eliza Furze's *Three Portraits*, nude photos of herself in the guise of famous clowns. And I observe no connection between my work and Bob Righteous' *Ursa Major*, a crudely sculpted London city centre, with every sky-scraper replaced by a soapstone penis. Patrons gasp and venture prods at it, love it because they get it on sight. Is that the measure of good art? Then what does that make me?

Pathetic. I shouldn't be here. I must empty myself and leave the body behind to allow interpretation. What's to interpret? I thought presenting the loneliest moments of my adult life to others would create some inversion, a public display of private moments to steal from loneliness' claws of suffering. To create a new expression of community. It says something similar on the plaque beside me, under my title for the month's remainder: *Veiled in Flesh*.

I have not yet created transcendence by shuffling about this plinth of a few paltry square metres in a scrap metal chastity belt of your construction, occasionally self-harming with the razor blades strewn around my feet when the urge strikes me. I've done it several times now, the public in awe of my bravery, but there hasn't yet been an organic impulse to do it. Private loneliness, I know now, on day three, cannot be expressed in public. Twenty-eight days more of a failed experiment to go.

*

You come in the night. Lynch's bed swells into the shape of us fucking. The timbre of my moan tells me it's after you told me about her. I'll never forget the strained sound of knowing you were in love with someone else. I told you it was okay to sleep with others, nothing more.

The mound of sheets falls as I leave the bed and return to my piece, leaving you there to tremble and weep. Beneath one lowly spotlight, the blood of those sheets becomes fresh again, eats up the light like a black hole. I whimper, breaking my vow of silence. I try to run to you, but I can't. They chained me to a rusty spike and it holds me back. I thought it was just cosmetic.

In the morning, your blood is still there, dried in a new shape. Who would know? A patron, visiting the gallery more than once? Were the guards so observant? Would the artist himself even notice?

*

Many nights pass and you don't visit. Not sleeping is part of my act, but who will stop me? I try to lie down, but the bulk of irregular steel at the back of my belt prevents me. Did you design it like this on purpose?

I try to lean on one side, but it's too much effort. The belt rocks forwards and I lie face down until the plinth's pressure against my knees gets too painful. I can't sleep and you know it, and when I sit cross-legged, you think me ready for your next piece.

You stalk out from behind *Ursa Major*. Your shadow walks over to the wall, to the clown portraits. Now I see you, see the coin-sized hole in your chest. It beats out heartblood that saturates the dirty white t-shirt you had on in the video of your demise. Blood soaks your jeans, drips down your legs, makes tributaries between your toes, flows to the floor. You look at me and hold out a hand to the portraits as you walk past them. With your touch, they turn to me, their make-up garish and grotesque, their straw hair curling to steel wool. They laugh silently. When you're beyond them, you dissolve back into the darkness.

*

Your fresh blood streaks across the floor, and now I know you were here. Visitors don't notice. I hear it squeaking beneath their soles, watch them collectively traipse a long, thick track of it that worms all over the linoleum.

You bought a gun and shot yourself in the heart. I saw the film of it for the first time at your wake's gallery. At your request, it played on multiple LCD screens, in black and white, in colour, slowed-down, sped-up, reversed. A projector on the ceiling washed a beam of it over us all. I was the only one who emerged from your funeral with any meaning still applied to the footage, as I assume was your intention.

They brought this "piece" out again, for my performance. No negotiation. Only for lack of tech did they not play it in the same room as me. I hear the gunshot all the same, every ten seconds or so. What, I wanted to ask, did my relationship with you have to do with my art?

The curator mentioned that you'd chosen your mistress to unwittingly record your death. She thinks it's not just the art itself that's important, but also who makes it. I'm wearing your belt, but I don't know if I agree. I do resent that she used *your* justification.

I'm using all my energy not to flinch. Your video seems to change pace. I can't predict the next shot. When the DVD ends, I have a minute of respite before it begins again.

*

I pick up a razorblade and slice a thin horizontal line beneath my bellybutton.

I spent days in my studio trying to give my blades authentic wear with various oxidising agents—citric acid, vinegar, hydrogen peroxide—and laid out sample after sample, on wax paper, across the desks and floor. I made several passes each day and disposed of the failures. I couldn't use those with rusted blade tips, else I risked doing serious damage to myself.

At the end of this painstaking experiment, I had nothing but a small cigarette case of falsely weathered props. Of my career, I put the most effort into them, and they mean nothing. It was hardly inventive of you to shoot yourself. Hardly took much effort either. A pull of the trigger and you were gone. But that seems to mean the most of anything either of us ever did.

They say you sacrificed yourself for art. After each gunshot, I hear a sigh as your last breath releases from your lungs. It strums your vocal cords on its escape. It sounds like you, but you're long gone. You were already dead before the shot, so there was no sacrifice, no suffering. Effort, energy, time, inspiration, imagination, suffering—they don't necessarily mean the resulting art is any good. But what does?

My blades are as unreal as my performance. Its veracity depends on the absence of me from my body. But here I am, waiting for you again.

*

You don't return, so I leave myself. I appear at the border of the spotlight over *Ursa Major*, whose stone melts into flesh. Each penis ejaculates blood with my touch, a motion-detecting fountain of red. My symbolism was never subtler than Bob's. I suggested to you that we sleep with other people because I already was, all over town.

Flies accumulate on the sculpture like a black fur, enamoured with the meat's rotten stink. The patrons smile as if it was still stone. The *crack* of gunshot after gunshot barrels through my brain. This is no exhibition; this is my funeral of art to mirror yours.

Two guards pass by me, bulky guys in matching black fleeces. One mentions that he finally fixed the projector upstairs. That at least on this, the last day of the exhibition, the public can see your footage. Your film wasn't playing; I still heard the shots.

I wail. A ripple of gasps emerges from the audience, catches my attention.

She's there, her blonde curls caught the sunlight, a starlet amongst the grey drudgers mulling around her. She looks at me, her mouth a crimson O of horror and awe.

I slice my wrist, deeper than ever before.

They think it's part of the performance. Maybe it is.

44

DELAYED DEPARTURE

Bruce Thomas

A man in a fluorescent orange waistcoat emerges from the cockpit with a clipboard. Seconds later the cabin crew perform a routine cross-check.

The doors are sealed.

I swallow deliberately to unclog my head as the cabin pressurises.

My teenage neighbour worships her phone, head bowed, nimble thumbs dart and stab, indifferent to a sombre announcement from the captain.

Three hundred kilometres away, a dense fog has swallowed Gatwick Airport. So we're grounded in Barcelona until our destination clears. Air traffic control have issued us a "slot" which means we're not going anywhere for God knows how long.

That's what the adolescent to my left doesn't realise.

The cabin is seething with highly-flammable Spanish teenagers.

They must be on a school trip to 'English-land.' Boys giggle at exposed bra straps while girls pout for selfies.

A woman waddles down the aisle. I'd describe her as 'fat' if it wasn't for the badge that reads 'BABY ON BOARD,' so I guess she's pregnant but fat enough to fly.

The conductor of our youth. She waves her arms and the teenagers quieten. With grammar-school English, she repeats the captain's news. Silence. Then again, in broken Spanish. The cabin erupts with a chorus of profanities. The chaperone waddles off.

Teenagers offline are basically crack-heads in withdrawal. Deprived of social media the itchy addicts spool out of their seats and wander the aisle, loitering to solicit approval. Designated seating gets shuffled so that friends and lovers can collude.

The volume has suddenly increased by two decibels.

The air tastes recycled and its temperature reminds me of a public swimming pool. Nice and warm, in a beige kind of way. I remove my tunic, and check my phone. Lucky me. The airport's public WiFi is in reach.

I grab onto it and check the EasyJet website.

The captain was right. London: -3°C, heavy fog. Severe weather warning.

I look past my neighbours and out, over the tip of the wing. It's a beautiful day outside. I hate London. I hate queuing. I hate cigarettes and I'm craving a smoke.

My neighbour flicks a glance at me, then preens her hair. I smile. I remember that phase.

She's pretty. Her T-shirt is creased by her bra, one of those stiff moulded bras, one cup size larger than its actual contents. She's not fishing for male attention just yet, she's defending herself … from the cruel scrutiny of her peers. I remember that phase too. If only she knew hundreds – perhaps millions – of men adore small breasts.

I look up to see her competition. Two aisles down. A murder of crows.

Another announcement extends our delay.

The air hostess follows up, with apologies and a peace offering, broadcasting that refreshments are now available for purchase; excluding alcohol.

OK that's it. I march to the toilet and locked inside I pull out my trusty e-vape, loaded with delicious oily nicotine syrup. Old-school rebel. I push the barrel in my mouth and suck a lung full of synthetic smoke. It curls out seductively. I check the mirror. A mid-life crisis looks back at me through lecherous foggy glasses. Where did I go?

I swallow another lung full of smoke, then another. Then knock, knock, knock. Shit. I wave the air frantically and pocket my nicotine gun and flush the toilet. KNOCK, KNOCK.

I'm caught. I unlock the door, ready to fight. There's no way in hell I'm paying a fine.

But it's just another passenger. Not what I was expecting. I recognise her. It's Miss 'BABY ON BOARD.' The chaperone. She's twitchy with a handbag clutched under arm. She smiles and apologises. The English live to apologise. An inexplicable cultural obsession. I call her bluff with a double apology, but she trumps me with a false smile. I fold.

The catering cart arrives.

"Anything for you sir?"

"Yes, um, a cuppa tea and a Kit-Kat."

I unfold the table and relax into the internet. After a couple of emails I swap over to BBC news, and as the page struggles to load I notice the group of girls, the ravens, whispering and giggling. I pretend to read.

Two tightly shrinkwrapped girls stand in the aisle beside a friend's seat. Wanton eyes hunting, they're not innocent. One girl notices me watching. A lipgloss whisper directs all their eyes towards me. I drop my eyes, betrayed by carnal curiosity.

My neighbour bows her head and gasps. Her knees snap together.

She looks up at me in absolute shame.

Her turquoise leggings blacken with blood, like a surgeon's gown. Her eyes are frantic. My heart breaks on her behalf, so I lean down and hand her my black tunic and nod. She looks up at the button, to call for assistance, and then at me.

I know what happens next, because it happened to me once, a lifetime ago. A trial by laughter. Teenage cruelty.

I have a plan. The catering cart is approximately three metres down the aisle, and the crew are all women. I press the attention button. The hostess notices and approaches, when she's about two meters away I whisper to my neighbour in pidgeon Spanish.

"I need you to trust me."

She nods.

I bump my lukewarm cup of tea into her lap, and leap up apologising frantically. She bursts into tears. Her trousers are drenched and dark, down to the knee. Her humiliation is in disguise. The air hostess arrives and in the commotion I manage to whisper.

"I think she's having her period, please … get a blanket."

I continue to serenade with melodramatic apologies, and open the overhead locker, so we have access to her suitcase. Her peers will remember this incident for the wrong reason, in the future they will laugh at her, but mostly they will laugh at me, and I'm proud of that.

The hostess returns with a blanket. I follow them with her suitcase.

The toilet is occupied.

The hostess knocks with authority.

No answer.

She knocks again and demands a response.

Silence.

Bang, bang, bang. The ultimatum.

Nothing.

She folds aside an aluminium flap, adjacent to the handle, which conceals a manual override.

She slides the bolt over.

The door swings open and the teenager screams.

The human ear is hard-wired to certain frequencies of sound. We can't ignore a crying baby, for example. These sounds penetrate the fabric of existence, and we respond by reflex. It's a pure sound. It cannot lie or deceive in the way language does. Its pitch describes the very essence of being, the nature of suffering, the extent of pain or the violence of rage.

Her pure scream described Armageddon.

A few female passengers suddenly began to weep, while others jumped up in terror. All 236 heads on flight EZ8527 were turned on us. I needed to vomit, but first I must stop her scream.

I guess it must have looked bad when I snatched the girl and gagged her gaping mouth. It must have looked really bad, like I was violating her. I just didn't want anyone to hear what we had seen in that fucking cubicle.

The hostess slammed the door, and took the hysterical girl into the rear reception area of the plane, and sat her down to console her. A massive man in the front row unbuckled himself. My judge, jury and executioner started to march towards me. I pressed myself against the toilet door and lifted my nicotine gun into my mouth.

"Good news ladies and gentlemen! We've been cleared for takeoff. Cabin crew, please prepare the cabin for departure."

The pilot's oblivious optimism was grotesque.

The air hostess unhooked the intercom, dialled a code on the keypad. I didn't hear what she said. Behind me, inside the cubicle a woman sat limp, on her chest a badge 'BABY ON BOARD,' her skirt hitched up, her panties around her ankles, mascara rivers running down her face. The toilet seat, basin, floor and walls were haemorrhaging blood.

When the door first opened, she was shivering. A torrent of blood ran down her inner thighs, meandered around her calves, over her ankles to reach the glossy red lake below. She wore sticky crimson evening gloves that stretched from finger to elbow, and cupped in her hands ... oh god ... in her hands ... forgive me, I can't describe what she cradled in her bloody hands.

She looked up at us, then down at the absurd landscape.

"I, I, I ..." her lips quivered, "I am so sorry."

Slowly she lifted her hands to her mouth, a lumpy purple umbilical cord dangled down between her legs and she kissed her aborted passenger goodbye.

She's still in there now. I'm against the door ventilating on nicotine. Judge Dread is almost upon me. My neighbour is wailing in the corner, with blood throbbing out of her groin and the air hostess is in the other corner, vomiting.

As the avenging stranger passes the lipgloss sex kitten in the aisle, she also expels that terrified gasp, folding forward as her ovaries collapse and blood floods into her crotch.

The alpha male arrives along with his verdict.

Crack! A punch in the head and I smash down next to the hostess. My face is bleeding, the teenager is gushing, and he steps in for strike two, but the air hostess raises a manicured hand in my defence.

He-man pauses confused. The penny drops.

He retreats and opens the toilet door, crosses himself like an altarboy, then weeps like a child as he tries to heave open the rear door to the aircraft.

The air hostess leaps up on high heels, trained to disarm, she grabs his massive shoulder.

"Excuse me sir, you can NOT do that."

But he's on autopilot.

"Sir, return to your seat immediate..."

Her unpronounced syllable made me look up. I watched her step back and look down at the floor where she was. A drop of blood, the size of a five pence coin, had stopped her. The next drop, fifty pence in diameter, opened her up.

Blood snaked down her leg, clotting in her stockings.

"Oh God no!!!!! What's happening to me?!"

The rear door popped open, an emergency slide exploded outward and inflated with a hiss.

A murmur from a woman, adjacent to the open toilet, cascaded down the aisles, infecting each row with panic, which erupted like a tidal wave.

I crawled over to shield my neighbour from the hysterical stampede.

Outside the sky was dense, with a sinister mist.

A month has passed since then.

"The bonus ball is … eighteen. That's: one and eight, eighteeeeee…"

Click. I change channel.

A handsome woman presents the news. Unemployment is soaring, and nobody gives a fuck. She smiles, the handover smile, she holds for two seconds before the weatherman appears, and if you look at her smile closely you can see the crack in the whole of humanity.

It's all gone wrong.

The ingredients are there: shiny eyes, bleached teeth, lips in a crescent moon. But it's sterile. Her smile is sterile. All woman have that same smile. It's the smile of infertility.

This lady hemorrhaged, just like all women hemorrhaged, except hers happened on prime time television, as she broke the story of her career. 'GLOBAL PANDEMIC' which featured footage of passengers, quarantined on a runway, in Barcelona.

The weather followed.

Fog. Low visibility. 94% humidity and a hay fever alert: 'extremely high' levels of pollen.

Armageddon was neither nuclear nor biological warfare. It was ecological.

Mother Nature's last resort.

By the time we figured it out, it was too late. An airborne spawn covered the globe, carrying with it a pollen based protein, designed to sterilise women. The abortion of the human race only took about three weeks, and nobody died.

Click. I change channel.

The world's youngest person is weeks old, today.

Click. I change channel.

Click. I'm killing time.

45

NO WASTE

T.R. Guest

I'm writing this so you know what happened.

I hope you don't mind, but I won't say my name. I'll just tell you what you need to know. I hope you'll see I'm a nice person. That I mean well.

I hope you like me.

So – one thing about me. I'm a bit messy. The house is a lot to keep on top of, so when it's too much I go out driving at night. I go away from the estate, into the lanes where my headlights are bright in front. It helps me think straight.

I've had the car a while now. It's got some paint missing, rust on the wheels, a bumper I tied on. I did my best, but people still stare. So now I only go out at night.

You probably think: "What does he do in the day?" I used to think that myself. Days would go and I couldn't remember. But in the last few weeks I've started making Christmas gifts for the neighbours – the ones who are nice, who say hello. Some of them wave. One even helped sort out the front garden. I just want to say thank you to them. And I love making things. I've made some lovely things.

But I'm getting ahead of myself. My mind jumps left and right some-times. I'm sorry.

It was a year back when it started. I was still driving in the day then. I'd passed a kid's bike, missing a wheel, just left out by the big shop bins. It stuck in my head. When I got home I was crying for it. I didn't know why. So I went back and got it. I used bits of the wheel as a climber for plants. I painted the frame, added a fancy trim and put it on the wall. It felt good. It wasn't wasted.

So I took to driving. Driving at night and collecting things. Making them useful.

A month back, I was out in the lanes, only a few miles off. It was all black ahead, with just my yellow lights. I braked almost before I knew what happened. It was that quick. A loud noise, a bang. I shot forward in the seat. I'd hit something.

I sat there for a bit, calming down. When I got out, there was black blood sprayed all over the front of the car. It was a badger. It was lying in the road, its mouth was open – all long, yellow and brown teeth. It twitched about a bit. I stared at it till it stopped breathing. Its blood around my shoes.

I'd heard on the radio about a man who lived off meat he found. I didn't want it to go to waste, so I dragged it in the boot. Nearly hurt my back. I got it home, put it on the floor.

I didn't know the names of the different cuts of meat, or where you're supposed to slice, so I just did it like I fancied. I didn't do a bad job. It tasted funny, the first bit I cooked. A bit like turkey. Stringy. Dry. But I got used to it. You can get used to anything. I tried fry-ing it, I roasted a bit. I even poached its cheeks in a bit of old milk. I think I had 10 meals from it. Maybe more. I even tried an eye.

I didn't want to waste the rest of it. Sounds funny now but I glued its claw on a bit of wood for a back scratcher. It took a bit of time for the smell to go. I skinned it, made a sort of cloak, but I won't wear it out. It's just for home.

So I started picking up other dead things I found at night. Eating them. Using the other bits. I got a rabbit once. I made a slipper. There wasn't enough for two. But you can't wear just one. But I won't go on about all the animals. There's been loads. But I didn't waste any.

Then last week, I went out past midnight. The Christmas lights in some of the estate houses. They really cheer the place up. I went out where it's really dark. It was cold, but that nice cold, so I had the window down. I drove fast. The car rattled, but I kept on. I enjoyed it, no one else about.

Then I was spinning. The car tyres screeched. It was really loud. I'd hit something big. This time I grabbed the spade, got straight out. Sometimes with the animals you have to hit them, or chop at the neck before they crawl off.

But it was a bloke. Only young. Fit-looking. He was twisted on the ground. He made a noise with his mouth, like a cry. His arm was twisted at a funny angle, and he looked like he had an extra elbow. His bottom half looked like it was going the wrong way. There was blood on his face. I didn't know what to do. So I looked at him, and waited for it to stop. Then he went quiet. But I couldn't be sure, so I did him with the spade.

He was too big for the boot. It took ages, but I got him on the back seat. I got home, dragged him into the house. He was wearing a shirt like someone in an office. I could smell drink on him. Must have been out. Maybe a Christmas party. I thought about who he might be. I stood over him for a bit. I had a think. I didn't want him to go to waste.

So I got the knife out. It's funny, but it was easier to cut than most of the animals. Maybe it's because I know the joints and which way they go, because I've got them as well. There were lots of bits. Fingers and things. And I did try some. I didn't want to at first, but it's a waste otherwise. Frying was best. Cutting it thin. I had to dab the blood off with an old towel, otherwise it took ages to dry in the pan and go cooked-colour. But I won't go on about all the meals I tried. I can tell you later if you want. Some of them were nice. About half's still bagged in the freezer.

But I need to speed up. The police came round today. About a missing man. I said I didn't know. They asked to look around, just routine they said, but I'd seen on TV they need a warrant or something, and they didn't have it. They went away again, but they looked at the car. One of them asked if I still drove it. I said no. They said they'd come back later, so I'm writing this now, just in case I can't later. I might be busy talking with them or something. Even though it's Christmas.

So I've left some of the gifts I've made for the neighbours on their doorsteps, just in case I don't get the chance tomorrow. They'll find them in the morning. It's not the same as a proper stocking, but it's still a nice surprise.

I stripped the skin off his fingers and fanned them out. I used a bit of wire and some old lace to make it pretty, and to make a kind of shape, for a lady's hair. Like for a wedding. I've left that for Mrs Bishop at the end. She always looks nice.

I got the bag from under his willy, and used a bit of cotton to make it a pretty purse for a young girl, so Kayleigh around the corner's got that. I put a surprise in it too, so it's like two gifts in one. I cut off the soft bits from his big leg bone, and put some wire around it with some lovely paper roses on, for a display. That's gone to the Peters family over the road. They're a nice family. I won't go into all the presents, but I think there'll be some smiling faces in the morning.

So I hope you understand. I found Greg's card in his trousers when I was going through everything. I recognised his last name. Knightley. So I found out the address. I just wanted to tell you your son didn't go to waste.

Happy Christmas.

46

BLACK INK

Penegrin Shaw

The man on the table shrieked. Then he blacked out. Again.

Victor took the opportunity to take a rest. He put the kettle on and whilst he waited, mopped blood from the floor in tiny circles. He turned the radio up and from it, *Nick Cave* sang a lullaby to the unconscious man, whose name Victor had forgotten.

Victor was about half-way through. Yesterday, the man had been face down. Today, he'd started at the man's feet, one toe at a time, then worked his way up to the knees. Now the man looked like he'd been dipped in tar, to the waist. Although he wore nothing, anyone walking into the room would assume at first glance that he was wearing tight-fitted trousers, minus a shirt. On closer inspection of course, his skin bled freely, where the needle had scratched and tore it, leaving a stain in the wounds in the one, perfect, single hue. Nothing was to be excluded. Even the shaft of the man's penis and his testicles, bled through. A flaccid member was difficult to deal with. The foreskin had to be taut. It had to be done right. Victor had a reputation.

He unfurled a roll of kitchen towel and placed it in squares over the man's lower body; marvelling as the pieces turned burgundy in an instant. It reminded him of science lessons. *Something to do with 'ph'.* He'd always been better at art.

Victor sipped his tea and listened to the radio.

*

The man was still unconscious when Victor resumed his work, but the man soon screamed out above the sounds of the needle as it hummed its electric chorus, changing pitch and note, whenever it met flesh.

"Please. Stop. *Pleasestoppleasestopitplease,*" the man begged and Victor turned the radio up even louder. Wails and sobs became a perfect backdrop to the creative arts and it made total sense to Victor.

The centre of the chest was always particularly painful. The needle would vibrate along the bones of the chest plate, so it felt like the ribcage was being pulled apart and then set on fire.

But Victor knew it wasn't the worst. The worst was yet to come. Even more than the penis and the testicles, because the man had been unconscious for most of that.

The man was lucid again. Pain surged across his skin as his blood seeped through mangled pores. He felt both hot and cold. He was dizzy, yet wired from the adrenalin his body was producing. Victor forced a donut into the man's mouth and he actually ate it, sensing that he needed the sugar desperately. *Instinct.*

"Sixteen hours," Victor said quite plainly, looking at the vinyl record-come-clock on the wall. The man tried to grab Victor with his restrained hand, but Victor swatted it away casually.

"Please stop. Please. I'm begging you. *PleasestopitpleaseIwilldoany-thing!*"

Victor started tattooing the man's lower neck, which he knew would be unpleasant. When he got to the Adams Apple, the man started to retch, before throwing up all over himself. Setting his equipment on the work bench, Victor had to move the man's head to the side to stop him from drowning in his own vomit, before unfurling more of the kitchen roll.

*

By the time Victor had another cup of tea, the man was whimpering quietly to himself. Inked entirely from his feet, to his cheek bones; now resembling a scuba diver, more than a naked man. Victor mopped the floor once more, emptying the rose-water within the bucket twice, before the floor looked clean enough for him to continue.

They shared a donut, (as they were nearly all gone) and Victor changed his needle for the last sitting.

He took great care completing the final piece. Victor gently stroked the man's face as he coloured it in, moving the man's hair from his eyes – all the while nodding to the man as if to show a deep empathy with his pain and the ordeal itself. He felt closer somehow. More akin.

Victor turned the radio down. The man lay quietly in shock. His teeth chattered, barely audible but enough for Victor to regard it and enjoy it. All that was left to do was the eyes. Tiny circles revealing what he'd once looked like beneath the ink that endured in his wounds and took hold like poison. Ready to blossom. Ready to alter the man into something else.

The man looked at Victor. He was surely broken, but somehow in his expression, he held a look of hope, as if Victor would stop and take the restraints off of his arms and legs. The man wanted to live, after all.

Victor pressed his foot on the pedal and the needle came to life once more, with a sickening sound as it ripped the surface of the man's eyelids. Victor held him firm with his elbow, pushing his weight onto the man to keep his head pinned down. *Not to spoil the work.* Madness came to the man finally, finding he couldn't escape the needle, as the very noise of it filled his skull and the pain reverberated in his head where there was no haven, nor safe room or sweet dream to behold so he could hide from it. His screams echoed from the walls of the studio, but he knew that no one would come. To Victor, the screams sounded like laughter. The man willed Victor to put more weight upon his skull. *Let it crack. Let it end. Let it go.*

When the noise and the needle ceased, the man could only see red before him. His face was a horror of ink mixed with blood, creating a new colour.

Victor marvelled at his work. He wiped the man's face and sprayed it clean. The man's eye balls were blood shot and his eyes themselves swollen and bruised. The ears were intricately painted, so every arch and curve of them was covered, like the rest of him. Victor studied the hands, which were inked around the thumb and finger nails and deep into the prints of the fingers and creases of the knuckles themselves.

The man tried not to cry anymore, as his tears were also fire and they ignited the rest of him as they trailed down the sides of his head.

Victor drank his tea and ate the last donut in front of the altered man.

Then, he took off the man's leg restraints and he unbuckled the belts around the man's arms. The man did not move or try to escape. He did not try to attack Victor.

Victor took out his phone and snapped pictures of his art from various angles.

He yawned, tired from his own ordeal of tattooing for so many, many hours. The last part had sapped all energy from him. Now he just wanted to go home and take a bath.

It was over. Finally.

Before he walked to the front of the shop, before he unlocked the shutters and entered the street towards the place where he'd parked his car, Victor leant over to the man lying above a pool of blood on the tiled floor and he said, "Now we're both *Black*, Motherfucker."

47

TINDER

Fiona Leitch

I'm not sure exactly when I realised the creature I was growing in my womb was a monster. Deep down I think I knew all along.

I met the father on Tinder. Don't judge me. I was 38, fresh out of yet another disastrous relationship and trying to fight the rising sense of panic, of running out of time. My biological clock wasn't just ticking; the alarm had gone off and no matter how many times I hit 'Snooze' the fucker wouldn't shut up.

He wasn't my type. I like fair hair, boyish good looks, but he was dark and swarthy, kind of Mediterranean or even Middle Eastern in appearance. Coal black hair and smouldering eyes lit from within by the fires of mischief... God, I'm making him sound like a fucking Mills and Boon romantic hero, but it was obvious just from his photo that it wasn't love he was looking for.

I swiped right.

We met up Friday night at the Fire of London Monument, near the hotel he was staying at for the weekend, and at first it played out like a normal date. We went to a tapas bar, where I drank a little too much to extinguish my nerves, and he barely touched a drop. Then we ate. Fiery *albondigas*, piquant meatballs that scorched my taste-buds; chilli-flecked *almejas*, tiny, succulent clams which took my breath away, both at their heat and at the sight of him flicking his tongue around their shells; and the hot, paprika *chorizo* sausage that made my eyes water. He laughed at my discomfort.

"If you think that's hot, I don't think you'll be able to handle what I've got for you," he smirked.

Oh my god. Anyone else, I'd have laughed at them and called them a dick, or just walked away; but not this time. Instead I took another bite of chorizo and stopped my eyes from watering by staring deep into his. He smiled.

I'd like to say that we went back to his hotel and made love all night, or even 'had sex' all night, but that implies that I had some say in the matter. I was just a hole – or, in the interests of accuracy, several holes. He pounced on me the minute we were through the door and then spent the whole night and most of the next day pounding and thrusting into me with a wild ferocity. In a daze, my mind floated above our sweat-slicked bodies and looked down. It looked more like something from the Discovery channel than consenting sex. After god knows how many hours of this I was bruised and aching, stinging, exhausted. I felt humiliated. A used up slut.

It was fucking amazing.

Finally, sometime early Saturday night, he left me alone long enough for me to fall into a deep and feverish sleep. Or I passed out. I'm not sure there's much difference.

I – woke up? came round? – around midnight. A cool breeze dried the sweat on my skin. The window had been flung wide open and a thin stream of moonlight pierced the room, narrowed and squeezed into a sharp point by the surrounding buildings. Even at this time of night there were voices in the street, buses and taxis crossing London Bridge, the rumble of trains. The real world was just outside, throwing the strangeness of this whole encounter into sharp relief.

I lay there for a moment, wondering how the fuck I'd got myself there and if now would be a good time to sneak away – before this man I hardly knew, this man who saw me only as a receptacle, came at me again with his fucking never ending hard-on or turned into an axe-murderer – until I suddenly realised that he wasn't lying next to me.

Off sharpening his axe I thought to myself. But then I became aware that there was someone – or something – at the end of the bed. I gingerly lifted my head to look.

Moonlight picked out the jagged contours of the strange creature perched by my feet, illuminating the barbed claws hooked into the bedclothes and highlighting spiky-tipped wings as they unfolded, wings big enough to engulf a full-grown man – or woman. The creature shook itself, and fine black feathers rained from those massive wings like ash.

It let out a low squawk and tossed its head in the air, light glinting off a serrated beak. There was something in that beak, something soft that wriggled and squealed, high pitched with terror. The bird creature shook its head again, tossing the squealer in the air and opening its beak to catch it. The squealing stopped abruptly. Something black and liquid in the moonlight, warm enough to steam in the cold night air, oozed from its masticating jaws.

I clenched my own jaws shut to stop myself screaming, tensing my whole body – *don't move, stay still, if you stay still it won't see you* – but my traitorous legs betrayed me. Feeling me shake, the monster turned its head towards me. I let out a low moan as I felt, rather than saw, its eyes travel up and down my body. It shuffled closer and peered into my face and I was shocked to see that mocking expression in its eyes that I'd seen hours before, in the tapas bar. Its beak opened slowly and the last thing that went through my mind before I passed out was, *your breath smells of almejas* –

When I woke up, it was Sunday morning. He sat by the edge of the bed, already fully dressed, smiling at me. I wasn't sure what to say but he spared me the bother.

"Well, that was fun wasn't it?" he said. My aching body wasn't entirely sure it agreed with him but I decided not to argue the point. "I have to go, but you can take your time. I've ordered you breakfast and paid the bill."

"Oh… thank you," I said. He smiled and bent in to kiss me – the first and last time he'd done that. I felt vaguely uncomfortable.

He stood up and headed for the door, then turned back with that mocking smile again. "Be seeing you." And then he was gone.

When I found out I was pregnant, I was overjoyed. I wanted a baby.

If I couldn't have one with a decent partner, I'd settle for having one with someone who was basically just a sperm donor. I made arrangements, bought a cot, painted the spare room...I did everything but take notice of that little voice in my head that kept saying the same thing over and over again. *Be seeing you.*

But as my baby grew, I couldn't ignore it. The heat inside my womb. Sometimes it felt like I was on fire in there. The feel of whetted claws scraping at my belly, desperate to get out.

The midwife and the doctor didn't believe me. And why should they? The scans looked normal. *But of course they look normal! HE looked normal at the time!* The other mums at my antenatal class all laughed about having baby brain and I wanted to scream at them, *leaving your fucking handbag on top of the car and driving off isn't the same as growing a monster in your belly!* But I didn't say anything because having a baby is meant to be a wonderful experience.

Pregnant women are meant to glow, but not literally.

And now I writhe on the hospital bed; my time is near, I can feel it. I scream at the fire in my belly. The drugs aren't helping, and neither are the platitudes uttered by the midwife and the doctor. They still don't fucking believe me. They will soon.

My waters break with a hiss of steam, scalding liquid pouring down my legs, burning my skin. The midwife stops her *it's nature, love, every mother in the world's been through this* in mid-sentence, because they've not fucking been through THIS. The last thing I think before the inferno of pain begins is *I finally realise what his last words meant...*

48

FINGERS

Lewis Rice

What have I become? What has my desperation driven me to? I had it all, but a few lapses of judgement have cost me dear. Look at me and what do you see beyond the spider web of bloodshot eyes, set far back into my skull beyond what is real; Tinkering on madness. A tattered Armani suit which no longer fits and festering fingerless stumps for hands, which when offered on meeting new people are rarely shaken. I've become a nobody. A waste of breath. My father should have squirted me into a tissue.

"You really are a useless piece of shit!" was my father's favourite catchphrase; those were the first words I can remember him saying whilst I lay in my cot as a toddler. I'd already given up crying, as no one would ever come. Then again when I brought home my first drawing from school, or school reports and medals for second place. That time that I brought a new girlfriend home and he and his friends forced her to watch as I was made to have sex with Old Agnes; they laughed and cheered as I sobbed afterwards. Each time those eight words.

When he finally overdosed, I helped to drag his body out of the back door and we left it for the police to find him in the back alley of 'The Fox and Hounds.' An hour passed, and the room in which he died was tidied up and ready for its first client of the day. I screwed my father's widow good and proper and then left the whorehouse in which I'd been raised and made my way over to St. Giles' church to get married.

'Was dumping his body the start of my woes?' I reflect, staring into steam-coated glass, graffitied with my own blood, looking for a shard of hope. There is none. I glance towards my last shrivelled-up finger, but it's sunk, lost beneath a blood-enriched basin of foamy water. I need to see it one last time, that accursed ring. Bid it a fond farewell before I flush it away. I submerge my head wholly, eyes closed, tongue probing for its location, avoiding lumps of vomit and sponges of bile. Acrid copper. My tongue clips both bone and flesh and I bite deep into the carrot-like fleshy digit and feel a phantom pinch where my finger ought to be. I pull my head up, shaking the excess water in triumph. The ring is there, located at the battered end. I shimmy over to the toilet, ready to flush the ring away, but fate intervenes once more, I slip onto the floor, knocking myself out cold and dreamt of my past.

*

A busy Middle-Eastern market, a bazaar maybe? Sweet-smelling spices infused with the even sweeter body stench of the hard at work. And I'm joined by Jackie my wife; so I must be dreaming of my honeymoon in Marrakech. We're bartering with a market trader over that ring. I didn't trust that one-handed fellow and wanted nothing from him, but Jackie was won over by his devilish charm. Despite my annoyance, we left hand in hand, with me wearing that smooth and perfectly fitting ring.

*

I'm standing at a bar alone entertaining dozens of tourists whilst Jackie's confined to bed with food poisoning. I'm partying with three fifty-somethings who are on a wine tasting tour. In a short while, I'll be smashing them all whilst their husbands sit and watch.

It's the next morning and my ring finger's throbbing and itchy and I suspect I've caught something. I pull and twist as best I can, but my finger has swollen too much and the ring's staying right where it is.

*

I'm in an English hospital surrounded by many doctors and experts, and they're looking rather perplexed over my finger. "Gangrene... We'll have to take it all off... He's lucky it's spread no further..." How many voices did I hear, all speaking at once?

I wake from a dream within a dream and Jackie's sitting at the end of my bed, sobbing. I look down to my hand and fight to get the bandages off to get a better look, but the nurses won't allow it.

*

Its several weeks later and I'm back at home on sick leave from work. I'm still coming to grips with the changes to my hand whilst pleasuring myself and can't help but stare at its new beauty. There is a knock at the door and I let in an escort who takes over from me.

Nearing the moment of climax my right index finger is hit head on by a sharpness shooting right through me. The escort looked at my face, mistaking my expression for joy and we screamed in unison as I explode inside of her. I withdraw the hand which I'd been using to pleasure her and it plungers out the blood and destroyed muscle which once made my finger. She panics and attempts to flee, but the remaining parts of my finger flop out of her, causing her to vomit over me.

*

It's a good while later and I'm unaware that buried beneath a mass of bandages, the ring had been placed on my left middle finger. Only when I felt a tingling in that finger following a special bed bath administered by one of the prettiest nurses that I'd ever met, I realise what's happened. I tear at the bandages, desperate to get to the ring and remove it. Jackie denies it even now, claiming that she never put the ring back on me. She reckoned that it was either one of my sick friends having a joke, or me. I look down at my middle finger and tug as hard as I can, but to no avail, it just won't budge. I watch as it crushes tightly, causing my fingernail to flick away. I open the bedside cabinet, gently shut it against the ring and pull back with my feet until finally it comes off. I hadn't accounted for the morphine affecting my hand, or even my fingers, so didn't even realise that I'd de-gloved the skin from my entire middle finger. I stand there gazing at my finger of bone and pulsing claret, before a panicked nurse close lined me back into bed. They couldn't save that finger, and at the request of my wife they disposed of the ring.

*

I'm at home, injecting morphine into my leg; soon after this I'll be moving onto something stronger. I'm housebound, and imprisoned, as Jackie believes I deliberately disfigured myself. Her status prevents her from seeking real help, which got her into a right spot of bother when I shoved my whole right hand into a tree shredder, hoping to ease the pain following the ring's return. One minute I was busy up to my nuts in guts with the pretty little female gardener, and I knew I had no ring on, and then it just appeared and the pain was like nothing I'd felt before. Panic and desperation set in and I shoved the whole hand in, only hoping to get to the one finger, but I was wrong, oh so wrong. It was at that moment when it dawned on me that it was all her doing! She must have known about all of my affairs and flings; her grandfather's Will meant that divorce would leave her out of her inheritance! She wanted me out of her way, or I suspect, better off dead!

*

I'm now committed and far away from prying eyes. Despite all that had gone on, Jackie told me that she'd stand by me, which must have been a decoy in order to get that ring on my last remaining finger, my small left one. But what about the other fingers? Perhaps I'd lost more and forgotten? Maybe Jackie had taken them in my sleep. Or maybe it was the tree shredder? I just don't know anymore.

I didn't even notice it at first, it was only when I was fingering one of the patients with my little pinkie, that I felt that tingle again. I pushed the harlot back, and noticed the ring on yet again. I ran to the bathroom and locked myself inside by wedging a chair against the door. I scanned for tools to use, but all I could see was soap and toilet paper, so was left with little choice but to bite down deep, and rip the thing off. The agony caused me to drop my finger into the basin and finally, fingerless, for the first time in a year I was free of that curse.

*

Recovery was slow, real slow. They fitted me with prosthetics and my meeting with my Doctor proved fruitful. I was well and truly on the mend and was released into the care of the ever-reliable Jackie. The hospital had made me come to realise that it wasn't her at fault, it was me. My unfaithfulness had caused my delusions, and I was using her to draw the blame.

Another year passed and our marriage was well and truly back on track. She was pregnant and her girlfriends threw her a baby shower, which meant a weekend away, and I being left in the care of Becky, my nurse. That evening a power surge caused me to take my bath by candlelight. As Becky helped lower me into the bath, I caught a glimpse of her ample bosom and felt a slight tingle down below. She gently massaged my feet and I became more and more aroused as her hand wondered along my legs and towards my crotch. I raised my stumps, grasping her head and raised my penis towards her mouth. Our eyes met, and she smiled the most devious of smiles. I felt a slight pulling of my penis and glanced down towards it. The ring had returned, but this time wrapped around my penis and balls. My gaze returned to Becky's eyes and I shoved my manhood deep into her throat for what would turn out to be the last time that I'd ever feel like a man.

49

WORMS

Emma Pullar

I grab my altered jeans from the arm of the couch, where Annastia left them. The boys are setting the table, or they should be. I walk in on them using the cutlery as swords.

"Boys!"

Smiles drop from their lips as do the knives in their hands, the metal hitting the tablecloth with a thump.

"Setting the table is boring," Thomas grouses.

"I know, but your mother's gone to a lot of effort, let's show her that we appreciate it by setting the table nicely." I ruffle Thomas's dark hair and he looks up at me like I'm a grumpy old fart who just popped his balloon. "Do you want her to yell at you?"

"No, Dad," he sighs.

Joseph raises his eyebrows in an angelic fashion. He always does when he's about to say something rude.

"I'm not eating it."

"Joseph, you promised," I say, eyes locked with his.

"It'll taste like poop."

He screws up his face and pokes out his tongue. Thomas slams a knife and fork down on the table and widens his eyes.

"You eat poop?" He points at his brother, accusingly.

"No I don't!"

Thomas turns the mockery in his voice to full volume and dances about chanting.

"Joseph eats poo, he gets it out the loo…"

"Thomas!" I snap.

Thomas purses his lips and stands still as a statue. Joseph's bottom lip trembles, he squeezes past the dining room chairs tucked up close to the wall and leans against me, hugging my leg.

"Just try and eat it," I say, stroking his fine hair. "For me."

"Okay, Daddy."

"Good boy."

I leave the room hopping on one foot as I tug on my jeans, and shoulder through the bathroom door; zip up, fasten the button, buckle my belt, and reach for the hand soap. There's a yellowy gloop in the basin.

"What's this down the sink?" I shout to Annastia.

"What?" she shouts back from the kitchen.

"Did you tip pasta down the bathroom sink?"

"Sorry." My wife's head appears between the door and the frame, floating, as if detached from her body, her big doe eyes pleading for forgiveness. "I was in a rush, I screwed up the water to milk ratio and couldn't find the sieve so I tipped the ruined pasta in the sink. I'll clean it up after I finish cooking, okay?"

And by 'cooking' she means throwing packet pasta in a microwave-safe bowl with milk and water, then dinging it for eight minutes. My grandmother used to say packet food would be the death of my generation – microwave meals, the beginning of the end. She was a marvellous cook. Everything from scratch. She was also great at sewing, unlike my wife. I nod to Annastia and her floating head disappears behind the door. I'm left dreading dinner and dreading what the lads from work will say about my uneven jeans. I bend over and tug down the left leg in an attempt to lengthen it. I let go and the denim springs back up, a clear inch shorter than the other leg. I sigh.

I can't go out tonight looking like this. I could have taken them up myself, I suppose, but my sausage fingers struggle to thread a needle let alone sew the fiddly hem of my jeans. I lean to one side to try and make the shorter leg look even with the other. Perhaps we should invest in a sewing machine.

I catch sight of myself in the mirror above the basin. My face is thin; shadowy stubble is peeking through the skin. I look like shit. That's it! I'm going to start insisting we go to Mum's for dinner on Sundays. It's the only decent meal I'll get all week. I place my hands on either side of the white porcelain and stare down at the sludge of macaroni. She obviously started heating it and then realised afterwards that she'd put in too much liquid. I turn on the cold tap and the plughole glugs, choking on my wife's cooking as I have many a night. I better get it out of there before it clogs the pipes.

"Gross," I huff, scooping out handfuls of slimy tubes and chucking them into the bathroom bin.

Why didn't she just throw it in the bin? The watery milk mixture is why; makes sense, I guess. If the kitchen sink wasn't full of dishes all the time she could have chucked it in there. I turn off the tap and stick my fingers down the hole, pulling out as much as I can. The built-up water rushes for freedom as I unclog globs of sticky cheese. For fuck's sake, this is disgusting. They say the way to a man's heart is through his stomach but that's not true for me. I grimace: *remember why you married her, Tim. She's a lover not a chef.* I feel a chill around my exposed right ankle. *Or a seamstress.*

I fish the last remnants of slippery pasta out of the pipe; the push-plug taken out because the kids keep getting it stuck. I peer down into the dark hole. I didn't get it all; a few remain out of reach. A quick burst from the tap flushes them away. Before I leave the bathroom, I take one last look at the basin. A stray macaroni elbow is in the bowl. *Just leave it there, Tim, the kids will flush it away when they brush their teeth.* My obsessive personality kicks in and I can't walk away.

"Dinner!" Annastia shouts down the hall to me.

I sigh and pick at the pasta with the tip of my finger, dragging it up the side of the basin.

"Tim!" she yells.

"I'm coming!" I yell at the door.

When I look back down at the basin the pasta is gone. I feel a strange sensation on my index finger. Look at it.

"What on earth?"

The macaroni is inching around my finger and towards my nail. I bring my finger closer to my face, astonished. It's not pasta, it's some sort of worm. Pain shoots up my cuticle as the worm forces its tubular body under it. Eyes wide, a rush of panic turns my blood to ice. I yell out to my wife and pinch at my finger. It's too slimy. I can't get a grip on it. FUCK! The worm pushes further under my skin. I grip my wrist in agony, blood from my nail running in between my fingers, drawing red lines down my bare arm. Under the skin the parasite caterpillars along my finger bone, making its way painfully down my hand; my stomach lurches, like there's a hundred worms inside it, wiggling around. I hold my hand away from me, as if this will stop the worm from digging deeper into my body.

"ANNASTIA!" I yell.

White-hot pain drives down my arm like a long needle being forced into my body. Eyes watering, I grip my forearm, and pinch the pink flesh. I'll stop it going any further! I swallow the pain, grit my teeth and squeeze harder.

"ANNASTIAAAAAAAA!"

Where is she, damn it!

"Dad! Dad!"

My boys come screaming into the bathroom, sending the door crashing into the wall. The five – and seven-year-olds launch their small bodies at me. I gasp and stumble backwards, falling into the cold, empty bath; legs dangling over the side, back shocked by the hard edge, rod of pain jabbing my spine. Little hands reach for me and my sons stagger towards the bath, faces wet with tears. The worms squirm and wriggle out of their nose, mouth and ears, and hit the floorboards in clumps, writhing about their small feet. My children whimper and rasp, their little faces sinking, skin sagging like a deflating bouncy castle.

"Stay there, boys," I say, my voice fractured. "Daddy will help you, just don't come any closer."

Thomas leans forwards and coughs bloodied worms into my lap. I scream and try to brush them away. They wiggle all over my crotch, trying to find a way in, under my skin! I grip the rolled edge of the bath and pull myself forwards, but pain in my exposed ankle causes me to drop back down. There's another one inside me! I lever my body out of the tub and sidle past my worm-ridden children. Thomas falls sideways into Joseph and they drop to the floor. Joseph's body convulses, projectile-vomiting worms and stomach lining, dark jelly, organs and God knows what, over the floorboards. My bottom lip trembles as I run from the bathroom. I want to help my sons but I can't. I have to get away! Get away from their worm-infested bodies.

"I'm sorry boys," I sob, and wipe the tears from my eyes.

I limp down the hall, my ankle throbbing, and as my hand grasps the kitchen door I feel a tingling on the tip of my dick. No! No! I rush to undo my belt, the relentless ache in my arm and ankle causing my fingers to shake and I can't budge the tight button on my jeans. Pain shoots down the eye of my penis and my breath catches in my throat. I clench my jaw, biting into the side of my tongue.

"FUUUUUCK!"

The pain is too much. It's burning — a searing fire iron forcing its way down my urethra. Red rises up my face, eyes bulging, the veins pop out of my neck. *Oh hell.* I drop to my knees, hands clasped over my crotch. I fall forwards and push the kitchen door open with my head, the hinges creak and the thick wooden door slowly, reluctantly, reveals my wife's body. She's spreadeagled on the chessboard floor, head facing the open door, she stares straight through me — at least she would if her eyeballs hadn't been eaten, hollow sockets dribbling with dozens of worms. As they eat her from the inside out, her face starts to collapse. The pain of worms burrowing into my own body is overridden by grief. Hot tears sting my eyes. This can't be happening. From my kneeling position, I allow one of my hands to let go of my groin and slap myself round the face.

"Wake up!"

I squeeze my eyes shut but tears break free and race from their corners. When I open them, the nightmare is still unfolding, only now my wife's body is a hollow sack; all that's left of her is skin and bones. Our marriage is far from perfect but I love her so much.

"Oh Annastia." I cry out.

The worms turn their attention to the fresher meat in front of them. They inch and roll along the checkered floor, wiggling over each other, fighting to get to me. The pain from the three worms eating me from the inside out returns tenfold and pushes bile up my throat — lava in my mouth. I cough and bright red sprays across a white tile. I blink. My eyes roll back, a sensation of falling comes over me and my shoulder slams down hard against the cold floor. I land opposite my wife — what's left of her. I manage to lift my eyes to the kitchen bench. I spy packets of macaroni, a worm wiggling out of the nearest one.

My father always joked that Annastia's cooking was deadly; little did he know it would be what killed us. The slimy little fuckers crawl all over my skin, burrowing in. I open my mouth to cry out in pain but as soon as my lips part, the worms pile in, choking me; some wriggling up my nostrils, towards my brain. Air cut off, I gag on the writhing mini-beasts sliding down my throat, and as my body shuts down my thoughts ring loud: *In the end, we all become worm food. Only, I'd expected this to happen after my death.*

50

INGROWING

Andrew Mark Perry

Terminal. Six months. Cancer. Regardless of how he rearranged the words, Robert couldn't come to terms with their meaning. Why hadn't he visited the doctor when the headaches began?

The cracked mirror fragmented his image in the sallow light. Week long stubble graced his cheeks and neck; pocked skin and cracked lips complemented bloodshot eyes. Robert clutched the hand basin, examining uncountable grotesque reflections. He should call his mother. No, not yet.

Maybe it was a mistake? No, not a mistake. He'd seen the scans. White mass, incongruous against grey brain. Unreachable, inoperable, fatal. He always said he'd never want to know if he was ever terminally diagnosed. When the mind gives up, the body follows, he believed. Yet, when the oncologist said 'terminal,' all Robert could say was 'how long?'

Glass and porcelain chimed as a freight train charged past Robert's apartment. He wouldn't sleep tonight. Another scan in the morning. What was the point? He'd call his mother tomorrow. Christ! How would she cope without him?

Robert passed his hand over his face; an angry spot throbbed, demanding his attention. He inspected his chin. Black stalks of hair sprouted from a pulsating lump. The boil erupted as he squeezed, spewing pus upon mirror and sink. A barbed hair remained, protruding from a bloody wound. Robert reached for the tweezers and tugged.

Teeth gritted, bile rising, Robert pulled. He stopped, panting; a finger-length coarse hair sagged from the gaping hole on his chin. Grabbing it in his fist, Robert yanked hard. A searing pain in his forehead screwed his eyes shut. He continued to pull. The agony forced him to his knees. Senses numbed, Robert gave a final effort. He felt his chin tear as the hair gave way. Robert vomited on the floor.

He woke hours later; congealed sick stuck to his hair and face. Entwined around his fist was the hair he'd wrenched from his face. Robert peeled himself from the floor and inspected the hair which terminated in a ball of flesh. The pain had subsided, yet a fogginess swam through his head. He mopped the floor and, as he showered, Robert watched the hair coil down the drain.

*

He'd get drunk tonight. Not before he called his mother. Maybe one drink. Robert lay on his bed, a half-glass of whisky reflecting copper crystals on the bedside table. No word from the oncologist since the scan a few days previous. Still, what news did he expect? Anyway, what would he say to his mother? 'Sorry, mum. You're on your own. First dad, now me.' She wouldn't last six months, not in her condition. The guilt wasn't even the worse of it. Bitterness and self-reproach at his own mortality fuelled his anger.

He'd ring her, but not tell her. Not yet. See how she is and gauge the situation. Maybe she wouldn't live long enough to find out. He cursed himself for the selfish fantasy and reached for the glass.

Midway through the bottle, Robert's phone rang.

'Mr Faldon?'

'Yes,' Robert replied.

'This is Dr Wilson. Sorry to call so late. It's regarding your scan. We've observed some abnormalities with the tumour.'

'Abnormalities?'

'Yes, something we weren't quite expecting. Are you able to come in tomorrow?'

'I guess, sure. But what are you talking about? Has the tumour spread?'

'On the contrary, Mr Faldon. It's shrunk. This is unprecedented, but we believe a course of chemotherapy may now be beneficial.'

Shrunk? Robert suppressed the optimism rising in his chest. One step at a time. Chemo to get through, then maybe they could operate. He allowed himself the first smile in weeks. No need to call mother now. Let's see first.

The wound on his chin had begun to heal, so Robert decided to shave. A delicate matter after weeks of growth. As he roughed the bristles on his face, he felt a lump and, parting the beard, found another spot. Robert grimaced; he couldn't face an episode like the other night.

A thought struck him. No, it didn't make sense. But the spongy, bloody pulp at the end of the... was it even a hair? He'd yanked it out and part of the tumour had come with it. It couldn't be... could it?

Seating himself at the mirror, he shaved carefully to avoid the bulbous boil on his cheek. Then, using the same action as before, Robert squeezed. Sure enough, another barbed, black hair-like growth splintered his skin where the spot burst. Robert breathed deeply. Whisky is what he needed. Dull the senses first. He took a couple of slugs and bit down on the handle of his toothbrush, holding the tweezers over the barb. The night train sped past, rattling the mirror and his grip. 'Steady now,' said Robert to himself and pulled.

The whisky nulled the pain, but still a razor blade raked his brain as he wrestled the hair from its root. He was going to be sick again, or pass out. No, he had to keep going. He pulled and tugged, ignoring the numbness enveloping his body. He watched his skin split as the hair climaxed in a black, bloody bolus.

Holding the offending growth to the light, Robert raised himself from the chair. He found his left leg had no feeling and gave way. Robert's jaw cracked against the basin as he fell before darkness consumed him.

*

The distant echo of a train faded as Robert prised open an eye. Hazy sunlight fogged his apartment. What time was it? He pulled himself upright and flopped against the bathroom wall like a discarded puppet. His left leg was devoid of feeling and utterly useless. A result of the fall? No. He played back what he remembered; the leg caused the fall. He rubbed his aching jaw, feeling a tender lump.

He found his phone. Midday. Missed calls. 'Mr Faldon, we're just ringing to confirm the time of your appointment... Mr Faldon, are you able to call us to rearrange... Mr Faldon, this is Dr Wilson. It's important you call me...'

They were wrong. Clearly, the cancer was already affecting his body. Why else would his leg fail? Across the bathroom floor, Robert saw the bloody mass he'd dragged from his skull. Could he really be pulling out the tumour piece by piece? He ran his hand over his throbbing head, down across his face. More lumps. One on his forehead, another on the other cheek; both in addition to the one on his jaw.

If he could get more of the tumour out, maybe the feeling in his leg would return. He would go to the hospital and show them what he'd done. If a scan showed the cancer shrinking... this could be a breakthrough. Robert dragged himself across the apartment collecting water, pain killers, mirror and tweezers. This would be safer on the floor. Swallowing a handful of pills, he positioned the mirror and waited for analgesia to kick in.

The crack of a train threw Robert from his reverie. The light bulb danced, casting shadows against the pallid tiles. Robert broke the boil on his jaw. Discharge dribbled down his chin, leaving a shiny spike that glinted black in the swaying light. His jawbone bulged as, inch by inch, he drew the hair. Nerves desensitised, he felt a burrowing which seemed to tickle the back of his eyes and throat. Despite the pills, a warm pain embraced his body as the sore on his chin gaped, then ruptured. Robert found himself holding a crimson ball of meat, dangling between bloodied fingers. He tore it apart, like a sneezer inspecting their tissue. Black matter smeared his palms. He dry-retched and, finding himself unable to swallow, poured water down his throat.

One down, two to go. He repeated the motion with the lump on his cheek. Pain; less intense, yet more acute, rose in his chest. It culminated in a euphoric head rush that numbed his entire body as the second gory pulp pulsed clear from his cheek. No more. Not today. Sweat chilled his back against the cold tiles. He needed a drink and to sleep.

Reaching for the basin, Robert hauled himself up. He slipped and fell, smashing his elbow against the porcelain tiles. His lungs filled with a silent scream. Both legs were numb. He jammed the tweezers into his right thigh. Blood oozed between metal prongs. No pain. Lying prone, he crawled for his phone and called the hospital.

'Dr Wilson's office?'

Robert issued a guttering growl.

'Hello? This is Dr Wilson's office; how may I help?'

Robert tried again, but nothing but a curdling collection of phlegm formed in his throat. The phone went dead. He sobbed, silently. Dumb and paralysed from the waist down, he was out of options. All hope gone... Apart from the last boil on his head. What did he have to lose? Maybe removing it would fix everything; it could be the final piece of the tumour.

Robert dragged himself back to the bathroom, collecting the whisky and using it to swill down the last of the painkillers. He spat metallic mucus, rinsing his mouth with the remainder of the bottle. He burst the final boil on his forehead. It blistered open in a rainbow of yellow and orange flecks. He positioned the tweezers over the barb. When the mind gives up... he wasn't ready to give up, and pulled.

At first, nothing. Robert's head pulled forward as he twisted the hair from its root. Movement. A fraction of an inch maybe. The hollow of his head felt like it was being dragged inside out. Another fraction. His sinuses swelled with acid. An inch. Tongue and tonsils fought for permission to explode. An impasse. Robert strengthened his grip. Pain had no meaning now. Another pull. He felt every tooth wrench from his skull. His eyes wept blood; he watched it waterfall over the crescent of his nose, parting like a red sea over white lips.

He was nearly there; he couldn't feel anything, but he knew. One last pull. His breath fogged the mirror, already claggy with saliva and pus. He held his breath, waiting for the mist to clear. Pain accompanied a sucking sound as Robert's head propelled backwards into the hard tiles. Whatever it was, it was out. Blinded by the pain, he traced the hair, feeling an orb between his fingers.

Robert took in air, running his tongue over splintered teeth. He opened his eyelids and attempted to focus. Staring back at him was his own eyeball. He began to laugh. Muted chuckles became empty, maniacal roars. He crushed the eye in his fist; jelly spewed between clenched fingers. He smeared it across his mouth and face.

Another hair. From the chasm of his eye socket, he felt it. He followed it into the depths of the abyss. When the mind gives up... As Robert pulled, he was outside himself, watching the hair coil away from bloodied void. Grey matter seeped from the socket. The action was automatic. Robert watched as his body heaved, pulling the cancerous tumour from his skull. He watched as the poison left his being. He watched as, with it, the rippled mass of his brain spilled down his chest and groin, delivering him into timeless darkness.

A LITTLE BIT
MORE... TWISTED

Read more about Twisted50 at www.Twisted50.com where you can indulge in author blogs, listen to audio clips for Twisted vol 1, watch trailers and descend into the deep underworld of Twisted50.

Printed in Great Britain
by Amazon